Designed and Edited by Hal Schuster

STEPHEN KING

and

CLIVE BARKER

THE ILLUSTRATED MASTERS OF THE MACABRE

BY JAMES VAN HISE

PIONEER BOOKS, INC.   LAS VEGAS, NEVADA

ACKNOWLEDGEMENTS ➤

This book reviews all of the fiction of Stephen King and Clive Barker published to date. Most of this work is still in print or else in easily available back issues. The only non-fiction I have reviewed is **Danse Macabre** because it is a major work in the field. I have also taken a brief look at the films based on the works of both King and Barker, most of which are available on videotape.

Special thanks goes to Dr. Barry M. Brooks, 54 Woodside Avenue, Box 22, Winthrop, MA 02152, for his invaluable help in providing copies of rare King fiction from **Mystery Monthly** which I would otherwise have been unable to acquire for review.

Thanks also go to the many talented illustrators appearing in this book. Their work provides ample visual confirmation of the imaginative power of both King and Barker.

Library of Congress Cataloging-in-Publication Data
James Van Hise, 1949—
   Stephen King and Clive Barker: The Illustrated Masters of the Macabre

   1.   Stephen King and Clive Barker: The Illustrated Masters of the Macabre (literature)
I. Title

Published by Pioneer Books, Inc., 5715 N. Balsam Rd., Las Vegas, NV, 89130.

First Printing, 1990

JAMES VAN HISE writes about film, television and comic book history. He has written numerous books on these subjects, including BATMANIA, HORROR IN THE 80S, THE TREK CREW BOOK, STEPHEN KING & CLIVE BARKER: THE ILLUSTRATED GUIDE TO THE MASTERS OF THE MACABRE and HOW TO DRAW ART FOR COMIC BOOKS: LESSONS FROM THE MASTERS. He is the publisher of MIDNIGHT GRAFFITI, in which he has run previously unpublished stories by Stephen King and Harlan Ellison. Van Hise resides in San Diego along with his wife, horses and various other animals.

contents

THE HORROR KING

Although Stephen King may seem like that overnight success that every writer hopes to become, a closer examination reveals that all is not as it seems.

King sold his first short story in 1967. He worked on he college newspaper, graduated to find he had to work as a laborer in an industrial laundry before he could even land a teaching job. He sold **Carrie** in 1973 and that can be marked as the year when everything turned around for King in extreme ways. But between 1967 and 1973, a lot of hard work was done just to establish himself in the most basic fashion, and those short stories he was selling for $200.00 each went a long ways towards paying needed bills. There were also several unpublished novels written before he sold his first one. So when you just see the headlines about King signing forty million dollar contracts, remember that it wasn't always that way, and when he was writing his heart out to tell stories he wanted to tell, even Stephen King never imagined that it would come to what it has.

--JAMES VAN HISE

Dino De Laurentiis Presents
Stephen King's
"CAT'S EYE"
from MGM/UA Entertainment Co.

CE-6 Best-selling novelist and screenplay writer Stephen King poses with one of the feline stars and friends on the set of his latest motion picture.

Photo Credit: Dirck Halstead

The Man And The Writer

The world of Stephen King is a world of the uncommon intruding on the commonplace. A world where a small town in Maine becomes a hotbed of vampirism. Where a hotel in Colorado is the nesting place for decades of accumulated evil. Where a cornfield in the Midwest hides the inhuman god known as He Who Walks Behind The Rows.

It is also the home of memorable characters rich in identifiable human experience. Characters we come to care about on a human level so that we can fear for them and feel what they must be feeling when they come to grips with the supernatural. A careful blend of storytelling and characterization propels King's novels with an underlying sense of power, and carries us along for the wild ride. But who is Stephen King, besides being a writer with two-dozen books to his credit?

He came into the world on September 21, 1947, born Stephen Edwin King, the son of Donald and Nellie Ruth Pillsbury King in Portland, Maine. He was an unexpected child because Nellie King had been told she couldn't bear children. Thus when Stephen was born he already had an adopted brother, David.

Stephen never knew his father, Donald, as the merchant seaman left Nellie when Stephen was two, and never returned. To this day he doesn't know what became of him. In **Danse Macabre**, though, King muses:

. . . in 1964, during the troubles in the Congo, my mother insisted that she had seen him in a newsclip of white mercenaries fighting for one side or the other. I suppose it is just barely possible.

After his father left, Stephen and his brother were raised by their mother, who worked long hours in several jobs to keep things going. Over the course of the following nine years they moved around a lot but always ended up back in New England, finally returning to Maine for good in 1958. His grandmother and grandfather were then in their eighties and the other family members hired Nellie King to care for them in Durham, Maine.

An attic in an aunt's house nearby one day produced a box of books which once belonged to King's wayfaring father, and marked a turning point in the young boy's life. Among the books was an anthology of stories reprinted from the pages of *Weird Tales* magazine, and an early paperback collection of stories by H.P. Lovecraft.

In **Danse Macabre**, King explains:

That box of books wasn't my first encounter with horror, of course. I think that in America you would have to be blind and deaf not to have come in contact with at least one creature or boogey by the age of ten or twelve. But it was my first encounter with serious fantasy-horror fiction. Lovecraft has been called a hack, a description I would dispute vigorously, but whether he was or wasn't, and whether he was a writer of popular fiction or a writer of so-called "literary fiction" (depending on your critical bent), really doesn't matter very much in this context, because either way, the man took his work seriously. And it showed. So that book, courtesy of my departed father, was my first taste of a world that went deeper than the B-pictures which played at the movies on Saturday afternoon or the boys' fiction of Carl Carmer and Roy Rockwell. When Lovecraft wrote "The Rats in the Walls" and "Pickman's Model," he wasn't simply kidding around or trying to pick up a few extra bucks; he <u>meant </u>it, and it was his seriousness as much as anything else which that interior dowsing rod responded to, I think.

11

STEPHEN KING

Every writer has a moment when they encounter that one book or story which connects with vivid force and they know instinctively that more of this will never be enough.

King had encountered horror long before this in other forms, such as in 1953 when he eavesdropped on a radio drama his mother was listening to, an adaptation of Ray Bradbury's "Mars Is Heaven" whose climax consists of a man's brother turning into a Martian in the middle of the night and killing him. The first horror movie he remembers seeing is **The Creature From The Black Lagoon**, and his mother would read Classics Illustrated Comics to the boys, who found they particularly liked **The Time Machine** and **War of the Worlds.**

Reality intruded during a showing of **Earth Vs. The Flying Saucers** at a local theatre on Oct. 4, 1957, when ten year old Stephen was startled by having the movie pause half-way through so that the manager could inform the audience that the Russians had orbited the first space satellite, named Sputnik. To a child of the Cold War Fifties, that must have been a frightening revelation indeed.

As to whether his childhood experiences were reflected in what he later wrote as an adult, when Stephen was about 14 he walked into his grandmother's bedroom one day and found that she had died. Memories of this would resurface years later and shape themselves in the short story King titled "Gramma."

Stephen wrote as a child, particularly when an illness once kept him out of school for a year. At the age of twelve he seriously began submitting stories to such magazines as *Fantastic* and *The Magazine of Fantasy & Science Fiction* (a market he would not crack for another 15 years).

His now constant reading of horror stories finally brought him to the literary doorstep of Richard Matheson and the book **I Am Legend** where a man in Los Angeles has to barricade himself in his house every night because the city has been taken over by vampires. This could almost be described as a moment of epiphany for the young writer because it brought into focus something he had been unknowingly searching for, the idea that horror could happen anywhere, even in your own home, not just in exotic locales.

While attending Lisbon Falls High School, King began publishing his own stories on a press in his basement. Besides some originals (two of which survive to this day) he also wrote a twelve page "novelization" of the movie **The Pit and the Pendulum** and actually made a profit until he was told to cut it out because his aunt didn't think it was a seemly thing to do.

It was during high school that King's first story was published by other hands. "I Was A Teenage Grave Robber" appeared in a 1965 comics fanzine called *Comics Review*, published by another young writer named Marv Wolfman (who himself has been a published writer for two decades now, working for Marvel and DC among others). Even with the encouragement this must have given him, King never got very involved with the world of fandom or fanzines, feeling that it would be a distraction from more important things. In his case, he was no doubt correct.

He also completed an unpublished novel during this time, called **The Aftermath** (an after-the-bomb story), and wrote a parody of the school newspaper, which he dubbed "The Village Vomit." His efforts promptly earned him a three day suspension.

After graduating from high school in 1966, he began work on a novel of psychological suspense titled **Getting It On.** He would finish it five years later but it would not be published until 1977 when it was issued under the title **Rage** as the first Richard Bachman novel.

In the fall of '66 King attended the University of Maine at Orono. During his freshman year, he made his first professional sale, a short story, "The Glass Floor," which appeared in the Fall 1967 issue of *Startling Mystery Stories*. He also completed his first mature novel, **The Long Walk**, which was rejected by a first-novel competition and which he then lacked the confidence to submit to any of the major publishers in New York. It remained unpublished until King started releasing material under his "Richard Bachman" pseudonym in the late 1970s..

King's literary influences by this time had broadened to encompass such writers as John D. MacDonald, Don Robertson and John Farris. Another important influence was a poetry seminar King attended during which instructor Burton Hatlen asked if there was such a thing as a "white soul" since much was being made at the time of Eldridge Cleaver's novel **Soul On Ice** regarding the Black experience in America. King felt that the experiences which were unique to white urban America were significant in their own way and qualified for the definition of a "white soul." This realization is present at the heart of much of the fiction King has written since. Hatlen agreed to read **The Long Walk** and gave King a great deal of encouragement based on what he saw.

King became actively involved in the college newspaper, *The Maine Campus*, and wrote a weekly opinion column called "King's Garbage Truck." It was while at college that he met Tabitha Jane Spruce, who would later become his wife.

King graduated from college in 1970 with a Bachelor of Science degree in English and a teaching certificate qualifying him for high school level instruction. Shortly after graduation he sold the first in a long line of short stories, "Graveyard Shift," to *Cavalier*, a magazine which at the time published horror and science fiction which just needed to tell a good story and didn't need a sexual slant, unlike the demands of the magazine today.

In January 1971 he married Tabitha Spruce during her last year at college. Since he was unable to immediately find a teaching position after graduation, he settled for a job as a laborer in an industrial laundry, from which he drew the background for the short story "The Mangler."

King finished **Getting It On** in 1971 and submitted it to Doubleday, who encouraged him to do some re-writing, but ultimately turned it down.

In the fall of 1971, King began teaching high school English at the Hampden Academy in Hampden, Maine. He does not have entirely fond memories of the experience and once stated that if he lost everything and had to go back to working a regular job for a living, he'd sooner load crates in a Pepsi plant than teach high school.

During one winter weekend in 1971, King wrote **The Running Man**, which was rejected by both Doubleday and by Don A. Wollheim, then at Ace Books. Wollheim rejected it because the publisher wasn't interested in books about negative Utopias. In other words, the future had to be a spiffy place, considerably better than the present.

The Kings were living in a trailer at the time when their second child, Joe, was born. King had been working on an idea for a short story about a girl who got back at her classmates for a dirty trick they'd pulled on her, but he didn't think it was working out and threw it in the trash. Tabitha retrieved it and encouraged her husband to finish it. The result was **Carrie.** King explained how the idea expanded from a short story into a novel in an interview in *Rolling Stone*, "I wanted the reader to see that this girl was really being put upon, that what she did was not really evil, not even revenge, but just the way you strike out at somebody when you're badly hurt.

13

STEPHEN KING

"I had done four books before **Carrie**. They're all home in a trunk. (referring to the novels later published under the Richard Bachman pseudonym). None of them are horror stories. It never crossed my mind to write a horror novel because there were none being published. As I worked on it I kept saying to myself, 'This is all very fine, but nobody is going to want to read a make-believe story about this little girl in a Maine town. It's downbeat, it's depressing, and it's fantasy.' But as I finished the first draft, *boom*, along comes **The Exorcist** and **The Other**, and that's how it was pitched."

The book was sent to Doubleday where it was bought after King was asked to re-write the last fifty pages. **Carrie** was purchased for hardcover sale for the princely sum of $2,500 in the spring of 1973. On Mother's Day, Bill Thompson, King's editor at Doubleday, called to inform Stephen that New American Library had bought the paperback rights for $400,000.00, of which King would receive half. King was home alone when he received the call and when he told his wife, she was certain he must've misunderstood. She made him call Bill Thompson back and the good news was confirmed. **Carrie** was published in 1974, a year after it was purchased.

King was able to quit his job teaching to write full time and his wife quit her job at the bakery.

His second novel was **Salem's Lot** (1975), which is about the fictional town of Jerusalem's Lot and is very much patterned on the people and the town he grew up in.

This was followed in rapid succession by **The Shining** (1977), **Night Shift** (1978), **The Stand** (1978), **The Dead Zone** (1979), **Firestarter** (1980), **Cujo** (1981), **Danse Macabre** (1981), **Different Seasons** (1982), **The Dark Tower: The Gunslinger** (1982), **Christine, Cycle of the Werewolf, Pet Sematary** (all in 1983), **The Talisman** (1984), **The Eyes of the Dragon** (1984), **Skeleton Crew** (1985), **The Bachman Books** (1985), **It** (1986), **The Dark Tower II: The Drawing of the Three** (1987), **The Tommyknockers** (1987), **Misery** (1987) and **The Dark Half** (1989) with more on the way!

"Secrets of Stephen King"

by Stanley Wiater

As an interviewer, I have had the unique opportunity to interview Stephen King and Peter Straub not once, but on three separate occasions. These lengthy interview took place at the 1979, 1980 and 1984 World Fantasy Conventions. Portions of those interviews have appeared in various publications, the most extensive being in **BARE BONES** (1988), edited by Chuck Miller and Tim Underwood. However, even there the entire transcript of the combined three interviews did not see the light of day. In other words, some material with King remained unpublished and is now seeing print for the first time. (Where it's required for clarity, the year the interview took place is mentioned.)

WIATER: Why the recent popularity of the horror tale, which for so long has been relegated to the bottom of the paperback rack, but now can be found at the top of the hardcover bestseller lists?

KING: I'll tell you something—people have been asking me why there's been a boom in horror for all the years I've been publishing books. And there really hasn't been! **CARRIE** came in at the very end of the boom; it was not a bestseller in hardcover. It did well in paperback—after the movie came out. But there's never really been a 'boom' in it. There *was* a short one near the end of the Sixties and in the early Seventies: **THE EXORCIST, THE OTHER, ROSEMARY'S BABY**. Those three, and then what've you got in the middle?

You've got one book by Frank DeFellita (**AUDREY ROSE**), which I would argue isn't even a horror novel at all—and it even isn't that good of a book! And the other thing is, when the books do come on the lists, they don't demonstrate tremendous 'legs.' They don't sell and resell. **THE SHINING** was on the New York Times bestseller list in hardcover for one week. But Peter Straub's book (**GHOST STORY**) was on for nineteen weeks. It just rode and rode. One of the reasons **THE DEAD ZONE** got to number one was when the book came on the list there was nothing that was strong on the list at all.

I was convinced from the time I was a teenager trying to sell my first novel that, sooner or later, I'd break through and get published simply because they've got to publish something, and these old farts are going to die off! I mean, they're not farts, but they are on the lists forever.

WIATER: Yes, but why do you think horror finally took off as a truly contemporary genre? It's never really disappeared from the scene, except perhaps in the Fifties.

KING: Even if you go back to the 1950s, when this stuff was very—I mean, *Weird Tales* magazine died from lack of interest as much as anything—but horror was there, and it would crop up every now and then. There was **THE SEARCH FOR BRIDEY MURPHY**, which was the Fifties' answer to **THE AMITYVILLE HORROR**, and just as hoaxy, apparently. It's just that people gotta' have this stuff! You need it—like a little salt in your diet. I've always sort of worked in this field. But I was surprised when New American Library bought **CARRIE** for enough money to put me over the top, to be able to stop teaching and everything.

WIATER: Long before you made it 'over the top,' when your early novels were rejected and you were just starting to sell stories regularly, what was it that kept you going?

KING: For two reasons. The first reason is because, number one: you think you can do it. You think you have the talent to go over the top and earn your living that way. In a way, you feel that's what God meant you to do. You don't feel satisfied with what you're doing because you *know* that's not what you were meant to do. I won't say I've led a grim life, but it was—and still is—sort of a humdrum life. It isn't any big deal. I don't go out and ride around in a limousine, sniff cocaine with a babe on each arm. But it's *fun*. And it's escapism. It's why people watch TV. But this is like 'mind TV' or 'mind movies.'

The other thing that was always in play with me was that I was convinced—*deeply convinced*—that somewhere, deep inside me, was a money machine, waiting to be turned on. And that when I found the dials and the combinations, the money would just pour out.

WIATER: Which it clearly has, probably beyond even your own wildest dreams. But was there any motivation to write so as to say, finally, 'I told you so' to those early critics who didn't share that faith?

KING: (hesitates) Well. . . a little bit of that. But not much. It was never a question of that I felt I had anything to prove to anybody else. But, in a way, with those early (rejected) novels, I felt like a guy who was plugging quarters in the machine with the big jackpot, and yanking it down, and at first they were coming up all wrong. Then with the book before **CARRIE**, I felt I got two bars and a lemon. Then bars across the board—and the money poured out. But the thing is, I was never convinced that I was going to run out of quarters to plug into the machine. My feeling was, I could stand there forever until it hit! There was never really any doubt in my own mind. A couple of times I felt like I was pursuing a fool's dream, but they were rare. They were moments of real depression!

WIATER: How do you feel about the current state of the horror film?

KING: The thing about (horror) films is that there are as many good ones as there are! You wouldn't think there would be; there's such a tendency to play safe, isn't there?

WIATER: But isn't that what Stanley Kubrick did with **THE SHINING**? He went with the bankable stars like Jack Nicholson rather than the right actors to interpret the characters you had created.

KING (sighing): That's the only place that Kubrick falls down, because he's not very good at casting.

WIATER: Does it bother you when your fans seem to be more upset at the way your novels have been changed when they're adapted to the screen than you might be?

KING: I'm getting to the point now where I'm starting to get actively pissed when somebody walks up to me and says, "You know, they ruined **CARRIE**." And I say, "They did?" And they say, "Yeah—the town, it blows up in the novel, it goes up in flames." And I say, "Hey, Paul Monash was lucky to get that picture made at all!" He went to United Artists—it was like the third or fourth place he had gone—they had told him no soap at Paramount, they told him no soap at Warner Brothers and a couple of other places he went. And finally UA said yes, and we'll give you a shoestring budget—I think it was two million dollars or something like that. And that (director Brian) De Palma got to make the picture at all—I mean, how can you blow up a whole town with a budget of two million dollars?! These days it probably costs fifty, sixty thousand dollars just to have somebody fall down a flight of stairs!

WIATER: Would it be fair to say you began writing adaptations of your own works because you were dissatisfied with the results of other screenwriters?

KING: No, that wouldn't be fair at all. (It's done) because sometimes it's fun, and because I want to see what that's like. And a lot of times, I felt like a high school kid who is almost getting laid, but not quite. (Laughs) Like when you're a high school kid, and you say to yourself—if you're a boy!—you say that one of the major factors in wanting to get laid is that once you do it, you don't have to worry about *worrying* about it any more! I sometimes think that if I could get a screenplay that was actually produced—whether it was good or bad or indifferent—then I could say, "Yes, I *am* capable of doing that. (NOTE: This was before the making of **CREEPSHOW** in 1982, which was his first produced screenplay.) I don't have to worry about *that* any more!

WIATER: Could you tell us the origins behind your only non-fiction book, **DANSE MACABRE?**

KING: There was quite a bit of research involved in it, but I don't think it shows in the book a lot! That is to say, hopefully it shows in the sense that the facts are right, the facts are straight. What happened was Bill Thompson, who edited the first five novels that I did—CARRIE through THE STAND—went to Everest House. When I left Doubleday, Bill got fired. . . .

Anyway, he called me up later and said, "Do you want to do a book about horror in movies and on TV and radio and all this for the last thirty years or so?" And I said, "No." And he said, "How many times have you been asked why do you write that (horror) stuff?" And I said, "Billions." He said, "How many times have you been asked why do people read that (horror) stuff?" And I said, "Billions." He said, "Write this book. And whenever anybody asks you those questions, you can just say, 'I wrote this book.' And then you'll sell books and never have to answer those questions again!" So I said, "Okay, I'll write the book." I got into it in a very casual way, and found it very difficult to write.

It's got some autobiography in it because in discussions like this, they always want to go back to Freud; they want to know what your childhood was like. I told a story—this is in the book—at a convention, a mystery convention. And we were on a panel about Fear. There was myself, and there was Robert Morasco—who did **BURNT OFFERINGS**—and there was Janet Jeppson, who is Isaac Asimov's wife who is also a psychiatrist—a medical psychiatrist. So you know why *she* was there. And that shows where they come from, when they set that panel up!

Somebody in the audience said, "Did anything ever happen to you in your childhood that was really horrible?" And I told a story that I thought would satisfy them. I mean, it isn't anything *I* remember, it's something my mother told me. She said I was out playing one day with a friend of mine. I was about four. I came home, deadly pale, and I'd peed in my pants. And I didn't want to talk. She asked me what happened, but I went upstairs and closed the door and stayed in my room all afternoon. She found out that night that this kid I had been playing with had been run over by a train, okay? I can remember her telling me that they picked up the pieces in a basket. A wicker basket.

I don't remember anything about it; the chances are very good that he had wandered off on his own somewhere, and then I wasn't anywhere around. There's a small chance that maybe I *did* see it happen, maybe the kid chased his ball onto the tracks or something. So I told this story, and said, "I don't remember it at all," and immediately what Janet Jeppson said was, "And you've been writing about it ever since!!!" The whole audience applauded—because they *want* to believe you're twisted!

It's odd that it should work that way. One of the things that psychiatry—the Freudian brand—is supposed to do is to allow you to open up lines of communica-

STEPHEN KING

tion from your subconscious to the outside, where you can finally externalize it to the world. So, on the one hand, we say that psychiatry allows us to talk about our innermost fears, and that's wonderful. It helps you to get "normal." But if you do what I do, you must be "weird" because those channels are open. If they were closed, people would say you're normal, because you can't talk about your fears. Situation normal: all fouled up!

WIATER: So if you were ever to wake up "normal" one morning, you might not have any more stories to write.

KING: That, for me, is what's so frightening about what's happened to somebody like Ray Bradbury. I read his collection (**THE STORIES OF RAY BRADBURY**) because I reviewed it. And what happened is you begin with someone who's totally—apparently—messed up, if he had these imperfectly resolved conflicts, and I think he did. Little by little he works them out, and his fiction ultimately becomes very boring.

One of the things that has comforted me about my own work is that, in almost all cases, I've begun with a premise that was really *black*. And a more pleasant resolution has forced itself upon that structure. Like in **SALEM'S LOT**. I was convinced that everybody was going to die! That's what I wanted to happen in that book. But it didn't, and I didn't try to monkey with that fact because I knew in the end that it was right that they not all die. So that's okay, I think. It works both ways (with horror). It's the only place you can write any more, it seems to me, where you can still deal with romantic notions and not seem impossibly corny. You still have to be really careful though, or people will laugh.

WIATER: But are there any limits you've set for yourself as to how frightening or "black" a work can be?

KING: Yes, for me there is. I've just finished a novel which I've put away in a drawer. The name of the book is **PET SEMATARY**, and I'm not sure if I want to publish it, or have anything to do with it. (NOTE: This was in the fall of 1979 and it was published in 1983 only to settle a contractual dispute.) It's blacker than black, and by the end of the book, your worst imaginings are totally realized. Tabby read it, and I wasn't even sure she'd finish it. Well, she did finish it—she wept through the last half of it. And she brought it out and said, "You know how you said you were going to put it away in a drawer?" And I said, "Yes." And she said, "Put it away in a drawer." And so I did. Maybe I'll take it out some day. But it's a *dreadful* book. It's dreadfully grim and horrible, and there's no ray of light on the horizon. It's a dreadful, dreadful book. But when I conceived the book, it just seemed like a terribly exciting idea!

The idea was perfectly simple, based on two incidents. I've got a little kid who's two (at the time of the interview). And he's screwing around in the yard, and we live on a road that's really busy—we did at the time—and he ran out into the road. Well, he didn't know he was doing anything bad, just playing "Keep Away" or something like that. But my daughter's cat had been killed in that road, about a month and a half before. I'd picked him up and buried him in a Hefty bag, and I had to pick up this stiffened corpse with mud all over its fur and those two things kind of went together like (slaps his hands together) *that*!

And a whole book came up in my mind, with no bad thoughts or anything! I just said, "I do this, this, this, and this" and. . . I saw all the connections, and I was tremendously excited. I think that if this had been five years ago that what would have come out would have been something like **SALEM'S LOT**. But in reality, the characters became more fully fleshed and rounded and everything like that—and then it went straight down the hole! I mean it—it was *bad*. I didn't want to finish it, but I did. It took forever to finish the book, which is one of the reasons why I have such bad feelings about it.

WIATER: Critics are now reading all sorts of things into your work. Have there been some "underlying meanings" purposely placed in your work which readers might have missed along the way?

KING: I got a letter from David Morrell, the guy who wrote **FIRST BLOOD** and some other novels. I'm going out there to Iowa basically to meet him. (King and Morrell are now very good friends.) I'm going to do a speaking engagement because that way we can drink across Iowa and all the rest, which is a small price to pay! But he was talking about **FIRESTARTER**, and he said he enjoyed "the green motif" that ran through it, and I had not planned that. That wasn't anything that crossed my mind. For instance, an editor at Viking enjoyed the thing with Charlie McGee and Rainbird that's kind of unstated—to me, anyway!—an unstated (sexual) thing with her and Rainbird all through it. She has a dream where she's riding naked on a horse, and there's a fire, and Rainbird's up ahead and all the rest. And nobody's mentioned *that* to me at all! I loved it, and I didn't want to go any further with it because there's no sex in the book except for that. And that seems to me to be very powerful sex because it *is* unstated. It's just there, and if nobody notices it I don't care. I noticed it.

WIATER: I'm sure you're aware that when it was published, more than one reviewer compared **FIRESTARTER** to an earlier John Farris novel, **THE FURY**?

KING: Sure. I did read that—but one of the things that happened before that was we had a price tag on the movie rights to **FIRESTARTER** for a million dollars, and *that* was super cool. Then I heard that (producers) Zanuck and Brown were close to buying it, and then the next thing I heard was that Zanuck and Brown were in a screening room with 20th Century Fox watching (Brian De Palma's film version) of **THE FURY**. And I said, "Oh, oh, this is not going to happen." The telling of the tale is this: **CARRIE** came, and then (the film version of) **THE FURY** came, which is a lot like **CARRIE**, and then **FIRESTARTER** came. And to me, I saw a relation between **CARRIE** and **FIRESTARTER**, but I never thought of **THE FURY** in the course of writing my book, although I liked the (original) novel. I didn't care for the film very much at all.

WIATER: It's obvious that the vast majority of your short stories deal with horror in supernatural, rather than psychological, terms. Any reason for this preference? "The Man Who Loved Flowers" is one of the very few stories that fall into the latter category.

KING: I like to make stuff up! (laughs) There's a scene in (Peter Straub's) **SHADOWLAND**—it's my favorite single moment—where this guy looks up from an examination and there's this pencil floating in the air, and Delmar Nightingale sees it and snatches it away because he doesn't want anyone else to see it. But that's the essence of the attraction the supernatural story has for me: this pencil just floating there in the air. It's like those Magritte paintings where trains are coming out of fireplaces, Dali paintings where clocks are draped over branches. In "The Mist," for instance, the great attraction in a story like that to me was I really don't *care* what causes it, or anything else. The familiar juxtaposed with the unusual and the strange. That, to me, is the attraction. The psychological stories just seem nastier.

WIATER: In your introduction to **THE SHAPES OF MIDNIGHT** by Joseph Payne Brennan, you state that it's in league with Charles Beaumont's **THE MAGIC MAN** as a book "meant to be read not just once, but many times." It seems that Beaumont has always been one of the great unsung horror and fantasy writers, known mostly today due to his association with the classic **THE TWILIGHT ZONE**. It's clear you've read his stories. What did you think of him?

KING: I think he was great. I think he was wonderful, and I think—if he had lived—he would have been just an *amazing* writer. I just wish I had gotten to meet him sometime! **THE MAGIC MAN** and **NIGHT RIDE** and all that stuff. It was good.

WIATER: Since you must read horror as much as you write it, is there any writer who still is capable of giving you a chill or two?

KING: Well, I like Peter Straub's books better than anyone else's, so I guess I'm stuck with that! (laughs) I read a lot of horror novels, but I don't get a *frisson* from too many of them. Every now and then I get a book that scares me, that is not supposed to be "in the genre"—at least it *says* it's not supposed to be in the genre. But if it scares me anyway! I can't think of an example right now. Oh—like people ask me what the scariest book I've ever read is, and my answer has always been **LORD OF THE FLIES**. That's what scares me the most.

I (often) go to a movie—it's easier to get scared in a movie. But good writing in itself is a pleasure, and it can seduce you into the story. I'm not very concerned with style or anything like that, but I am concerned with the balance. Language should have a balance, and it should be a balance the reader can feel and get into, and feel a sort of rhythm to the language as it moves along. The language should be able to carry you into the story. And that's *it*. Because if the reader is seduced into the story, then it carries him away.

WIATER: You've stated elsewhere that you're not above "hurting the reader." That sounds more like rape than seduction.

KING: I *like* gross-outs. But every time I've done it—and I have had that impulse to do it—unerringly, an editor has cut that from the book. Every time! There was a scene in **SALEM'S LOT** with rats in the basement. And there have been rats in other things—one of the stories that was in *Cavalier*. And, by God, when they printed (it in) **NIGHT SHIFT**, they cut that part right out!

WIATER: Surely you're too important now to be censored?

KING: In fact, I've got a crime story in *Ellery Queen's* this month (December 1980), but it was a lot better crime story before they bowdlerized it! In some ways I wish I had just withdrawn it. It's a story called "The Wedding Gig" and it's about a fat Irish girl who gets married to a very skinny Italian. The narrator of the story is the leader of a small jazz combo and they play at the wedding reception. And the thing that made the story play is the piano player in the jazz combo—who is black. And everybody called him "boy," or they called him "spade" or "nigger. They cut all the pejoratives out of it!!! They wouldn't let anybody be called a "mick" or a "wop" or anything like that (either). I let them do it, and I wish I hadn't now.

WIATER: You haven't found many really good horror novels to read?

KING: I read a couple of good ones in the last year or so, but the best I've read lately is a book by Anne River Siddons called **THE HOUSE NEXT DOOR**. It's a haunted house, but it's a *new* house—that's the gimmick. And Siddons's a Southerner, and she's got a way of getting really, really *nasty* about these things, like Flannery O'Conner. There's this one guy who's very proud of his masculinity, and the house makes him sort of sexually "hot" for this other guy, and everybody's at this party, and these two people are making love! And the guy later—POW!—blows his brains out. Then there's a couple who've lost their teenage son in Vietnam, and who buy the house after the first group vacate. And they start to see their son on TV saying, "I'm still alive! I'm rotting in the jungle—why did you leave me?!" It's nasty; it's a nasty book. A NASTY BOOK!!!

WIATER: So in spite of all the demands on your time, you still find time to read?

KING: I read *all* the time! You want to hear something really gross? (laughs) You've heard of people who read when they go into the crapper—I read when I take a piss! I read when I brush my teeth, too.

WIATER: I think I've just found the appropriate headline for this interview! But, seriously, there's a scene in the film version of **SALEM'S LOT** where the young hero is shown to be "monster-crazy." At least in the sense that his room is filled with monster models, posters, and so forth. Was your room anything like that when you were that character's age?

KING: No. I think I had an Aurora (model) werewolf at one time that I put together, but that was all. I was trying to set up a situation where we would be able to believe in the kid dealing with this. I knew that there were kids who were—and are—big monster freaks. I received a couple of Polaroids from a nine year old in the mail the other day. The kid had read **SALEM'S LOT**, and he sent two Polaroids. One was of himself, this kind of chubby little blond kid with short hair. And the other one said, "Me as a Night Monster with a snake on my arm." It was the same chubby kid—only he had a rubber snake on his arm. That's all. But in his head, he *was* the monster; he was really *scary*.

WIATER: Everyone knows about your finished product—but few people know how you go about the sheer mechanics of writing, which you attempt every day of the year except Christmas and your birthday.

KING: I start at about eight-thirty—I try and get out and walk two or three miles first—and "write" as I'm walking around. A lot of times I'll see things while I'm walking that will turn up later that day at some point (in my work). I'll come back and have a big glass of ice water, and then I'll write from, say, eight-thirty until eleven o'clock. Then I'll stop, and then for the rest of that day and that night I'll go in there with two quarts of beer and rewrite for about two and a half hours.

The rewrite I'll do is always something else. What I'm working on in the morning is what I'm *working* on. The material that I'm rewriting, that's a different function altogether. That's a very—"mechanical" is the wrong word—but it's a very nuts and bolts operation. It's like adjusting the carburetor or something to make it right. That's what you do. But I always like to drink beer with that because it's fun, and it's not as demanding of something in me that says in the morning when I sit down: "I'm *really* working! Invent" That's *WORK*! (LAUGHS)

MAHLON L. FAWCETT©

THE LONG FORM

CARRIE

Carrie seems like it has been a part of the literature of terror for many years, but it first saw Print in 1974. This novel appeared on the stands amid the morass of **Exorcist** rip-offs which proliferated at the time and I overlooked it for that reason. The paperback was packaged to cash in on the crest of exploitation which followed in the wake of William Peter Blatty's best-seller. The cover carried the description of it as "A Novel Of A Girl Possessed Of A Terrifying Power" at a time when the word "possessed" was *de rigeur* on horror paperbacks. But while the **Exorcist** rip-offs have all but faded from sight, **Carrie** stands firmly on its own.

I saw the film years before I read the book, and as much as I enjoyed the movie, the novel stands as a much richer experience. The texture of this novel is quite unique. Even when it was first published, before the film was even a gleam in director Brian DePalma's eye, the reader is clued in that something monstrous is lurking down the road in the climax. The text is sprinkled with asides which are ostensibly excerpts from articles written on the tragedy of Carrie White and the horrors she wrought. Thus while we're meeting the characters and exploring their backgrounds, we're also experiencing tension and suspense, wondering what it's all leading up to, as well as who will survive the coming tragedy.

In the novel we can savor the details of Carrie's life which the film didn't go in to. Surprises not present in the film await in the novel. The climax of the novel goes far beyond that portrayed in the movie. In many ways the climax of . the book possesses not only more power and intensity, but more emotional impact as well. Here, Susan Snell (the sole survivor of Prom Night in the movie) finds Carrie dying. In a very human and evocative scene, Susan feels Carrie die in her mind.

The horrors of high school lie at the core of this book. King later returned to comment on them in other works, such as in **Danse Macabre,** where he states that high school is a place of "bottomless conservatism and bigotry." This is really what **Carrie** is about, even more than her TK power and her insane mother. King worked as a high school teacher in Maine in the early and mid-Seventies while writing both **Carrie** and **Salem's Lot.** After **Carrie** sold to a paperback house for four hundred thousand dollars, King turned to writing full time. King has remarked that if he ever faced going back to teaching for a living, he would sooner load crates in a Pepsi plant. This novel encapsulates the insensitive caste elements present in high school where many are ostracized for very superficial reasons. The lives of these people turn into years of misery due to daily cuts that wound unseen. High school is very much a microcosm of society. Very few of those caught in its rigid caste structure realize it at the time. They are caught up in the day-to-day fads, the "in-crowd" syndrome and all the rest. Few appreciate that their social life is meaningless. The in-crowd and all the other cliques become ordinary people with little social advantage once they graduate and leave high school behind. High school social structure vanishes upon graduation day. Years later, those considered most popular find themselves driving trucks or grilling greaseburgers at the local fast food emporium with all of the pomp and circumstance of high school changed into meaningless memories. When **Carrie** lashes out against the injustice, she is crushing all of them literally, just as they had been crushing her spirit figuratively for years.

The depth of human experience in **Carrie** is just as touching as the imagination is delightful. King polishes ever facet to render depth to the experience, including the TK concept. For instance:

CHAMBERLAIN, MAINE (AP)
STATE OFFICIALS SAY THAT THE DEATH TOLL IN CHAMBERLAIN STANDS AT 409, WITH 49 STILL LISTED AS MISSING. INVESTIGATION CONCERNING CARIETTA WHITE AND THE SO-CALLED "TK" PHE-NOMENA CONTINUES AMID PERSISTENT RUMORS THAT AN AUTOPSY ON THE WHITE GIRL HAS UNCOVERED CERTAIN UNUSUAL FORMA-TIONS IN THE CEREBRUM AND CEREBELLUM OF THE BRAIN. THIS STATE'S GOVERNOR HAS APPOINTED A BLUE-RIBBON COMMITTEE TO STUDY T:HE ENTIRE TRAGEDY.
—page 238

King's work is fun to read because of his turn of phrase. Even in this, his first published (but by no means first written) novel, passages ring true to the style we've come to find familiar.

Billy's car was old, dark, somehow sinister. The windshield was milky around the edges, as if a cataract was beginning to form.
—page 129

King skillfully concocts very on-target, yet very queasy, metaphors.

At another point, one of King's characters comments on Hollywood when she discusses the inevitable film which arises out of of unusual tragedy.

From My **Name Is Susan Snell**

They finally made a movie about it. I saw it last April. When I came out, I was sick. Whenever anything important happens in America, they have to gold-plate it, like baby shoes. That way you can forget it. And forgetting Carrie White may be a bigger mistake than anyone realizes. . .
—page 98

Oddly enough, when **Carrie** was filmed it did depersonalize the story by ex-panding the significance of the religious fanaticism of Carrie's mother to the point where it twisted the climax out of shape. In the novel Carrie disposes of her mother almost as an offhand gesture during her rage of destruction in the town. In the film, the death of Carrie's mother is the focal point on which the film's climax hinges as though the death of a religious fanatic requires retribution on a Biblical level.

Even if you've seen the movie, you still enjoy the book immensely as it' s a deeper, richer story. One with new background and a powerful experience all its own.

SALEM'S LOT

The vampire novel is more popular than ever these days. But when **Salem's Lot** was first published in 1975, Lycanthropy was a fallow field badly in need of til-ling. Most contemporary horror dealt with possessed children or offspring of Sa-tan. Although the hardcover didn't create a stir, the filmed version of **Carrie** in 1976 brought film-goers flocking into book stores looking for another good scare from King. They found the paperback of his second book. And the readers have been returning ever since.

Michael R. Adams

What new readers found was a story in which the town of Salem's Lot slowly fell under a spell of terror and agony. Friends became strangers who became rabid killers roaming the night until the entire town fell victim to supernatural plague.

The plague began after the arrival of Barlow, the king of vampires. Clearly forged in the Dracula mold, Barlow was a powerful and terrifying presence who proved his menace time after time. Forget the teevee version of Barlow— that was someone's misplaced homage to the bizarre vampire makeup of *Nosferatu*. In the novel he projects emotional presence when he talks of the fate in store for Salem's Lot. His deadly personality and horrific image could have emerged out of a Frazetta painting—King describes him in just such terms.

In time-honored tradition, Barlow commands a human servant almost as frightening as himself. The servant's image came to screen life perfectly played by James Mason in the television movie.

In this version, the fate of the Glick children is handled differently than in the novel. In the book, one boy is kidnapped and sacrificed to allow evil to enter Salem's Lot while the other returns from the dead as a vampire. In the telefilm the kidnapped boy returns from the grave to infect his brother. The notion of a child vampire was probably considered too daring by the network.

A terribly effective scene in the novel was left out of the film because it was considered too strong for timid television audiences. The event set at the funeral of the boy who returns as a vampire. In the middle of the service the dead child's father goes berserk, hurling himself on the coffin while screaming, "Danny, you stop it now! You got your Momma' scared!" Needless to say, the funeral party becomes hysterical after that.

Effective stories always possess more than just a good plot. **Salem's Lot** is more than just a horror novel. k offers many fully realized characters. The story is really about love, friendship and strength in the face of adversity.

King inspired other writers with his claustrophobic tale of a town slowly destroyed by supernatural evil. Several have written their own variations on the theme. Peter Straub used this premise to underlie both **Ghost Story** and **Floating Dragon** while Robert McCammon adopted both the theme and the vampires to bring about the downfall of Los Angeles in his highly effective **They Thirst.**

Although for a time King had considered writing a sequel to Salem's Lot, he has reportedly abandoned those plans. He doesn't want to set it a decade after the original because he wants to write about the 13 year old boy who survived in the original story while the character is still a boy. One wonders why he couldn't just tell the story as a flashback since that's the form that **Salem's Lot** is told in.

King *has* written a short story sequel to **Salem's Lot** showing that you can go home again (Thomas Wolfe not withstanding). The story, "One For The Road," appears in the **Night Shift** collection. It deals with the aftermath of **Salem's Lot** but not with any of the original characters. It's a good little story which stands well on its own .

THE SHINING

The haunted house story is one of the oldest in horror literature. So King went that one better and came up with the haunted hotel. Claustrophobic feelings run amok as Jack Torrance, his wife and young son become caretakers at the closed Overlook Hotel during one winter in Colorado.

STEPHEN KING

The Torrance family arrives as the Hotel is closing for the winter season. We meet Dick Halloran, the black cook who recognizes that young Danny has a special talent which the boy doesn't understand yet.

As the Torrances settle in for the long winter things seem okay on the surface, but we quickly learn that Jack is a former school teacher who lost his job when he injured a student caught slashing his tires. Jack keeps turning this incident over and over in his mind, blaming it for all his problems, including the financial woes which have forced him to take this job. This underlying tension and bitterness emerges in a flashback that reveals Jack's tendency towards violence when he is pushed to the edge by his underlying frustrations.

He always feels remorse, but it is partially over the act and partially over his ability to commit such violence. Once when his son, then only about two, had ruined part of a manuscript, ~ack had violently grabbed the child's arm, breaking it. All of this boils around in his head during the suffocating winter in the hotel. This brings about the books only flaw in pacing and structure. In order to show Jack's weaknesses and how he can be manipulated by the forces which lurk within the hotel, King keeps returning to the incidents which trouble Jack Torrance. After the third detailed flashback of the same incident, I felt the point was belabored. Early in the book, it becomes clear Jack has an unhealthy fixation on these past events that he can do nothing to alter. He feels like a failure. The rage bums unquenched within him, eating away at him. The powers loose in the hotel tap into this, manipulating him and giving his rage direction, pushing his precariously balanced sanity over the edge. He finally feels his family is at fault.

This book bursts with memorable scenes. The story is very visual. When it moves, it really packs a wallop. The main characters capture our interest, while Halloran is particularly powerful. King infuses Halloran's journey back to Colorado from Florida with tension and suspense, particularly when he is on the road to the hotel and hears Danny's mental S.O.S. choked off. Terrific stuff!

Halloran is a fully realized and important character in the book. Kubrick chose to kill him off in the film (he doesn't die in the book), demonstrating his lack of understanding of the material. Halloran only knows of Danny's psychic power but possesses a similar power, in much weaker form. This establishes an important link between the two characters in the reader's mind even though Dick is absent throughout most of the book until the long climax.

The book builds to such a wild, fever-pitch that it remains a classic of the form no matter how many other horror stories you've read. Because it features more characters and incidents, **Salem's Lot** works better as a whole. But **The Shining** boasts the finest climax of any King book for sheer power and imagination. It delivers a one-two punch which carries the reader straight through to the conclusion with pile-driver intensity.

In the June 17, 1980 issue of *The Boston Phoenix,* King was interviewed about Kubrick's version of **The Shining.** The author revealed his reactions to it, "I think the movie is brilliant, and at the same time I wanted *more."* Then King finally explained what bothered him about the translation of his story to the screen. "And actually, it's on the story level the movie bothers *me* the most. The movie has no heart; there's no center to the picture. I wrote the book as a tragedy, and if it *was* a tragedy, it was because all the people loved each other. Here, it seems there's no tragedy because there's nothing to be lost. And yet, the movie as a whole is scary. The camera angles and the use of the Steadicam are very upsetting and unnerving to me. So even though the family relationships are all screwed up in terms of storytelling, there's something uneasy about the whole film. And I'm not sure that what the movie achieves, it could possibly have achieved if it had gone a more commercial route."

King got the idea for **The Shining** while on a long vacation in Colorado. He had read an article about a house which supposedly stored the evil of events which transpired within. This gave him the inspiration for the haunted Overlook Hotel. What he did with those very basic ideas is a shattering experience in the literature of horror and deserves to be called one of the most frightening books ever written, right up there with Richard Matheson' s **Hell House.**

THE STAND

It was things like Howard Duck, he thought, that made you believe the world was maybe just as well off destroyed.
—*page 628*

This book works best on its second reading. The first time around you want King to get on with it already so you can see what' s going to happen next. The second time through you appreciate his diversions into the individual lives of his characters and the explorations.

This book presents a lot of interesting and memorable characters, some of whom stand out in memory long after details of the plot become elusive. The two most interesting characters in the book are the two most unlikely candidates for those positions.

Nick Andros and Tom Cullen steal the show. They make reading the book a memorable experience because they steal *all* the best scenes. Nick is a deaf-mute and Tom is mentally retarded. Both are grown men and thus have learned to deal with their handicaps. When they meet and team up, King's portrayal of their touching friendship is a genuine tour-de-force. In many ways, these-two people are more interesting than the normal, physically healthy souls they associate with. We care about these two and the tragic fate that befalls one of them. One of the most fascinating characters in the story is Harold Lauder. We first encounter him when he's a lanky, childish, over-weight sixteen year old, and then see his personality shape and develop just as a real person grows. We even understand when he makes an emotionally overwrought decision that alters his own destiny as he chooses whether to be humane or vengeful. He chooses when someone fails to live up to the fantasy he had worked out for them to participate in with him. His personality has many sides, and he becomes as two-faced as can be. We watch with interest as he becomes a secret viper in the midst of his former friend~ people who still trust him. As he becomes more spiteful, Harold becomes more interesting than the characters around him. The only off moment King has handling the character is when Harold finally decides to exact revenge, it's not referred to again for fifty pages. This is maddening. When King returns to the revenge act, I no longer remember anything that happened during those fifty frustrating pages. But I sure remember what Harold did!

Harold is just a flunky in the scheme of things. The real villain of this sprawling novel is Randall Flagg, otherwise called The Dark Man or The Walkin' Dude. Flagg stands in the background when the virus escapes the germ warfare lab to decimate over 90% of mankind. He then comes forward to organize a band of followers from the tough survivors. We learn few things about him, such as his links to the JFK assassination and the kidnapping of Patty Hearst, but little more. Clear-

THE STAND

ly evil personified, his great powers are merely hinted at. For most of the book he seems just a mysterious, awesome figure wandering the backroads of America. When he finally emerges into the foreground late in the book, his awesomeness diminishes. He appears no more unusual than an organized crime boss. While genuinely portrayed as an agent of Satan, his strength fades under close scrutiny. His characterization becomes superficial and not at all as frightening as what we had been led to expect. King has stated that he did this purposely to show that up close, evil doesn't loom large.

It doesn't work for me. I've been brainwashed by too many movies and comic books to expect a larger than life villain to look like Darth Vader or Doctor Doom when you get close up to them.

The Stand is a peculiar departure for King in that he treats religion differently than in other books. Instead of portraying religion as embraced only by the intellectually impoverished, he shows it to be unquestionably real. Mother Abagail, an old Black woman is the focus of the forces of good. She experiences genuine heavenly visions and unquestionably holds a direct link to God. She is not portrayed as crazy or ridiculous. Whether you swallow the unleavened religion depends on your own world view. She becomes the spiritual leader of the community in Boulder, Colorado (which signifies purity while the community in Las Vegas run by Flagg symbolizes evil). She tells her people what they must do because God told her so.

The main problem with this book, other than it's protracted length (Pacing? What's pacing?), is that the end-of-the-world saga is trite in both literature and films. In such a familiar setting we need unfamiliar events. The concept of an ultimate battle between Good and Evil represented by the conflict between Boulder and Las Vegas is an interesting new wrinkle, but it's never brought off We expect a final conflict and instead find things contrived and tossed off in a low key fashion with a *deus ex machina* Sodom and Gomorrah climax. We expect conflict on the order of the **The Shining** in which the stored evil in the Overlook Hotel sought to consume all. In the end that hotel appears far more powerful and threatening than Randall Flagg and his cronies.

When tackling a concept as broad and all-encompassing as Good versus Evil, the denouement must overshadow all that has led up to it. There must be sharp resolution, like a thunderclap following lightning.

Plus King competes with himself. Great expectations are brought to the book by readers who've read his other stories. He must at least equal what he's done before. In this case the book doesn't measure up to the expectations. An 800 page buildup shouldn't end on an anticlimax.

In 1989 plans are in the works for an expanded version of **The Stand** to appear with the 300 manuscript pages restored that King's editor had caused to be removed from the earlier version. It remains to be seen whether this addition makes the story better, or just longer.

THE DEAD ZONE

Only Stephen King could write a novel whose main character is named John Smith. And he makes it not only compelling, but moving and genuinely haunting. Johnny Smith is just a regular guy—a high school teacher with normal parents and a girl friend. One night he attends a carnival and experiences a bizarre run of luck on the Wheel of Fortune. His luck runs out when that night, after dropping off his

Michael R. Adams

lady, Smith suffers a traffic accident which leaves him comatose for the next four and one-half years.

While films treat a coma as just another way of looking at sleep, King documents the medical aspects, describing the techniques used on Johnny Smith in the hospital to prevent him from developing bedsores and severe ligament problems. When he finally awakens, we feel the pain he undergoes retraining his body to walk and move normally.

Johnny encounters other, more unusual, problems upon awakening. His brain now possesses a fully activated psychic ability. It enables him to know personal details about someone's past, present and future just from touching them.

Smith's experiences with this ability include a combination of hiding from the rest of humanity and confronting reality to help other people. Once he tracks down a brutal killer. Another time he saves dozens of lives when he foresees a deadly nightclub fire.

These incidents combine to force him to make a moral decision when he meets a politician. He foresees Armageddon should the man become president of the United States. It is apparent the man is well on his way to realizing his goals unless something should tip the scales. A wild card. Something unpredictable. This finally forces Smith to make the most fateful decision of his life.

King rarely approaches the exact same theme, so instead of being a horror novel, **The Dead Zone** is more accurately a bizarre mystery. The main character not only demonstrates additional talents to aid in his problem solving, but becomes part of the mystery himself.

The "dead zone" of the title is an eerie reference Smith occasionally makes when he discusses holes in his memory. Certain scattered memories disappear in the part of his brain that was bruised in the accident. Smith refers to his lost memories as being in the dead zone.

After featuring a woman in **The Stand** who has genuine divine visions, in **The Dead Zone** religion takes a drubbing in the form of Smith's mother. After his accident, Johnny's mother slowly goes insane and (like in **Carrie**) the insanity manifests itself in the form of religious fanaticism. This goes beyond religion to include most forms of unfounded supernatural belief including astrology and *National Enquirer*-**style** psychic prediction. When Smith awakens, she informs him that this is all part of "God's plan," and that his powers were given to him for a purpose, in much the same way Ellen Burstyn's character is pressured in the excellent film **Resurrection**. This makes it more difficult for Smith to separate his own abilities from the phony mysticism.

The Dead Zone is an excellent drama filled with eerie and even touching moments. This King novel sneaks up on you in small and unexpected ways instead of with the huge horrors of **Salem's Lot, The Shining** and **The Mist.** The deeply compassionate characterizations King writes so well are all here.

He just tells a little bit different story with them this time—but not *too* different.

Since you have seen the film, you probably figure the ending of the book is a foregone conclusion. But the book captures a feeling that's impossible to transfer to the screen.

STEPHEN KING

FIRESTARTER

This book was inevitably compared with **Carrie**. It deals with a young girl with a wild talent. Beyond that the two stories are totally different. **Carrie** is the better book. It is more inventive in large ways, but **Firestarter** is nonetheless very interesting.

Firestarter is a rewarding story. You don't have to wait for the end to see what young Charlie McGee can do with her power when she cuts loose in pitched battle. That occurs in the first third of the novel. In many ways that scene is more gripping than the climax.

Not a horror novel at all, this is even more of a contemporary science fiction set piece than **The Dead Zone.** The wild talents cause the characters to lead extraordinary lives, yet they remain fragile human beings.

Charlene McGee is the eight year old daughter of Andy and Vickie McGee. Her parents met during an experiment they volunteered for in college, the only test ever conducted on human beings of a powerful mind-expanding drug. The drug releases dormant psychic abilities.

Andy McGee exhibited the ability to "push," or to plant psychic-hypnotic suggestions in a person's mind—a basic form of mind control.

Vicky manifested a rudimentary form of mind over matter. Their daughter, Charlene (Charlie for short) was born with pyrokinesis—the ability to start fires. Andy and Vicky didn't know that the agency behind the testing continued watching and studying the survivors.

The agency, a secret government outfit called The Shop, is not above using strong-arm tactics to achieve their goals. Personal liberty comes second to achieving their goals; torture and murder are tools they're very quick to employ.

The father/daughter relationship between Andy and Charlie is well defined during their run from Shop agents. They quickly come across as real human beings. Even the supporting characters are all quite different, with little quirks and tics as well as genuine moments of heart-warming humanity, all too rare in this story of human exploitation.

King often reveals he's a fan of fantasy and science fiction, just like many of his readers. His books contain references to Frank Frazetta and E.C. comics. In **Firestarter** he reveals such roots quite unexpectedly when he draws upon unique metaphors to describe one of his antagonists: "Rainbird was a troll, an orc, a balrog of a man." (Page 87). The character described so vividly is a Shop hitman named John Rainbird. He's a dangerous man, Indian by descent, and missing his left eye. A runnel of scar tissue down his face offers physical reminder of an explosion in Viet Nam caused by his own side. Death fascinates Rainbird. Whenever he commits a murder, he stares into his victim's eyes in an attempt to understand what his victims witness as death overtakes them—what glimpse of the other side comes through to them. It's almost as if he expects to see that vision reflected in their dying eyes. Rainbird looks forward to performing this same experiment on Charlie McGee.

Like all of King's best works, many little details add up to support the larger story. Little things like the after effects of Andy using his mental "push." This not only includes piercing and potentially deadly headaches in himself, but effects in others, too. For instance, when he tells a cab driver that a one dollar bill is actually a five hundred dollar bill, there is a residual effect on the currency. Other people who touch the dollar have a startling, momentary flash of seeing it turn into a five hundred. Then there's the Shop agent whom Andy "pushed" to sleep and who didn't wake up for two weeks and then continued to follow the suggestion whenever anyone spoke the word sleep.

Another effect is what Andy calls a ricochet, in which a mind "pushed" too hard may begin to come apart because a secret fear forced into their conscious mind dominates all coherent thoughts. This ricochet causes one man to go mad, dress up in women's clothing and commit suicide by sticking his arm in a garbage disposal. Another becomes paranoid about non-existent snakes and his sanity slowly disintegrates. Usually Andy can control the ricochet and undo it, but when he's dealing with his enemies he isn't able to stick around long enough to indulge in that luxury.

The only cavil I have with this book is that it shows elements reminiscent of **The Fury** by John Farris (which was made into a fair movie by Brian DePalma). **The Fury** details the internecine conflict between two secret government agencies over the acquisition and exploitation of a boy who possesses vast psychic powers. The the boy's father, an agent himself, tries to undermine the efforts of both groups and rescue his son. The similarities may be only thematic but they're still cut from the same cloth in much the same way that two werewolf stories might be compared for employing similar basic themes. The two books might be read together as bookends on the same idea—government exploitation of people with psi powers as both stories climax in catastrophes.

CUJO

While this book offers interesting scenes and some very funny bits in the first half, the second half is bloated and drawn out. It comes across as a puffed up short story.

The story involves a man who split from the New York advertising scene to open his own business in Maine. The first third of the book includes a darkly humorous subplot about their biggest client, a cereal company, who considers dumping them when a batch of their raspberry-flavored cereal has an unpleasant (but harmless) side effect. It turns some people's excrement red. The character in the television spots used to advertise the product becomes the butt of nationwide jokes (including bits by Johnny Carson and George Carlin), and the two ad men have to scramble to save the account and their careers. This part works wonderfully, but the primary plot offers little more than subplot material. A man's wife and young son get trapped in their car by a rabid dog for *days and days*.

The book falls to the ground. Prior to this prolonged, pointless sequence we are carefully introduced to all of the characters, including the dog, Cujo. We even meet the dog's owners, marvelously portrayed small town people. They are more interesting than the book's main characters. The advertising man has a six year old son whom we come to know quite well. We also come to know that a malevolent spirit lives in the little boy's closet—the spirit of Frank Dodd, the Castle Rock Killer from **The Dead Zone.** The character of the little boy is well depicted, particularly since he's only six years old. That's the set-up.

Once the boy and the mother become trapped in the car the plot grinds to a screeching halt. This sequence grinds on with one repetitious scene after another for one hundred and fifty pages~ Only occasional plot asides relieve the tedium. The scene just goes on and on until a bitter, ugly resolution. Just as they're rescued, the little boy dies. Although King seemingly didn't intend it that way, the death comes across as the mother's punishment for leading a sordid, extramarital affair. It's all the more frustrating because although the baleful ghost appears now and then throughout the story to tease and tantalize, nothing is ever done with it. What was the point of including it in the story at all? It's a very obvious dangling plot thread.

I've enjoyed and admired a great deal of King's fiction, but this one he really fumbled. Disposing of the child like that causes the whole book to unravel at the end.

A keen disappointment.

CYCLE OF THE WEREWOLF

Although not really a novel, this novella appears as an individual story in a single volume illustrated by Berni Wrightson.

Told in twelve chapters, each section takes place in a different month beginning consecutively with January. Each month the werewolf appears and kills in a different way. All of the crimes are horrible. The worst is the slaughter of an eleven year old boy. Only the werewolf holds the story together for the first six chapters, the continuing thread being the bloody murders it commits. Little by little the townspeople come to believe that something extraordinary is loose.

The first person to see the killer and live is ten year old Marty Coslaw, a boy in a wheelchair. When the Fourth of July celebration is cancelled, Marty takes his firecrackers and decides to have his own holiday. The werewolf shows up as an uninvited guest. Through boldness Marty drives it off, but now he knows the truth. Now he knows what killed his friend, Brady, even if no one will quite believe what he saw. No one but his uncle. Then the war of nerves begins. The war in which Marty has to discover who the werewolf is and then use himself as bait in a trap.

This is a very effective little story although it's somewhat unbalanced since the protagonist isn't introduced until halfway through. I would have liked to have seen much more of Marty earlier on but the quirky structure of the story prevents that. (This was remedied when King adapted the story for the screen as **Silver Bullet.**) As interesting as this story is, the front end is your typical werewolf tale punctuated with such interesting bits as a man coming into a cafe and soon turning into a werewolf and slaying the patrons. There's even an unusual scene in which a lonely woman fantasizes that the werewolf is some lover come to her, even as it murders her. But in the second half of the story, when Marty starts sending threatening notes to the beast's human form, things become interesting.

This certainly doesn't do for werewolves what King did for vampires in **Salem's Lot,** but it's still a lot of fun. The writing style is looser and more straightforward, almost as though it was a documentary. That adds to the overall moodiness of the piece.

The accompanying artwork by Berni Wrightson is very good, particularly the black and white pen work, but then the whole point of King writing the story was so that Wrightson could illustrate it.

PET SEMATARY

This is the novel King, at first, found too terrible to publish. He finished it and put it aside. Actually King has written much stronger stories. This one is disturbing in that the focal point becomes the death of a young child and how it changes the lives of everyone in his family.

Louis Creed is a doctor who moves with his family from Chicago to a small town in Maine. Part of the reason he does this is to get away from his wife's parents—particularly her father who has always hated Creed and never approved of his daughter's choice for a husband. Creed's new home in Maine rests by a thick woods which contains an odd burial ground for children's pets, with a crudely lettered sign by it which reads PET SEMATARY. Through the woods and up a hill lies another, much older burial ground, one dating back to the time of the Micmac Indians who originally settled the region. Creed hears legends about that burial ground, how those buried there can return from the dead. Creed tries an experiment when the pet cat, Church, is killed. Then when his young son is struck by a truck, Creed's grief overcomes his better judgement. Desperately, he digs up his son's body.

The plot of this novel is predictable, the ending infuriating. We want to know what happens next because the ending doesn't offer a proper resolution. It reads as if a chapter is missing.

The best parts of the story involve Louis Creed's relationship with Judson Crandall, an elderly neighbor. Creed's father died when Louis was just a boy so he really takes to this man. It's annoying when the character is later dumped unceremoniously instead of employed in a dignified fashion the way Halloran was in **The Shining.** In fact, King gets rid of Crandall in the same misguided way director Kubrick got rid of Halloran in the filmed version of **The Shining.** Good scenes include the fight between Creed and his father-in-law at the little boy's funeral, and the chapter which convinces you all the horrors Creed underwent were just a dream, until he actually wakes up and learns they were all too real.

One scene exemplifies the core problem of this book: when Creed goes to the cemetery to dig up his son's body. This scene is telegraphed early in the book. Otherwise the journey to the ancient burial ground won't follow. Yet King spends twenty pages describing how Louis breaks into the cemetery, digs up the body and carries it back to his car. Since it was obvious this is what he was going to do and nothing surprising happens along the way, why use twenty pages when far less would have worked more effectively? Too many pages describe too little in this book, and yet, at 374 pages, it is one of King's shorter novels. It doesn't hold together. Ideas aren't explored or developed very well. Perhaps even King realizes that parts of it don't work as he has reportedly revised the story in adapting it into a screenplay for the feature to be filmed by George Romero.

THE TALISMAN
(with Peter Straub)

This isn't really a horror novel (in spite of the cover blurbs), but rather a fantasy adventure. The story jumps back and forth between our world and the parallel world known as The Territories. Everyone in our world has a counterpart of themselves in the other, except for 12 year old Jack Sawyer. He's special, but it takes him awhile to learn just how special. The forces out to stop him aleady know and hunt him on his journey across America. His goal is to locate a talisman which will save both the life of his mother (who is dying of cancer) and the Territories version of his mother—the Queen of that other world. Along the way Jack is victimized by evil both in our world and in the Territories.

The hundred pages in which Jack is held prisoner in a home for wayward boys grips our attention. He is held in our world by a man who calls himself The Sunshine Gardner. This harrowing encounter is all the more interesting because Jack has a traveling companion with him, a werewolf from The Territories. Only in The Territories, this werewolf clan is honor-bound never to harm humans. Finally, when the time of the month comes around, Wolf can no longer tolerate imprisonment. The result is a deadly and poignant confrontation.

This excursion into fantasy works much better than the Gunslinger stories do. It is better thought out and we don't have to invent motivations for the main character. In The Gunslinger saga, after five stories we still don't know what's so important about the quest! While **The Talisman** is longer than it needs to be, it fits better into 770 pages, and is far more satisfying, than Pet **Sematary** is at half that length.

The hero, Jack Sawyer, is the modern day descendant of such literary boy heroes as namesake Tom Sawyer. Jack even has an Uncle Tommy, but he's dead before the quest begins. Unlike other boyhood adventurers, Jack lights out because he's forced to, not because he's footloose and fancy free. A grim determination to see it through, no matter how bad things fuels his adventures. And things do get pretty bad. This is King's second quest novel (**The Stand** being his first), but it's of a very different kind. And unlike the climax of **The Stand,** the final confrontation between Good and Evil takes place between the principal characters. It is fought without any divine intervention. While The Talisman plays a key role, Jack controls it and decides the outcome.

A very satisfying book, it was King's longest until he embarked on his third quest novel, one which encapsulated some of the author's favorite themes all in one story.

IT

In the autumn of 1957, It began to kill again. This time people noticed that the deaths were more than just the actions of a random killer. There was method in the madness. This was by no means the first time such violence had struck the town of Derry, Maine. It has struck approximately every 27 years since Derry existed. This time someone plans to confront it and stop its murderous rampage. All seven of those uniting against It could easily number among It's victims as they're each eleven years old.

This is another quest novel, but of a different variety. Two stories run concurrently. The first tells how the seven youths met and finally came to understand what was going on in Derry, and what to do about it. The second story shows a parallel to the first but takes place 27 years later when the killings start again. Those who had left Derry (all but one had) return to face It again—they hope for the final time.

We learn a great deal about the seven (six boys and one girl) as well as about their enemies. Their life in 1957 recalls the characters in "The Body," as well as in the film version, **Stand By Me.** In fact the film and this novel came out so close together that comparisons can be easily drawn. One might even call this *Stand By Me Meets The Monsters.*

What makes the creature, It, unusual is that we don't see its true form until the climax, but we do meet It many times. It often appears as a strange man named Pennywise who is garbed as a clown. When he confronts his victims, It is usually as a fearsome image pulled from their minds. Since children fear monsters, It ap

"The Boogeyman"

STEPHEN KING

pears as such cinema demons as the Creature from the Black Lagoon, Frankenstein and the Wolfman. It almost never appears as the same creature twice.

This book offers more than just a story of a monster on the rampage. At 1,138 pages it's an epic novel about the dark underside of a rural community in Maine. While Derry is fictitious, its history is not always so. Incidents explored include the firebombing of a black enlisted men's club in the Forties as well as the massacre of a criminal gang ambushed by a number of Derry's law-abiding citizens in the Twenties. We meet the people of Derry and learn they're not as different from big city folks as they'd like you to think.

While incredibly long, It tells an interesting story, although I did find myself hitting a wall around page 800. I needed my second wind before I could continue. The structure King uses infuriates as it is by no means sequential. Just as we're captivated by the older versions of the group (who call themselves The Losers because they were all outcasts as kids), the plot drops back to 1957. Then just as we're engrossed in that earlier time, it flips to the future again for a couple hundred pages. While it becomes evident why King's doing this near the end of the book (the two story's climaxes are inter-related and similar in many ways. Except the first time, when they face It in its lair, they all get out alive).

Plans are underway to turn It into an ABC mini-series. It should translate well into film as the complicated story will only have time to unfold its essentials. If adapted well, the mini-series will tell a much leaner, tighter story. Due to its length, the novel never builds a continuous head of steam. It fails to move along under its own power such as Peter Straub's **Floating Dragon** does. The latter is also a novel of a small New England town under siege by an ancient evil. The many small details of **It**, while interesting in themselves, prevent the sprawling story from forming a cohesive whole. King seems not to have wanted the novel to end. He wanted to keep on telling and keep coming back day after day to plunge once more into that well of nostalgia, rich depths he created for his characters to travel in.

THE EYES OF THE DRAGON
(Reviewed by Kevin Mangold)

The Eyes of the Dragon is probably the most bizarre book I have ever read. King starts the book by dedicating it to his daughter. It seems he had a classic fairy tale in mind at the start, but as he wrote it changed to a story for an older audience. **The Eyes of the Dragon** delights the reader. It's a love story, a fairy tale, a tragedy, a devotional and, among other traits, imparts a bit of wisdom. I compare this book to **The Little Prince** by Antoine De Saint Expury. **The Little Prince** is a most effective work so full of wisdom one can't help but heed its teachings and apply them to life. **The Eyes of the Dragon** is much the same; a story about a royal family in a place called Delain. Roland, the King of Delain and his wife, Sasha, had two children, both boys, Peter, the eldest, and Thomas. The story tells the tale of their lives. From the start, Sasha teaches her first son that the two natures of man are GOD and DOG. He promises her he will follow the ways of God and will use his napkin. Sasha told Peter to always do the right thing, and she used the etiquette of using a napkin at the dinner table as a metaphor to following God's word.

The book continually reminds the reader of the travels of Jesus in Jerusalem, teaching his disciples to do the right thing. Much like Jesus, after delivering her message to her son, Sasha died, leaving Peter to survive with the few teachings she had delivered onto him.

The relationship between the family members was strange even at the beginning. Roland wanted children so he would have an heir to his throne but he had no desire for his wife whatsoever. In fact, he had to get drunk once a month just to sleep with her. Finally two sons are born. Peter, the eldest, should rightfully be the heir to his father's throne but Flagg, the King's magician, is determined to see that Roland's youngest son, Thomas, is crowned instead. This is where the story begins.

The book contains everything a good fairy tale should: A deceivingly simple structure with lots of dragons, wizards, castles and heroes. The book is difficult to put down. It captivates with fast-paced story- telling. King doesn't waste a lot of time on detail, but rather covers a lot of ground. Still, of course, King's writing style is present in every word.

I would have to be a much better storyteller than I am, I think, to tell you how it was for Peter during the five years he spent at the top of the Needle. He ate; he slept; he looked out the window, which gave him a view to the west of the city; he exercised morning, noon, and evening; he dreamed his dreams of freedom. In the summer his apartment sweltered. In the winter it froze.

During the second winter he caught a bad case of the grippe which almost killed him.

Peter lay feverish and coughing under the thin blanket on his bed. At first, he was only afraid he would lapse into delirium and rave about the rope that was hidden in a neat coil under two of the stone blocks on the east side of his bedroom. As his fever grew worse, the rope he had woven with the tiny dollhouse loom came to seem less important, because he began to think he would die.

This example illustrates the faster than normal pace he keeps while preserving all of his style. **The Eyes of the Dragon** is different from any other King has written. He seems to have had a lot of fun with this one and it shows he can handle other types of writing. There are even a few works of poetry in this book. The book is nicely illustrated by David Palladini.

The Eyes of the Dragon is a powerful experience that will stay with the reader.

MISERY

Paul Sheldon was a novelist who had been in an auto accident. A nurse by the name of Annie comes to his aid. . . to aid him in a nightmare. Annie tells Paul that she is his biggest fan and that she is there to encourage him to continue his writing. What Paul doesn't know is how far Annie will go to see his next book finished. Annie not only wants another book, but his best work ever. And she wants it all for herself.

This story begins with a little bit of discomfort and proceeds to sheer terror. **Misery** is written in classic King style. It both scares and presents some very solid characters. King once again shows that he has the ability to shock, and to hold the reader on the edge of their seat. It is one of those books that will stay with you. Evidence the following excerpt:

I won't scream!

He sat in the window, totally awake now, totally aware that the police car he was seeing in Annie's driveway was as real as his left foot had once been.

Scream! Goddammit, scream!

STEPHEN KING

He wanted to, but the dictum was too strong—just too strong. He couldn't even open his mouth. He tried and saw the brownish droplets of Betadine flying from the blade of the electric knife. He tried and heard the squeal of axe against bone, the soft flump as the match in her hand lit the Benz-O-Matic .

He tried to open his mouth and couldn't.

Tried to raise his hands. Couldn't.

A horrible moaning sound passed between his closed lips and his hands made light, haphazard drumming sounds on either side of the Royal, but that was all he could do, all the control of his destiny he could seem to take. Nothing which had gone before—except perhaps for the moment when he had realized that, although his left leg was moving, his left foot was staying put—was as terrible as the hell of this immobility. In real time it did not last long; perhaps five seconds and surely no longer than ten. But inside Paul Sheldon's head it seemed to go on for years.

Once again, King tells the story of a person who has been taken. He gains our sympathy and pulls us close to the characters as if they were in our own lives.

THE TOMMYKNOCKERS
(Reviewed by Phil Gardner)

Stephen King consistently weaves wonderful stories out of the most basic ideas. Starting out with an old, used loom like an everyday alien invasion story, he shuttles the yarn (pun intended) back and forth, skillfully tieing all of the ends together. In **The Tommyknockers**, however, the picture on the tapestry at the end leaves a little to be desired. Like **The Stand, The Tommyknockers** has some very well written and memorable scenes. Unfortunately, none of them are anywhere near the end.

The story centers around a strange artifact found, nee, stumbled across, in the woods behind Bobbi Anderson's house. When Bobbi starts to dig it up, thinking that it is perhaps just a can or something, she finds that it is a lot larger than she had at first thought. She continues to dig it up as strange things start to occur.

The artifact affects first Bobbi and Peter, making them healthier and smarter, and then, as more and more of it is dug up, the entire town. Soon everyone is running around inventing strange Rube Goldberg devices and 'becoming.'

Unfortunately, 'becoming' does not seem all that conducive to human health. James Gardener, poet, alcoholic, wife-shooter, and friend to Bobbi, shows up just in time to catch a frail, wasted Bobbi when she collapses from exhaustion. After getting the story from her, he agrees to help dig up the ship.

King continues to weave a brilliant story, bringing us into the lives of those affected by the ship, until the final third of the novel. The ending is very weak considering the vast potential of Gardener and the ship. In order to make room for this ending, King kills off three of the most memorable characters in the story, one of whom was just introduced in the flesh a mere thirty pages before. Surely Anne Anderson could have been used more effectively if she had been brought around beforehand instead of being trundled out in the end to be used as cannon fodder.

As always, the characterizations of the major protagonists at the beginning of the story are excellent. For instance, Bobbi Anderson's love for her dog, Peter, is suggested so strongly that you start to feel her agony over his eventual death. And when he disappears from the story the reader is left feeling, just as Gardener, that something was not kosher with Bobbi.

The actual physical, mental, and emotional changes in the cast are an interesting twist on the old 'Invasion From Space' theme. When the people begin to invent 'gadgets' to do various and sundry things, from heating water to electrocuting their husbands, the reader is left wondering what could be done for humankind if a scientist had been there to be affected. It soon became apparent, however, that the gadgets would not be the end of the affair. The people of Haven, good, solid, hardworking farmer-salt of the earth type of people, actually started to become violent, flying into acts of rage and revenge for the tiniest little things. Not the type of people one would like to bring home to mom. Eventually the townspeople start to change, becoming a sort of half breed between humans and whatever the ships original owners were. It became, in fact, apparent that the ship was 'alive' and that the original 'souls' or ghosts of the 'Tommyknockers,' as Gardener called them, were still hanging around to possess the people.

The conclusion of the story is not only weak, but very predictable. Even that predictability would not have mattered much if the ending had not been so poorly written. The reader is left with a feeling of disappointment, of having wasted time reading the last two to three hundred pages.

King has always written fascinating stories with amazing skill. To take as simple an idea as a buried spaceship and twist it into a mind and body altering, haunted spaceship was brilliant. Even though it suffers from a poor ending, this is definitely a ghost/horror/science-fiction/alien story well worth the reading.

THE BACHMAN BOOKS

Sometimes you find that certain book that, for one reason or another, just seems to hit you with a wallop. This has proven to be the case for me with quite a few books by Stephen King. It seems that King's name is almost synonymous with horror, but there is another side to the writer that is responsible for such masterpieces as "The Body," the novella from which came the unforgettable movie **Stand By Me***. The side of Stephen King to which I am referring shows its face in only a few of his works, but to me these are among his best. These stories tell of the trials of the underdog, and the injustices of the world. Much like* **Stand By Me***, the Bachman Books tell the story of a character who has been smitten by the more fortunate and less caring. The realism of these stories is the best part. The good guy doesn't always win, and the less than good do not always get their just reward. This is the theme that stands out, to me, in all of the Bachman Books .*

RAGE
Review by Kevin Mangold

"The morning I got it on was nice," was how Stephen King started the first of *The Bachman Books*. As the boy, Charles Decker, threatened the lives of his classmates,the reader finds himself asking, "And why shouldn't he?" This is one of the powers that King has. He has a way of grabbing the reader by the collar and forcing self evaluation. Quite often the reader is surprised by the answer. I remember when reading **The Shining** I stopped in the middle of the page and realized that I was actually cheering when Jack Torrance stalked his own son.

King can slowly manipulate the reader into rooting for a killer, which was the case in **Rage** . Charley Decker became a representative of all the children in the world who have had sand kicked in their faces by the big guys, both literally and figuratively. I wanted him to get even with Ted Jones. Ted exists in the memory of each of us. He *was* a lot of us. Ted is the kid who had everything. He was the popular, good-looking never-to-fail type. The type that tore out the hearts of others without meaning to. The type who out-did everyone without putting forth a bit of effort, when others would give their lives to have just a little bit of what he had. Ted wasn't a bad person. In fact, he was quite a good kid. He was the pride of the school, the pride of his parents. He seemed to make all the right decisions. Ted was exactly the product the adults in his life had formed him to be. Charles wasn't and that's why Dicky Cable beat him up years ago.

He was laughing. He grabbed my head and slammed it into the ground like a whiffle ball. "Hey, pretty boy!"

Slam. Interior stars and the taste of grass in my mouth.

Now I was the lawnmower. "Hey pretty boy, don't you look nice?" He picked my head up by the hair and slammed it down again. I started to cry.

His day starting normally, Charley Decker sets fire to his locker, eventually shoots his teacher and holds his classmates at gunpoint. The storyline was really a clever way for King to tell the story of each kid in the class. Yet there is still plenty of the typical King gore and suspense. One memorable section of the story tells of when a bullet from the barrel of a sharpshooter's rifle tore into Charley's chest.

The impact of the slug knocked me straight backward against the blackboard, where the chalk ledge bit cruelly into my back. Both of my cordovan loafers flew off. I hit the floor on my fanny. I didn't know what had happened. There was too much all at once. A huge auger of pain drilled my chest, followed by sudden numbness. The ability to breathe stopped. Spots flashed in front of my eyes.

This action came at a time when the reader begins to feel that Charley is regaining his dignity and his sanity. The reader is again rooting for the madman when they shoot him. Throughout the pages of **Rage**, King develops each character to emotionally involve the reader. This is the side of Stephen King that works best, the in-depth character studies. The kids finally learn they each have their own problems and the story is allowed to fold to a close. **Rage** is best enjoyed by anyone who has ever felt a bit cheated, a bit angry.

THE LONG WALK
Review by Kevin Mangold

Perhaps King's best work. **The Long Walk** is a story that will stay with the reader for a long time. After finishing this book, a reader will pay much closer attention to relationships and the things in life that are taken for granted. The premise of this story is bizarre and terrifying, and full of emotion. The reader becomes more and more attached to the kids involved in an outrageous competition.

The Long Walk is a competition in which death is the competitor's only way out. As the teenagers tread the asphalt path, careful not to drop below the designated minimum speed, they grow attached to each other. The last remaining walker is the winner. Winner of what? Good question. Whatever it is, is it enough to justify watching your friends die beside you? Of course to most of us no prize could ever be great enough to pull us into such a competition, but these kids believed they had nothing better to do with their lives. I hated this story and I loved it. I hated it because I saw children being tortured by their own minds. They grasped at a way out of the gutter in which they lived. One kid winning this competition meant that another had to lose. It's a pity, but this is often the nature of competition. The losers didn't have to worry about ridicule, because after this race, there is only one survivor.

The story is about Ray Garraty, a boy who shares a lot of the qualities of Charlie Decker. Garraty was the son of an alcoholic father. He had little more in his life than Jan, his girlfriend, back home. Garraty had promised Jan that he would return, though she pleaded with him to stay away from the competition. Garraty knew that he had no other way to provide Jan with the type of life he thought she deserved. Each kid in the race comes from the same background, and they are all determined to win.

The Walkers were a typical bunch of kids, complete with raging hormones and uncertain opinions. Garraty, at one point, ran up to a spectator, grabbed her breasts and escaped with a kiss before the soldiers could issue a warning. At another point, much later in the walk, he is faced with a situation of another kind. As Garraty continued to walk, one of the other boys, McVries, started the following conversation:

"You're all crazy," Parker said amiably. "I'm getting out of here." He put on a little speed and had soon nearly disappeared into the blinking shadows.

"He thinks we're queer for each other," McVries said, amused.

"He what?" Garraty's head snapped up.

"He's not such a bad guy," McVries said thoughtfully. He cocked a humorous eye at Garraty. "Maybe he's even half-right. Maybe that's why I saved your ass. Maybe I'm queer for you."

"With a face like mine? I thought you perverts liked the willowy type." Still, he was suddenly uneasy.

Suddenly, shockingly, McVries said: "Would you let me jerk you off?"

Garraty hissed in breath. "What the hell...."

"Oh shut up," McVries said crossly. "Where do you get off with all this self-righteous shit? I'm not even going to make it any easier by letting you know if I'm joking. What say?"

Garraty felt a sticky dryness in his throat. The thing was, he wanted to be touched. Queer, not queer, that didn't seem to matter now that they were all busy dying. All that mattered was McVries. He didn't want McVries to touch him, not that way.

"Well I suppose you did save my life...." Garraty let it hang.

McVries laughed. "I'm supposed to feel like a heel because you owe me something and I'm taking advantage? Is that it?"

"Do what you want," Garraty said shortly. "But quit playing games."

"Does that mean yes?"

"Whatever you want!" Garraty yelled. Pearson, who had been staring, nearly hypnotized, at his feet, looked up, startled. "Whatever you goddam want!" Garraty yelled.

McVries laughed again. "You're all right, Ray. Never doubt it." He clapped Garraty's shoulder and dropped back.

The boys were real. Again, this storyline is an exciting way to meet a lot of interesting people. They seem to go through every stage of life. They start out being very selfish and competitive and throughout the ordeal slowly change their ways until they find sympathy for their opponents. Some actually offer to die in the place of another. I found myself really feeling bad for these guys as they came to realize exactly what they had gotten themselves into. Of course, there was no backing out once the Walk was under way, although many tried. The losers didn't simply get walked off the road either. They were taken care of right on the spot.

Suddenly Curley screamed. Garraty looked back over his shoulder. Curley was doubled over, holding his leg and screaming. Somehow, incredibly, he was still walking, but very slowly. Much too slowly.

Everything went slowly then, as if to match the way Curley was walking. The soldiers on the back of the slow-moving halftrack raised their guns. The crowd gasped, as if they hadn't known this was the way it was, and the Walkers gasped, as if they hadn't known, and Garraty gasped with them, but of course he had known, of course they had all known, it was very simple, Curley was going to get his ticket.

The safeties clicked off. Boys scattered from around Curley like quail. He was suddenly alone on the sunwashed road.

"It isn't fair!" he screamed. "It just isn't fair!"

The walking boys entered a leafy glade of shadow, some of them looking back, some of them looking straight ahead, afraid to see. Garraty was looking. He had to look. The scatter of waving spectators had fallen silent as if someone had simply clicked them all off.

"It isn't-"

Four carbines fired. They were very loud. The noise traveled away like bowling balls, struck the hills, and rolled back.

47

Curley's angular, pimply head disappeared in a hammersmash of blood and brains and flying skull-fragments. The rest of him fell forward on the white line like a sack of mail.

There's a whole array of Long Walk stories from years past. Tales of the winners as well as the losers. This story would make a wonderful movie so long as Stephen King has control.

ROADWORK
Review by Kevin Mangold

Again King tells the story of a child who has been dealt some bad cards. Only in **Roadwork**, this child is living in the body of an adult. What does a person do when all that he has worked for in his life is jeopardized by something called "progress?" Again, King puts the reader into someone else's situation. What would the reader do in the circumstances? Perhaps the same thing that Barton George Dawes did. He started his diary with the purchase of a thousand dollars worth of weapons and ammunition. While in the gun shop, he tells the owner that the construction of the 784 extension is giving them one year to find a new house.

Throughout the story the reader learns about the long list of injustices that have been shoveled at George Barton. Among them, the loss of his wife and son. The roadwork that tore Barton's life apart was not only the construction outside, but also the roadwork that God had decided to do on his son's brain. **Roadwork** is the story of a man who, much like Charlie Decker, is trying to regain his pride and his sanity.

That night sitting in front of the Zenith TV, he found himself thinking about how he and Mary had found out, almost forty-two months ago now, that God had decided to do a little roadwork on their son Charlie's brain.

The doctor's name had been Younger. There was a string of letters after his name on the framed diplomas that hung on the warmly paneled walls of his inner office, but all he understood for sure was Younger was a neurologist; a fast man with a good brain disease.

He and Mary had gone to see him at Younger's request on a warm June afternoon nineteen days after Charlie had been admitted to Doctors Hospital. He was a good-looking man, maybe halfway through his forties, physically fit from a lot of golf played with no electric golf cart. He was tanned a deep cordovan shade. And the doctor's hands fascinated him. They were huge hands, clumsy-looking, but they moved about his desk— now picking up a pen, now riffling through his appointment book, now playing idly across the surface of a silver-inlaid paperweight— with a lissome grace that was very nearly repulsive.

"Your son has a brain tumor," he said. He spoke flatly, with little inflection, but his eyes watched them very carefully, as if he had just armed a temperamental explosive.

George finally gets what he wants, but as in the typical King novel, the ending astonishes.

THE RUNNING MAN

Forget about the movie. Just drop-kick it out of your immediate perception because all that film has in common with the book is the title, the name of the main character and the death hunt gameshow called "The Running Man."

Thus far, this is King's only run at a full tilt science fiction novel set in the next century. It has all the trappings of such fare and reads like it is about the tenth such novel the writer has done because the texture and the everyday details of life in the year 2025 flow so convincingly on the page.

The world King portrays is what we fear the world 35 years from now might be like if certain trends continue unchecked. The population has risen and with it the vast poverty-stricken underclass. Pollution is taken for granted and television (called Free-Vee) is piped to the populace to keep them quiet, indoors and out of trouble as much as possible. Television has literally become a tool of quiet government suppression because with so many people out of work, they have nothing else to do. The Free-Vee keeps people from thinking too much about their status in life. This unfolds gradually throughout the story, but the kind of world that Ben Richards lives in, and the crushing poverty which drives him to volunteer for the often deadly game shows (like "Treadmill To Bucks" and "Swim The Crocodiles"—big prizes with big risks) is described in a nutshell in one scene. Ben Richards is on his way to the Games Building to try to earn money for his sick baby and to keep his wife from having to prostitute herself any more to make ends meet.

A rat trotted lazily, lousily across the cracked and blistered cement of the street. Across the way, the ancient and rusted skeleton of a 2013 Humber stood on decayed axles. It had been completely stripped, even to the wheel bearings and motor mounts, but the cops didn't take it away. The cops rarely ventured south of the canal any more. Co-Op City stood in a radiating rat warren of parking lots, deserted shops, Urban Centers and paved playgrounds. The cycle gangs were the law here, and all those newsie items about the intrepid Block Police of South City were nothing but a pile of warm crap. The streets were ghostly, silent. If you went out, you took the pneumo bus or you carried a gas cylinder.

He walked fast, not looking around, not thinking. The air was sulphurous and thick. Four cycles roared past and someone threw a ragged hunk of asphalt paving. Richards ducked easily. Two pneumo buses passed him, buffeting him with air, but he did not flag them. The week's twenty-dollar unemployment allotment (old bucks) had been spent. There was no money to buy a token. He supposed the roving packs could sense his poverty. He was not molested.

King emphasizes the anger Ben Richards has towards being poor. He'd quit the one regular job he'd had working at General Atomics because he knew the constant exposure to radiation would make him sterile, and he wanted a family. He was labeled a trouble-maker after that and work became increasingly hard to find until finally there was none at all.

The unspoken undercurrent of this story is that with a population too large to adequately support itself, life becomes cheap. Ergo General Atomics doesn't care that their workers are being irradiated. Plenty more where they came from. The government doesn't care if people engage in harmless pursuits like dope and illicit sex because it keeps the poor happy on meaningless levels and thus prevents widespread anger which would lead to rebellion. There aren't even newspapers any more because almost no one cares about reading when they can watch the Free-Vee.

Ben Richards carries his anger with him ill disguised. When he's in the Games Building and is in a line being herded along by police (some prospective contestants become violent when they don't pass muster) the following scene takes place:

There was a line of perhaps twenty applicants waiting at the elevators. Richards showed one of the cops on duty his card and the cop looked at him closely. "You a hardass, sonny?"

"Hard enough," Richards said, and smiled.

The cop gave him back his card. "They'll kick it soft again. How smart do you talk with holes in your head, sonny?"

"Just about as smart as you talk without that gun on your leg and your pants down around your ankles," Richards said, still smiling. "Want to try it?"

When Richards is chosen for the top rated show, "The Running Man," he knows that at least his family will be provided for. The object of the show is to go on the run and avoid being killed by the Hunters for 30 days. But while one would think that people would side with Richards the way they would with any underdog, the show fills the in-house studio audience with people who scream for the contestant's blood, and the show does its best to make the runner look like the worst human refuse. Someone who deserves to be hunted down and crushed out. So Richards cannot expect to find much help on the street.

He's given an advance on his winnings (he earns $100.00 for every hour he stays alive and for every hunter he kills) and a head start. He proves his resourcefulness time and again, staying just ahead of the hunters and sometimes barely eluding them in violent confrontations. We learn more about the society of 2025 from the people he meets and those who help him. When one of them wises up Richards to the way that air pollution is killing people because the government won't bother providing cheap noseplug filters for them, Richards tries to warn his fellow members of the great underclass, but is unsuccessful. This shows the broad characterization of Richards so that we can see that he cares for his fellow man in spite of some of the things he's driven to do to stay alive.

When he kidnaps a woman in her car in order to escape a roadblock, the differences between the rich and the poor become evident. The woman he's kidnapped doesn't believe anything Richards tells her, but when the police try to kill them both to keep Richards from getting away, the woman finds her whole concept of reality breaking down. She's a hostage, but the police don't care. They tried to kill her because life is cheap, as the woman realizes with shocking suddenness and which King captures expertly in the following passage:

The mask of the well-to-do young hausfrau on her way back from the market now hung in tatters and shreds. Beneath it was something from the cave, something with twitching lips and rolling eyes. Perhaps it had been there all along.

Richards contacts the press to announce that he has a hostage and which route he'll be taking. The police won't chance trying to kill the hostage to get him if there's witnesses, so an uneasy standoff results as Richards and his hostage cruise down the road in her car, on the way to an airport, while people are lined up on either side watching him, including hundreds of policemen. Here too we see the disparity between the rich and the poor:

Here on the right, folks, we have the summer people, Richards thought. Fat and sloppy but heavy with armor. On the left, weighing in at only a hundred and thirty—but a scrappy contender with a mean and rolling eyeball—we have the Hungry Honkies. Therein are the politics of starvation; they'd roll Christ Himself for a pound of salami. Polarization comes to West Sticksville. Watch out for those two contenders, though. They don't stay in the ring; they have a tendency to fight in the ten-dollar seats. Can we find a goat to hang up for both of them?

This continues as Richards pulls off a bold bluff in order to get an airplane, and continues up under the watchful gaze of the police who want very much to grease the car and its occupants but can't do what they want, what they'd ordinarily do, because the wrong people would see them do it.

The service ramp described a rising arc around the glassine, futuristic Northern States Terminal. The way was lined with police holding everything from Mace-B and tear gas to heavy armor-piercing weaponry. Their faces were flat, dull, uniform. Richards drove slowly, sitting up straight now, and they looked at him with vacant, bovine awe. In much the same way, Richards thought, that cows must look at a farmer who had gone mad and lies kicking and sunfishing and screaming on the barn floor.

King is harder on this book than he need be. Written, astonishingly, in 72 hours, he states in his introduction to the omnibus volume **The Bachman Books** that the novel is, *"nothing but story—it moves with the goofy speed of a silent movie, and anything which is not story is cheerfully thrown over the side."*

And yet as swiftly paced as this novel is, the details which create a willing suspension of disbelief are in great abundance. Characterization, a hallmark of King's books, may be lean in **The Running Man**, but it is not absent and if anything is more tightly focused and quickly nailed down. We may never learn anything about the background of Ben Richards' wife, but that doesn't reduce her importance as a key person in the main character's life.

This is the kind of book to read and reread because a writer can learn a great deal about the structure and pacing of a book from this, and about how to tell a rich, solid story.

THINNER

This was the last novel to appear under the Richard Bachman pseudonym and is the one which finally broke it all open. Unlike the other four "Bachman" books, this was not one of King's pre-**Carrie** unpublished novels, but rather a new book written specifically to appear under the Bachman name. It reads like a modern work of King's even if it does include a reference to King himself when the main character remarks that what's happening is like something out of a Stephen King book.

This is the only Bachman book which truly falls into the horror category. Also unlike the previous Bachman books (which were written at a time when King was still a struggling writer trying to make ends meet) the worldview is not quite as pessimistic. But then as Bob Dylan once remarked, "It's hard to be a bitter millionaire."

The main character, William Halleck, is very much in the typical King mold as he's a white, urban professional (this time a lawyer), around forty, with a wife and daughter. He's overweight, as people who become prosperous often tend to get, and this forms the crux of what happens to him.

When Halleck's wife attempts to perform oral sex on him one day while he's driving, Halleck is distracted just long enough from the road that he fails to see an old gypsy woman stepping into the path of his car until it's too late. She's run down and killed. But because she was just a gypsy (and such folk tend to be unpopular in wealthy Connecticut suburbs), and Halleck is well connected and well

STEPHEN KING

liked, particularly by the judge, charges of vehicular manslaughter are dismissed. But Gypsies take care of their own and an old man pronounces a curse on Halleck, stating, "Thinner"— just that one word, while his finger brushes Halleck's cheek. The old man who cast the curse is the father of the woman Halleck ran down.

Halleck starts to lose weight, a pound or so a day, but it's non-stop. The inevitable result will be that Halleck will diminish in weight until he dies. When Halleck cannot get the curse lifted through pleading, he declares war on the Gypsies and they finally capitulate.

The theme running through this book is that everything we do is connected to everything else we do and leads to an inevitable and inescapable result. It's not quite the same as fate, but rather that things happen beyond our control. We choose to turn left instead of right and have to deal with the consequences of that even though we didn't realize that it was a mistake. What finally happens to Halleck is a result of this philosophy of connected events.

This was originally called "Gypsy Pie" and started out as a short story which grew into a novel. King decided to make it Bachman's next book. **Misery** would have also been a Bachman book.

THE SHORT FORM

NIGHT SHIFT

This was King's first short story collection. It didn't sell well in hardcover but hit bestseller status with the paperback edition. That it hit bestseller status is a tribute to King's popularity. Short story collections are notorious hard sells. King's fans decided to give it a try because they liked his novels. They weren't disappointed by what they found.

These stories nearly all sold to men's magazines like **Cavalier** during the period before King became a successful novelist. They were written in his spare time to supplement his income. The stories are nearly all horror tales while his novels explore other areas as well. Some real beauties reside here.

"Jerusalem's Lot" is the longest story in the volume, and definitely one of the best. The only story which backs away from contemporary horror is a very conscious Lovecraft pastiche. For nearly fifty years, other writers have followed in the footsteps of H.P. Lovecraft, sometimes in imitation and sometimes in *homage*. The stories rarely stood on their own. Thankfully "Jerusalem's Lot" carves new territory.

Choosing the epistolary form of storytelling (best known from Bram Stoker's **Dracula),** King weaves a convincing tale of one hundred thirty years ago in New England. Since both Lovecraft and King draw on their familiarity with the countryside in their fiction, this offers King a strong base to work from.

Charles Boone moves into his inherited family estate and proceeds to encounter bizarre mementoes from the past. He also unearths unpleasant secrets about his ancestors. The townspeople shun him because he is a Boone who lives in the cursed house of Chapelwaite. Picking up clues from various sources, he finally finds an abandoned nearby village which bears the name Jerusalem's Lot. This village is tied to the fate of many of his ancestors. Boone discovers a cryptic diary which he manages to translate. It leads to more discoveries. One of these discoveries involves what he finds living in the walls of his house.

Both a good horror story and a Lovecraft tribute, "Jerusalem's Lot" at first appears to suffer the same self-conscious errors other homages have. King starts off a bit heavy-handed when, on the first page, he uses three words Lovecraft often used for effect: distended, obscene and miasmic. Only one truly inculcated in Lovecraftiana would recognize this, but when King refers to "the obscene little cherrywood table beside the door," surely even the most casual reader must wonder at the choice of wording. How many obscene tables have you ever seen? After this King gets down to business. Other obvious references to Lovecraft are rare, such as describing Chapelwaite as a "shunned house," as well as the inevitable description of "rats in the walls," (both titles of Lovecraft stories).

King proves there is plenty left to be mined in the Lovecraftian vein if one know how to use the tools properly.

"Graveyard Shift" is a very moody little horror piece. The simple plot concerns the cleaning up of a factory and the exploration of tunnels underneath it to exterminate a rat's nest. The descriptions of the workmen's routine and everyday life in the factory is quite convincing, unpleasantly so if, like me, you once held a job much like that. King often draws the most gritty details from his personal experiences to ground a story in contemporary realism. This doesn't stop him from introducing horrific elements to jolt the reader out of the complacency the familiar setting might lull them into.

Something had happened to the rats, some hideous mutation that never could have survived under the eye of the sun; nature would have forbidden it. But down here, nature had taken a ghastly face.

The gigantic rats grew as high as three feet tall, their rear legs withered, their eyes blind as those of moles, like their flying cousins. They dragged themselves forward with hideous eagerness.

"**Night Surf**" is a portrait of a small group of people slowly dying from a mutated flu virus, much the same as the one which annihilated most of mankind in **The Stand.** It's a bittersweet character study of people dealing with the end of their lives while nature carries on uncaring around them. An interesting change of pace story, it appears after two heavy horror entries.

"**I Am The Doorway**" is a bizarre science fiction tale of an astronaut who begins to metamorphosize five years after returning from an orbital run to Venus. Crippled on re-entry in an accident which killed his co-pilot, he had retired to Florida. One day he notices that his hands are growing eyes and those eyes have an intelligence of their own which attempts to control him.

For pure, undisguised, stand-up-and-scream horror, "The Mangler" takes the prize. Without revealing too much, which would diminish the effect, I'll say that it involves black magic taking place by chance, and a machine. But this is no ordinary machine. It seems cursed. People keep getting caught in it, but that's just the start. The story sets you up right from the opening paragraph and makes it clear that this one will carry a wallop.

The plant itself was empty; the big automatic washers at the far end had not even been shut down. It made Hunton very wary. The crowd should be at the scene of the accident, not in the office. It was the way things moved—the human animal had a built-in urge to view the remains. A very bad one, then. Hunton felt his stomach tighten as it always did when the accident was very bad. Fourteen years of cleaning human litter from the highways and streets and the sidewalks at the bases of very tall buildings had not been able to erase that little hitch in the belly, as if something evil had clotted there.

There's some pretty rough stuff in this story, so rough that you may have to come up for air a couple times. That's Stephen King's power. King writes realistic horror, in focus right down to the smallest detail. His terrors won't go away no matter which way you tum. Like The Mangler of the story, King' s writing is too strong to be swept away or weakened upon examination. Detailed realism provides its strength.

"**The Boogeyman**" is a very atmospheric story which I found very predictable, like numerous comic book stories I've read over the years. It captures the fear of something lurking in the dark quite well, but is burdened with too obvious an ending.

"**Gray Matter**" opens with a few old gents sitting around in Henry's Nite-Owl, a twenty-four hour convenience store in a small town. In the dead of winter, a young boy runs in with a wild tale about his father—and what he' s changed into.

In other hands this story could have easily degenerated into farce because it's about a man who starts changing into something *not quite human* after he drinks a can of contaminated beer. The man develops an aversion to light and sits in the dark drinking beer all day until his hunger turns towards refreshments of a non-liquid variety—but that's just half the problem.

The story is told from the point of view of some of the old gents. It almost seems like a tall tale, sprinkled as with salty language and odd colloquialisms.

These, although generally humorous, root the story in the reality of the small town atmosphere which King is able to achieve so well. The story tells of strange and inexplicable things happening without real reason. They just happen.

In a chilling aside, the narrator explains how he knows that the world can be a lot crazier than people give it credit for:

I once knew a fella named George Kelso, who worked for the Bangor Public Works Department. He spent fifteen years fixing water mains and mending electricity cables and all that, an' then one day he just up an' quit, not two years before his retirement. Frankie Haldeman, who knew him, said George went down into a sewer pipe on Essex, laughing and joking just like always and came up fifteen minutes later with his hair just as white as snow and his eyes staring like he just looked through a window into Hell. He walked straight down to the BPW garage and punched his clock and went down to Wally's Spa and started drinking. It killed him two years later. Frankie said he tried to talk to him about it and George said something one time, and that was when he was pretty well blotto. Turned around on his stool, George did, an' asked Frankie Haldeman if he'd ever seen a spider as big as a good-sized dog sitting in a web full of kitties an' such all wrapped up in silk thread. Well, what could he say to that? I'm not saying there's any truth in it, but I am saying there's things in the corners of the world that would drive a man insane to look at 'em right in the face.

And with these few words King tells another complete story as an aside. In the process he adds considerably to the mood of the main story by pointing out that if one strange and seemingly impossible thing exists, others might be possible.

"Battleground" is an odd little fantasy about a hit man set upon by the creations of one of his targets. The inventions consist of a box of toy soldiers which are more than they seem. The toybox, called a Vietnam footlocker, contains miniature surface-to-air missiles and an even bigger surprise. Murderous toys is an old idea but King adds some new, and very contemporary, twists.

"Trucks" didn't strike me as possessing any new twists on its old theme at all. It's the revolt-of-the-machines plot. In this case all motor vehicles spontaneously acquire minds of their own and besiege humanity. When King turned this story into his feature **Maximum Overdrive** he attempted to explain how and why all this happens. In the short story, it just happens. Nobody knows why, including the reader. The story proceeds without a reason and thus without point.

While King has written many types of horror stories, his specialty are those which deal with people, personalities and emotions—in which the horror touches the lives of real people. Rod Serling's *The Twilight Zone* offered early, and excellent, examples of how these stories could be done. One of Serling's finest contributing writers was Richard Matheson, a writer who has influenced King more than any other in the weird fiction genre.

"Sometimes They Come Back" is a story which perfectly exemplifies the kind of special horror story which King has truly made his own. It deals with an English teacher named Jim Norman. Norman suffers tormenting memories of his brother's murder sixteen years before at the hands of street punks. Now with helplessness and terror Norman realizes that the same three teenagers who killed his brother are, one by one, turning up in his classes. There is no mistake. They're the same kids, transfers from a Milford High School. When he phones that town, he learns that the only thing there named Milford is the cemetery.

King's powers of portraying a detailed, contemporary atmosphere come fully into play. The genuinely human characters that people this story combine with the contemporary atmosphere to make it far more than just a story. They create an unforgettable experience as powerful as the impact of "The Mangler," but in a very different way. Truly Stephen King writing at the top of his form.

"Strawberry Spring" is a curious little story about a Jack The Ripper style killer, but with a little twist. Strawberry Spring refers to a specific type of springtime weather which involuntarily causes the killer, nicknamed Springheel Jack, to go into action. The different viewpoint of the story make the ending quite effective.

"The Ledge" is a totally contemporary thriller. It features no fantasy elements but remains one of the most intense and suspenseful stories in the book. Imagine, if you will, being forced to walk a very narrow ledge all the way around a building 43 stories above the ground on a cold and windy night —minus any sort of safety devices. Starting to feel dizzy already? After reading this, *you'll* feel as though you walked the ledge with him! A very good adaptation of this appeared in the movie Catseye, although the internalization of the story you gain from reading it gives the written version an extra edge.

"The Lawnmower Man" is a *really* strange story. It's a darkly humorous horror piece full of strange people and stranger events. In it a lawnmower runs over little animals and a man with cloven hooves and green pubic hair follows behind the lawnmower eating the grass cuttings! You'll shake your head in wonder where King *ever* could have gotten the idea, especially since he wrote it when he was sixteen!

"Quitters, Inc." is another exercise in black humor of a very different sort. It deals with an organization for people who want to quit smoking, only it's run like the Mafia! The organization enforces your promise to quit. You keep the pledge or pay a penalty. . . Only it isn't always the smoker who pays the penalty—it may be one of your family! Imagine the Schick Center run by Vito Corleone.

"I Know What You Need" concerns a woman who falls in love with a psychic. She doesn't realize his difference at first, but finally learns the truth and realizes just how she was manipulated by him, including his murder of her former boyfriend. It's not all one-sided, though, because the character of the psychic is revealed to be spiritually stunted; a person who would be a nobody without his ability. Even as a child it was only his power that made his parents care about him. An unusual treatment of a familiar theme.

"Children of the Corn" combines a lot of diverse ideas. There's a society run entirely by children, a god of the harvest, life ending at a mandatory age and even religious fanaticism as the glue which binds it all together. Enter a middle-aged, bickering couple who wander in to this strange Nebraska hinterland. They soon discern just how crazy things are in this small community but when they attempt to flee they find themselves confronting the power of He Who Walks Behind The Rows.

This is the most intriguing story in the book, leaving room to explore still more ideas within that setting. Turned into a feature film, they padded it unmercifully while ignoring the significance behind the themes. Some ideas loom too large to be treated adequately in a short story although what's here fascinates.

The following description of what the main character finds in the church in that tiny town of Gatlin, Nebraska gives an idea of the concepts the story explores:

The space behind the pulpit was dominated by a gigantic portrait of Christ, and Burt thought: If nothing else in this town gave Vicky the screaming meemies, this would.

The Christ was grinning, vulpine. His eyes were wide and staring, reminding Burt uneasily of Lon Chaney in The Phantom of the Opera. In each of the wide black pupils someone (a sinner, presumably) was drowning in a lake of fire. But the oddest thing was that this Christ had green hair. . . hair which on closer examination revealed itself to be a twining mass of early-summer corn. The picture was crudely done but effective. It looked like a comic strip mural done by a gifted child—an Old Testament Christ, or a pagan Christ that~ might slaughter his sheep for sacrifice instead of leading them.

This may not be the most horrifying story in the book, but I think it's the best one and has more than it's share of thrills and chills.

"The Last Rung on the Ladder" is a very troubling story, a horror story about life and how people inadvertently lose touch with one another. In this case, a brother and sister. The characters seem terribly real and the events which touch them more than fictional. The story tells of a brother and sister who grow up and move to different parts of the country. The brother has been too busy to send his sister his new address whenever he moved, although he always intended to get in touch with her and get together again. She commits suicide and days later he receives a forwarded letter she had written which would have brought him running had he received it in time. This launches him into a reverie of their past, and recalls an event from early in her life which came to mind as she approached her end.

"The Man Who Loved Flowers" is so short, it's almost a vignette. It concerns springtime, love and how a young man's fancy turns to twisted thoughts of homicide while all around him view his pleased expression as first love. Only for this young man it's not the first. King paints a rich portrait of city life with clusters of people and activity. You can almost hear the sounds and feel the fresh springtime.

"One For The Road" is a sequel to **Salem's Lot** in short story form. Originally appearing in *Maine Magazine*, it was probably written on request. No doubt, it adds considerably to the state's folklore.

Vampires may be one of the oldest staples of the horror story, but King shows that they can still be vastly entertaining. The simple plot succeeds because the deep mood of the story establishes an atmosphere of dread; a feeling of claustrophobia and tension which never lets go.

One night during a howling snowstorm, a stranger staggers into Tookey's Bar. He'd made a turn into an unplowed road and gotten stuck, forced to leave his wife and child in the car while he went for help. The unplowed road leads to Jerusalem's Lot (known to the locals as Salem's Lot), a town which mysteriously burned down two years before. The two men in the bar decide to help this tourist get back to his car. There still might be time to prevent the worst from happening.

Only someone who has experienced heavy snowstorms can appreciate the menace, and King captures the sensation perfectly.

Maine blizzard Ever been in one? The snow comes flying in so thick and so fine it looks like sand and sounds like that, beating on the sides of your car or pickup. You don't want to use your high beams because they reflect off the snow and you can't see ten feet in front of you. With the low beams on, you can see maybe fifteen feet. But I can live with the snow. It's the wind I don't like, when it picks up and begins to howl, driving the snow into a hundred weird flying shapes and sounding like all the hate and pain and fear in the world. There's death in the throat of a snowstorm wind, white death—and maybe something beyond death. That's no sound to hear when you're tucked up all cozy into your own bed with the shutters bolted and the door locked. It's that much worse if you're driving. And we were driving smack into Salem's Lot.

King uses words to make the reader experience the sense of fear.

"The Woman In The Room" is a very sombre, thoughtful note on which to conclude **Night Shift.** It's about euthanasia. Mercy killing. A man's aged mother is slowly dying of an incurable disease. She will never be whole again. Her life lingers from medical efforts which sustain her pain without offering hope. The main character examines his feelings about himself and his mother and about what is truly important—whether life is still life when it becomes just lingering pain. Whether it is cruel to end her life or more cruel to allow the suffering to go on and on. It is troubling in the way that "The Last Rung on the Ladder" is troubling. Unlike vampires and machines which come to life, this can't be shut out and dismissed by closing the book. The bitter truth lingers.

The stories in **Night Shift** offer both a cross-section of the genre of horror and of the writing of Stephen King. We are shown a world comprised not just of ideas, but of life itself. King captures all the nagging little details and idiosyncrasies we know so well but often fail to contemplate until they're used to color the background of a story. The world in the stories of Stephen King comes very close to home many times, in many ways. It's difficult to forget the stories. We return for another encounter time after time.

THE DARK TOWER SERIES

Two volumes in this series have appeared thus far and King has indicated that it may run into as many as seven volumes. The stories in the first volume, **The Dark Tower: The Gunslinger,** first appeared as a series over a period of three years or so in *The Magazine of Fantasy & Science Fiction.* Only the first of the stories, "The Gunslinger," was cohesive in any way. It read like a bizarre riff on Westerns. The other stories in volume one didn't work at all as individual stories since it was really a novel being serialized with as much as a year between installments.

This series takes place in a future when civilization has crumbled and history is regarded as a set of myths. As King puts it in a preface:

"The dark ages have come; the last of the lights are guttering, flickering out— in the minds of men as well as in their dwellings. The world has moved on."

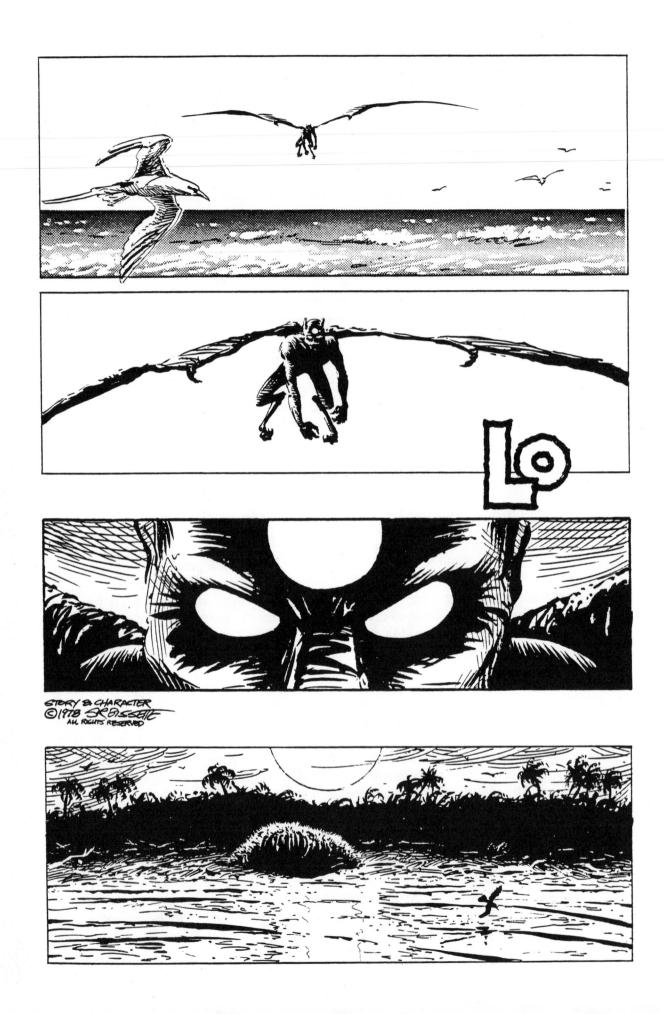

The main character is Roland, the last gunslinger, who wears a pair of six-guns and trudges through a world which is a huge version of America in the 1800s. But horses are rare and the stagecoach is the most modern means of transportation, as though time is slipping backwards from the 20th century and running down.

Through this wilderness, Roland searches for the mysterious Man In Black who is a sorcerer and an emissary of evil. Roland's quest is not so much the Man In Black as it is the information the man possesses about a place called The Dark Tower.

THE DARK TOWER: THE GUNSLINGER

The short stories **"The Gunslinger"** and **"The Way Station"** are the first two chapters in this novel. They show only a small part of Roland's determined tracking, and while we see the type of deadly traps the mysterious sorcerer can leave in his wake, we still don't know how or where the tracking started and learn very little about who Roland is.

"The Way Station" provides a touch of Roland's background while introducing a new character—a nine year old boy. Under hypnosis the boy reveals that he remembers being killed in New York City in ancient times by the Man In Black. Then the boy awakened in the desert in an old Way Station, where Roland found him. There is a strong implication that the boy, Jake, is another trap left by the sorcerer. But the Gunslinger accepts the boy's companionship anyway, thereby revealing more feeling and humanity than had been hinted at in Roland's character up to that point.

These stories are unusual in that they're science fiction with elements of fantasy and horror. They are unlike anything else King has had published and a lot of possibilities are left as to where these stories could go.

"The Oracle and The Mountains" finds the pair escaping the desert and entering an oasis-like area of grasslands at the foot of a mountain range. There they encounter an oracle which gives Roland needed clues, such as that the boy is the gateway to the Man In Black and that the sorcerer is the gateway to the three obstacles which will lead Roland to the Dark Tower. A few more hints are given to Roland's background, but no involved flashback such as contained in "The Way Station" appears. The Gunslinger finally faces the Man In Black in this story, but the sorcerer eludes him while Roland remains just minutes behind his quarry at story's end.

"The Slow Mutants" is drawn out, aimless and has Roland doing things that are inexplicable because we understand so little about his motivation. We are learning slivers of the big picture, but not enough to explain the underlying importance of the quest or why incredible sacrifices are justified. We're not allowed to care about events as deeply as Roland does, and while the flashbacks to his childhood are interesting, they're too distantly removed from what's happening to him in the main part of the story and thus carry no discernable weight or significance. King is still not letting us in on what is really going on; everything that happens seems murky and senseless. The plot advances, but to no real purpose that we can discern. The characterization of Roland shifts inexplicably from one moment to the next. First he claims to love Jake, and then suddenly acts as though he cares nothing about the boy at all. When he's forced to make a choice between the boy and going after the Man In Black, we have no idea from whence his decision arises or why the quest is so important.

The final chapter in book one, **"The Gunslinger and the Dark Man,"** is filled with riddles in which Roland finally has it out face to face with the Man In Black and learns how to find the Dark Tower, and what he'll need to do to get to it. It is just a set-up for the second book.

THE DARK TOWER II: THE DRAWING OF THE THREE

In this novel Roland deals with three obstacles and the book divides neatly into three parts and is a more cohesive story.

As this book is nearing completion the third volume in this series is imminent. More books in this series are forthcoming, but King has not yet written the third.

DIFFERENT SEASONS

Unlike King's previous collections, this consists of novellas, not short stories, and none of them previously appeared anywhere else.

"Rita Hayworth And Shawshank Redemption" is the story of an innocent man who spends nearly thirty years in prison. It's sort of a modern day **Count Of Monte Cristo,** but that implies adventure elements which the story lacks. Instead this is a story of coming to grips with a cruel fate.

Andy Dufresne is sent to prison for murdering his wife and her lover. He's innocent but all the circumstantial evidence points to him and so he's locked away to begin a new life behind bars.

The narrator of the story is an old man who'd already been in prison for ten years when Andy is sentenced. We see the story from the viewpoint of this old lifer who witnesses some things first hand and pieces other parts together.

The portrait of prison life is chillingly believable, but it's the human story of Andy Dufresne that holds our interest and keeps us fascinated from beginning to end. The depiction of prison life bristles with background details. Yet one doesn't get the impression of the ever-present brutality that is usually associated with such a story. Early in Dufresne's prison career, the concept of homosexual rape is dealt with. That overcome, Andy's life actually seems rather tranquil. I can't help but recall the searing. dehumanizing conditions of the turn-of-the-century prisons portrayed in Jack London's last book, **The Star Rover,** or the more contemporary situations in the Texas reformatory in the movie *Brubaker*. While Andy Dufresne seems to have it comparatively easy, this is still a fascinating story of a condemned innocent man. It possesses an imaginative and rewarding climax.

"Apt Pupil" is the backstory we never hear when we read about a senseless crime. It examines how an obsession can change a person and finally push them over the edge.

Todd Bowden, a typical thirteen year old boy, one day discovers his *one great interest* while looking through old true war adventure magazines. Todd is fascinated by the grim goings on in the Nazi concentration camps. Many children find fascination with the grotesque (check out the letter columns in *Fangoria* sometime), but Todd's interest is more than just historical; it's unhealthy.

The story fails to explore what makes Todd *hunger* for the grisly details the more sedate history texts gloss over. We never learn why he finds sadism so at tractive. Only the expansion of this fascination into the realm of obsession is portrayed, not the origins of his capacity for malevolence.

Todd had problems even before he began looking into the horrors of the holocaust. He felt compelled to learn more of the sick details, even to the point of blackmailing an aged Nazi war criminal. This last seems farfetched, but King makes it work.

In nearly 200 pages we see a strange, parasitic relationship develop between Todd and the old Nazi, Kurt Dussander. At first Todd threatens to expose him unless the man tells him, in detail, of the horrors he participated in, especially the many instances of torture. As time goes by, Todd finds himself trapped by his own scheme. Each slowly corrupts the other as Todd forces the past to come alive again for the old man while the old man feeds Todd's hunger with more and more emotional decay.

The sequences where Todd experiences nightmares brought on by the stories are well handled. It's all unnervingly believable. For whatever reason, even when Todd almost completely disassociates himself from the old man, the taint of the contact remains, festering and feeding until Todd's humanity transforms into a superficial mask he wears to hide his insanity.

Everything builds to a tragically inevitable bloody climax. Afterwards we still wonder what drew Todd into the awful abyss to begin with. We're left wondering why it all had to happen this way just as we are when we read about a bizarre and inexplicable murder rampage in the daily newspaper. We understand the history of the deadly explosion, but there's still something left hidden and untouched.

"The Body" has become the most famous story in this collection due to its sensitive adaptation into the recent movie *Stand By Me*. It's a tale of both lost innocence and recaptured memories.

Back in 1960, four twelve year old boys in Castle Rock, Maine learn the whereabouts of the body of a missing boy. Those who found it were afraid to report it because they'd been out joyriding in a stolen car at the time. The four younger boys concoct a plan to walk the thirty miles or so to where the body rests and then report it so they can becomes heroes, of a sort. They've never seen a dead body and more than a little excitement underlies the quest. One fleetingly recalls Todd's fascination with the morbid in "Apt Pupil" but these boys aren't the type to break into funeral homes to see more corpses. Yet the concept of seeing a dead person for the first time intrigues them.

The plot is actually quite complicated and involves their experiences during their little quest, some of them hair-raising. Events begin drawing a demarcation point in their friendships as two of the boys begin to understand more deeply what living is all about.

All of the boys are precisely portrayed. None come from what could be called average, happy, middle class families. The narrator comes closest, but his brother had been killed in an accident some months before. Worse, it had come heavily home to him that his older brother had clearly been his parents favorite as they both walk zombie-like through the day and treat their remaining son almost as though he were the invisible man. King deliberately writes of the narrator not only growing up to be a writer, but an English teacher as well. This leaves us with the impression that at least some of the story is the author purging himself of personal childhood horrors. If that doesn't nail the narrator down tightly enough he even says that three of his novels were turned into films.

By the time we finish this story we not only feel that we've met real people, but that the reader has gone through a cathartic experience as well. There's a lot of emotional cleansing in this story, and a lot of truth.

"The Breathing Method" is the only horror story in **Different Season.** It's dedicated to Peter Straub and his wife. The prose style reminds one of Straub's writing. It's no doubt dedicated to Straub partially because of the framing device involving a club where old men get together and swap stories, not unlike the Chowder Society of **Ghost Story.** King gives his society a peculiar twist all his own.

The Breathing Method of the title is just what it sounds like—a method women use to deal with the contractions encountered in pregnancy and childbirth. One of the club members recounts a tale of his younger days as a physician back in the Thirties when he treated a young, unmarried pregnant woman. The horror and the weird element arrive at the time of childbirth.

The story within a story is handled well enough, but fails to convince.

The setting of the club captures the reader's attention. Hints are dropped which lead us to expect the alien. The narrator reads marvelous books in the club library by authors and publishers he's never heard of. When he tries to track down copies or even just basic information about the books through the New York Metropolitan Library, he draws a blank. It creates a strange and surreal atmosphere which leaves the reader wondering if we'll be visiting that society again.

In **Different Seasons,** King displays varied talents. Although outside the realm he's known for, these stories succeed on many levels. Most importantly, they touch us where we live.

SKELETON CREW

This is the second mass market short story collection from King. While **The Dark Tower** also collects short stories which first appeared elsewhere, it is a small press publication never available in a mass market edition. **Different Seasons** collects novellas or novelettes that never appeared anywhere else first.

Like **Night Shift, Skeleton Crew** collects a wide range of published fiction and prose showing many facets of King. It leads off with one of his most powerful stories.

"The Mist" encapsulates everything King does well: well defined characters, interesting settings and fantastic horror presented realistically. The story quite literally takes us for a roller coaster ride through tension, suspense and imagination. The burgeoning feeling of claustrophobia achieved in **Salem's Lot** and **The Shining** is present, but much stranger than in either of those novels.

The plot concerns a small country community in Maine transported to another dimension by a mysterious thick fog which emanates from a secretive government installation in the nearby mountains. It's known only as the Arrowhead Project. The accident which triggers the bizarre phenomenon is brought on by a violent thunderstorm which rocks the entire area one summer night.

The main character, David Drayton, a commercial artist, lives by a lake along with his wife and five year old son, Billy. The storm badly devastates the area with fallen trees and disabled power lines. The morning after, David goes into town to get supplies and takes his son with him. They're in a huge grocery store when the strange fog sweeps down over the community and strands everyone where ever they are at that moment. Initially people refuse to believe that anything is wrong, but then the evidence mounts, along with the death toll.

The story centers on a supermarket where Drayton, his son, and many other people find themselves stranded. It's a useful place to be stuck and the story makes much of that aspect. Outside the supermarket, weird and obviously alien life forms lurk in the thick, ever-present white mist. The strange creatures are deadly in unique and hideous ways. There are 14-legged spiders, creatures which fly, others with tentacles and huge beasts heard roaring but never seen, except by their victims.

This story offers a convincing portrayal of ordinary people trapped in a hideously extraordinary circumstances, and how some people deal with it while others refuse to confront the truth. The narrative begins innocently enough but then builds, layer upon layer, trapping the reader as well as the characters. While the horror mounts the characters battle both strange creatures and each other while trying to come to grips with their new situation. Emotions are convincingly portrayed as events follow along logically. While certain aspects of the plot smack of cliche, they work when you encounter them because King gives them a hard rub and polish to turn them into something new and shiny. In the process he shows why other stories which tried similar things didn't really pull them off right.

"The Mist" gives the reader all that he expects, and more. I made the mistake of starting this one evening, and I can't begin to describe the strange dreams which visited me that night. I finished reading it the next day by the comforting afternoon *light*.

While describing this story to a friend of mine, he remarked that he wasn't sure if he wanted to read it. It seems he *liked* going out into the fog and mist. I explained that, oddly enough, it isn't mist which takes on new characteristics in your perception, but shopping centers. Supermarkets are even more mundane than mists. To imbue them lingering menace is quite a trick. Even now when I look at one with its tall, front windows I remember what happened there in "The Mist."

In reviewing the story in *Locus*, the reviewer observed, "If you can't feel safe in among the Froot Loops, where can you feel safe?"

"Here There By Tygers" is new to this anthology. It's about a little boy who discovers a man-eating tiger in his elementary school lavatory. The very short story reads much like a daydream, albeit a disturbing one.

"The Monkey" has all of the elements that a reader expects from a Stephen King story. It offers shuddery horror in the modem vein. The plot hearkens back to *The Twilight Zone*. It involves a strange little old wind-up toy monkey (you know, the kind which has a pair of cymbals). The origin of the toy is unknown but it seems impervious to destructive intent. No one can say the same regarding its intentions. Whenever this little contrivance is wound up, or whenever it spontaneously starts up, its cymbals come together and somebody dies.

This involved short story features several characters and spans twenty years, employing flashbacks to the main character's childhood when the toy first wrecked havoc and brought death. When the story opens, the main character's children find the toy monkey in the attic, even though he had thrown it down an old well twenty years before. The mood of this story is set right from the start. One line on the opening page says more than pages of other stories, "Outside a cold gust of wind rose, and for a moment lips with no flesh blew a long note through the old, rusty gutter outside."

For a short story the characters are quite well developed. We really learn to care about these characters and feel the turmoil Hal Shelbum experiences, both in his fear of what may come and in his recollections of the tragedies of his youth.

One especially eerie scene presents a skillfully conceived dream sequence described so visually it literally springs to life from the page. This excellent story keeps you on the edge of your seat right up to the last stroke because, literally *anything* can happen!

"Cain Rose Up" is another short-short original to **Skeleton Crew,** an interlude showing a college student snapping under the pressure and living out his darkest fantasies by shooting people from his dormitory window. Although quite short. it's disturbingly real.

"Mrs. Todd's Shortcut" is another one of those stories which gives Maine a mythic quality. Ophelia Todd is obsessed with finding shorter routes between her home and Bangor—routes which avoid the interstate freeway. The story is told from the point of view of Homer and a friend, Homer Buckland

being her caretaker. Amused by all this at first, Homer becomes concerned when she describes strange sights along her drives. After one of them, when she's made seeming impossibly good time, Homer sees that Mrs. Todd had hit something with her car, something still stuck on the front.

There was some kind of a animal half-smashed onto the radiator grille, just under where that Mercedes ornament is— the one that looks kinda like a star looped up into a circle? Now most small animals you kill on the road is bore right under the car because they are crouching when it hits them, hoping it'll just go over and leave them with their hide still attached to their meat. But every now and then one will jump, not away, but right at the damn car, as if to get in one good bite of whatever the buggardly thing is that's going to kill it—I have know that to happen. This thing had maybe done that. And it looked mean enough to jump a Sherman tank. It looked like something which come of a mating between a woodchuck and a weasel, but there was other stuff thrown in that a body didn't even want to look at. It hurt your eyes, Dave; worse'n that, it hurt your mind. Its pelt was matted with blood, and there was claws sprung out of the pads on its feet like a cat's claws, only longer. It had big yellowy eyes, only they was glazed. When I was a kid I had a porcelain marble—a croaker—that looked like that. And teeth. Long thin needle teeth that looked almost like darning needles, stickin out of its mouth. Some of them was sunk right into that steel grillwork. I looked at it and knowed it had a headful of poison just like a rattlesnake, and it had jumped at that go-devil when it saw it was about to be run down, tryin to bit it to death.

This is by no means a horror story, but a touching fantasy with an edge about a world where the inexplicable happens. Where people disappear for years only to return just in time for a happy ending. It's both unusual and touching, the kind of story you might want someone to read who really doesn't like horror but is still curious about King. It's a "'safe" story which presents interesting characters touched by events beyond the norm. It's Twilight Zone time, folks!

"The Jaunt" is a rare excursion for King into the realm of science fiction set in the future. Three hundred years from now a family plans a trip to Mars using that great new labor-saving teleportation device, The Jaunt (named after a similar abil-

ity described in Alfred Bester's **The Stars My Destination).** While waiting in the airport-like setting to be "launched" through the teleporter, Mr. Oates tells his children the history of The Jaunt, how it was discovered and why people using it must be asleep for the seemingly instantaneous journey.

This discovery is portrayed as possessing both wonder and terror. With hints, King conveys the sense of unimaginable vistas waiting just beyond our normal perceptions—waiting for us to take The Jaunt. More than just a travelogue, this story illustrates terror.

"**The Wedding Gig**" is a seriocomic tale which starts off like a comedy but then by degrees takes tragic turns.

It all takes place in 1927 from the point of view of a jazz musician whose band is offered $200 to play at the wedding of a gangster's sister. The racketeer, Mike Scollay, is fiercely proud of his heritage and painfully embarrassed by his sister's superstructure. When the band sets up, they see why.

You've heard about Jack Sprat and his wife. Well, this was a hundred time worse. Scollay's sister had the red hair he was losing, and it was long and curly. But not that pretty auburn shade you may be imagining. It was as bright as a carrot and as kinky as a bedspring. She looked just awful. And had Scollay said she was fat? Brother, that was like saying you can buy a few things in Macy's. The woman was a dinosaur—350 if she was a pound. It had all gone to her bosom and hips and thighs like it does on fat girls, making her flesh grotesque and frightening. Some fat girls have pathetically pretty faces, but Scollay's sis didn't even have that. Her eyes were too close together, her mouth was too big, and her ears stuck out. Even thin, she'd have been as ugly as the serpent in the garden.

Then there's the description of the groom to complete the image of this happy couple.

He could have put on a ton hat and stood in the top half of her shadow. He was about five three and must have weighed all of 90 pounds soaking wet. We was skinny as a rail, and his complexion was darkly olive. When he grinned around nervously, his teeth looked like a picket fence in a slum neighborhood.

This story was the first time King wrote anything about underworld characters tinged with either humanity or tragedy. His other stories about gangsters just portrayed grim characters on a collision course with a destiny of their own contriving. The people occupying center stage in this piece are very vivid elements in the tragedy. They play out their roles as history sweeps them inexorably into the dust.

"**Paranoid: A Chant**" is a free form poem, a song without music, about a character convinced that the world is out to get him.

"**The Raft**" is one of those contemporary tales of terror that King does so well. A very effective story although the main characters fail to interest the reader. I felt distanced by what happens to them.

The four characters, two men and two women college students, go for a romp one fall night down to a remote lake closed for the season. As they swim out to the raft anchored in the middle, one of them notices a dark blot moving through the water, towards them.

A classically structured story of people under pressure as they become trapped on the raft by a shapeless monster, the blob seems right out of the late, late show. It even dissolves the flesh and bones of its victims, particularly in one especially graphic and horrifying scene. Aside from moments of imaginative, graphic horror, the story isn't all that unusual. The ending leaves something to be desired and King indulges his penchant for introducing bizarre manifestations without the slightest nod towards explanation (i.e. "The Crate" and "Suffer The Little Children"). It's an interesting story, but unlike such stories as "The Monkey" and "Children of the Corn," it doesn't draw the reader back for a repeat experience.

"**The Word Processor of the Gods**" is an update on the old theme of a magic typewriter whose words can alter reality. These stories generally follow an established pattern, such as in the old Jerome Bixby story, "The Magic Typewriter." Richard Matheson created a spin on this idea in the **Twilight Zone** episode "A World Of His Own" in which a Dictaphone can create whatever the author speaks into it. King updated the idea still further and transported it body and soul into the computer age. An inexplicably effective word processor built for a man by his nephew as a surprise for his birthday performs wonders. The catch is the boy and his family were killed in a horrible accident three weeks before the gift was to be presented. Thus the writer, Richard Hagstrom, acquires the gift under tragic circumstances.

These stories follow a basic pattern and try for irony where the reader isn't interested in finding any. King abandons the cliche ending where the reader and all concerned get slapped in the face by fate. Instead he plays our emotions, summoning tension and suspense as he realistically portrays Hagstrom's pain and inner turmoil over the cruelty of fate. What King accomplishes here isn't a fantasy dealing with things on a cosmic level but rather ones which touch us on a very personal level. Afterwards we're glad to have encountered this story and the experience it provides.

"**The Man Who Would Not Shake Hands**" is just a story of a man living under a curse and how he inevitably ends it. It's interesting as far as it goes but isn't particularly memorable.

"**Beachworld**" is a science fiction story about a visit to a world where the sands are alive. It has its moments but the idea isn't developed as well as it might have been.

"**The Reaper's Image**" is the earliest published story appearing in **Skeleton Crew.** It appeared in *Startling Mystery Stories* in 1969 and employs the theme of the cursed mirror, a familiar one in horror. Examples of this kind of story include "The Trap" by Henry S. Whitehead and "The Painted Mirror" by Donald Wandrei (the latter turned into a ridiculous **Night Gallery** episode starring Zsa Zsa Gabor).

Despite how early a story it is, King evokes real sensations drawn from a vividly portrayed background.

They climbed the third and fourth flights of stairs in silence. As they drew closer to the roof of the rambling structure, it became oppressively hot in the dark upper galleries. With the heat came a creeping stench that Spangler knew well, for he had spent all his adult life working in it—the smell of long-dead flies in shadowy corner, of wet rot and creeping wood lice behind the plaster. The smell of age. It was a smell common only to museums and mausoleums. He imagined much the same smell might arise from the grave of a virginal girl, forty years dead.

The setting is a museum, once the home of a wealthy man who collected junk that he was convinced was art. Along the way he acquired genuinely priceless items, including a mirror made hundreds of years ago in Europe. The mirror possesses a curious history.

This story deserved to be resurrected from the dust of King's early efforts where it languished out of print from 1969 until 1985.

"Nona" is a psychological terror tale about a man who goes on a murderous rampage at the urging of a mysterious woman. It's more captivating than most glimpses into the mind of an insane killer. Flashbacks reveal his less than happy childhood and his bad experiences with women. These climaxed at a college dance where he believes that he saw all of the women change into huge rats. This strange story offers a convincing portrait of the mind of a psychopath.

"For Owen" is another exercise in blank verse but this time on a touching, personal theme—King walking and talking with his young son.

"Survivor Type" is a simple, one note story about a doctor marooned on an island. In order to survive, he begins eating his own flesh. Although populated with character detail and some odd ideas, nothing beyond the obvious is done with it. Even people who think they'd love reading something like this will be disappointed. This story is essentially from the doctor's journal, but whenever he decides to hack off and consume another piece of his anatomy, it's done off-stage. He states that he cut off his foot, but in spite of being a surgeon, he doesn't describe the surgery. Whatever horror and revulsion King hoped to evoke only affects those who made queasy and light-headed by the mere idea. The details are left to the imagination.

"Uncle Otto's Truck" is a simple revenge story in which a villain is done in by an old truck. End of story. A rather weak, very predictable entry.

The next two stories are related, but only by their strangeness.
"Morning Deliveries (Milkman #1)" is a paranoid's delight as it details a milkman taking advantage of his unsuspecting customers by leaving deadly surprises (cyanide gas, Nightshade) in with the deliveries.

"Big Wheels: A Tale of the Laundry Game (Milkman ~2)" tells about the milkman's friend, Rocky, and something strange which happens to him. He's out on a bender with a buddy when they meet an old friend who runs a two-bit gas station. The story is all decked out with the appropriate sights and smells and painted in the best Richard Matheson tradition of looking at reality through a gimlet eye. King does that very well. While some fantasy and horror writers have chosen to emulate Lovecraft or Howard, King found his inspiration in Matheson. He took that inspiration and ran with it. Readers familiar with Matheson's work won't be too surprised when, at the end of the story, it does a backflip into surrealism and super-reality to the degree that we feel as though we've just stepped off a sidewalk into a dream. The best part, though, is that it all works. Sometimes strangeness is its own best excuse.

"Gramma" is a very wordy story told as the internal monologue of an eleven year old boy left alone in the house with his aged grandmother on the night that she dies. This is no ordinary grandmother. She's a witch who covets the little boy's young form so that she can live on and begin her life all over again. Gradually the boy begins to suspect the truth about her, including her plans for him. It's mostly a mood piece as not a lot happens. Although it's only a short story, it's still too long. It translated much better to another medium when Harlan Ellison adapted it as an episode of the new **Twilight Zone.**

"**The Ballad of the Flexible Bullet**" is a very strange story about a man who believes that there's something alive inside his typewriter. Even his editor finally comes to believe it. It's all very strange and a bit drawn out, but certainly unusual.

"**The Reach**" was first published under the title "Do The Dead Sing?" and is about the last months of the life of Stella Flanders, the 95 year old resident of Maine's Goat Island who lived there her whole life and never visited the mainland. The story has many recollections of her past and is one of the most real and moving portrayals of life I've ever read. While slice of life stories can, and do, too often dwell on the tedium of everyday existence, King touches on the pulsebeat of humanity with an underplayed yet devastating touch.

Although a simple story, it weaves a complex tapestry of emotions which carry it swiftly along from one fascinating scene to another. And those of you who are drawn to King's work for his unique brand of weird fiction, well find a climax which is both haunting and touching. This won the World Fantasy Award for Best Short Fiction of 1981.

SHORT FORM: UNCOLLECTED

"**Before The Play**" appeared in the long out of print special Stephen King issue of the small press publication *Whispers* 17/18 in August of 1982. Actually the opening section to **The Shining** which the editor asked be removed to cut the page count down slightly, this several thousand word opening is the history of the Overlook Hotel. It tells what happened prior to the arrival of Jack Torrance as the new caretaker. The story reveals how the hotel came to be built and that it was cursed from the day it opened. It's a fascinating and eerie history, but the most important part of the tale is about Jack Torrance at age six, and how his father was a drunkard who beat his children. It's a haunting prelude with realism more frightening than the parade of deaths forming the rest of the story.

"**The Blue Air Compressor**" (*Heavy Metal*, July 1981) is one very strange story. In my review of "The Wedding Gig" (**Skeleton Crew**) I quote a passage in which King runs riot describing an obese woman to hilarious effect. In this story he goes outright berserk describing one. The story concerns a writer who rents a cottage from an old lady. As soon as he meets this corpulent soul, his imagination runs riot in his descriptions of her. He decides to write a story about her, but one day he comes home to discover that the landlady has found his story. She think's it's hilarious, as in hilariously awful. That is when the writer spots the blue air compressor...

The writing fluctuates from hyperkInetic stream-of-consciousness to intrusions by King himself describing how he came to write a story grounded in the E.C. Comics tradition. It's fractured style fIts right in with *Heavy Metal*'s tilted perspective and it's the most experimental style of writing that King has had published to date.

Whenever King indulges in writing bizarre humor he proves very successful at it. Readers can only benefit when he stretches his imagination in other directions.

"**The Cat From Hell**" (*Cavalier*, June 1977) is a story which starts out strange and then turns both weird and horrifying. It involves a hitman who is hired by an old, crippled millionaire to murder a cat. The cat is responsible for the deaths of three people, and the millionaire believes he is in line as victim number four. Hints of a dark origin for the beast are left to be considered. The best part of the story is the long climax in which the hitman is trapped in his wrecked car with the cat, which is now trying to kill him. If you don't think a story about a little tabby can have a weird and horrific conclusion, then you're in for a big surprise!

"**The Crate**" (*Gallery*, July 1979, adapted in the film **Creepshow***) was originally rejected to *Playboy* because, well, there's a creature in it that King admitted was a thinly disguised version of the Tasmanian Devil (of Warner Brothers cartoon fame). *Playboy* harumphed and deemed it not *their* kind of story. *Gallery*, on the other hand, likes twonky things like that. The interesting little tale tells the story of a one hundred year old crate found beneath the stairs at a university. A janitor discovers the dust covered crate and when he pries it open something yanks him roughly inside and eats him! The beastie is described as of brown fur and teeth, not very large, and yet capable of gobbling up human beings, bones and all, in no time flat—albeit with quite a bit of mess and bother.

A forgotten expedition which never returned sent this crate back during their journey. The only survivor of the modem day rediscovery decides to put it to personal use before disposing of it.

This is more of a tongue-in-cheek horror tale, sort of the kind of horror which the old E.C. Comics sometimes indulged in. It would have been nice, though, if there had been some sort of explanation as to how this creature could survive boarded up in a crate for a hundred years!

"Crouch End" (New **Tales of the Cthulhu Mythos,** 1980) is a Lovecraftian tale set in London rather than New England. It concerns a section of London called Crouch End where strange events occur because the region borders another dimension. An interesting but eerie mood piece where the couple chased by a monster pass stores with names like Alhazred. Really little more than a tip-of-the-hat homage, it's a very little story.

"Dolan's Cadillac" (*Castle Rock* #2-6,1985) deals with underworld characters and the revenge theme. Pretty soon King will have enough of these to put in a book by themselves.

"The Fifth Quarter" (*Cavalier*, April 1972) appeared under the pseudonym John Swithen, King's only pseudonym outside of Richard Bachman. E.C. used to call these "crime suspenstories." Most people still call them "potboilers." A quick read in which the story flows quickly from one scene to another. The story entertains without containing any human touchstones or anything beyond superficial characterization.

The plot involves a man out to avenge the ambush murder of a former prison cellmate. Four men had pulled off an armored car robbery and then hidden the loot because the bills were too new. They'd buried the money on an island and then divided the map into four quarters so that no one of them could find the cache without the other three. Soon a double-cross followed. The story moves so swiftly that only later do we stop and ask why if these four guys buried the loot, they needed a map to find it again. They *know* where it is! If King had not acknowledged the story as his, I doubt anyone would have ever guessed.

"The Glass Floor" (*Startling Mystery Stories*, Fall 1967) is King's first professional sale. An editorial notation which appeared with this story is interesting to read now, twenty years later.

Stephen King has been sending us stories for some time, and we returned one of them most reluctantly, since it would be far too long before we could use it, due to its length. But patience may yet bring him his due reward on that tale; meanwhile, here is a chiller whose length allowed us to get it into print much sooner.

Although written within a year of his fanzine story ("I Was A Teenage Grave Robber"), the style and craft of King appear much more evident in this story. The psychological terror tale tells of a man who visits the home where his sister recently died. He demands to see the room where she died—a room with a mirror for a floor. The story makes much more of the mirror concept than I think reasonable, but therein hangs the tale.

"**I Was A Teenage Grave Robber**" (*Comics Review*, 1965) was written when King was 17 and later reprinted in another fanzine under the only slightly less sensationalistic title, "In A Half-World Of Terror." Danny Gerard, left moderately wealthy when his parents die, is bilked out of his estate at the age of 18. He becomes so desperate to make a living that he takes a job offered by a fellow bar patron. All he has to do is rob a grave. For whom? A mad scientist, of course. And why? The scientist conducts experiments on human flesh. But these experiments have less to do with the flesh than they do with what is found on the flesh after the body molders in a grave. There's also the usual business of boy meets girl, boy rescues girl and the inevitable happy ending. The whole thing is heavily influenced by very recognizable horror movie cliches.

The writing is competent, but characterization sketched in the broadest of strokes. The kind of story you'd expect to find in a fanzine, complete with typos (Danny picks up his girl to go to a movie at 7:30 AM). Competent, but no surprises.

"**The End Of The Whole Mess**" (*Omni*, October 1986) is a story more fascinating in the telling than in the denouement. A man discovers something which makes people nonviolent and spreads it through the water all over the world. The characterizations of the two brothers is quite good, particularly the scene when the younger brother, at age 8, invents a successful, makeshift glider. Unfortunately the contrived twist ending isn't up to the rest of the tale.

"**It Grows On You**" (*Whispers*, August 1982) is one of those stories where weird things happen and hang the explanation. It's written in such an interesting fashion that it draws you in, and it can't help but achieve just what the title claims for it.

King writes about Maine like he not only knows the state like the back of his hand, but every person in it! In story after story he weaves a convincing mythological history of the state surpassing even what H.P. Lovecraft wrought for Massachusetts. This story adds to the richness of the history King has been creating by telling a strange tale about the inexplicable happenings around a certain house. Much is left to the imagination, but it works like a charm. The story is thick with description, despite its brevity.

"**Man With A Belly**" (*Cavalier*, December '78) is another tale of the underworld about a hitman and the odd kind of hit he's called upon to make by an aging Don. It seems that the gangster's wife has been humiliating him by gambling his money away shamelessly. To avenge his honor, the Don wants his wife roughed up and raped-and then told why it was done. The story takes some odd turns after that, but crumbles into pointlessness at the end. If it's supposed to be a character study of the cold-blooded, heartless hitman, it just doesn't gel.

"**The Night of the Tiger**" (*Fantasy & Science Fiction*, Feb. '78) is one of King's lesser stories although it contains some interesting ideas. It takes place in a circus and involves a lion tamer, his rival, and a tiger named Green Terror. In the bizarre, supernatural climax, the vicious lion tamer reverts to his true, beastly nature in a fight to the finish with Green Terror, the beast he had tormented. The final battle takes place during a fierce thunderstorm.

"**Skybar**" (**The Do-It-Yourself-Bestseller,** 1982) is just the opening and closing paragraphs of what is supposed to be a novel. The book it appears in also includes such set-ups and conclusions by Isaac Asimov, Colin Wilson, John Jakes, Irving Wallace, and Alvin Toffler. The fragment opens with a recollection about an old amusement park, the Skybar, where twelve boys snuck in once after the place closed, but only two came out. The closing describes the boy's adult memories of the corpse of a boy who had been thrown from a roller coaster, and killed, but who still shambled after them in the funhouse.

"**Squad D**" (**The Last Dangerous Visions,** publication date uncertain) is about a Vietnam vet from Castle Rock, Maine, the sole survivor of his squad.

"**Suffer The Little Children**" (*Cavalier*, Feb. '72) is a story that concerns evil children reminiscent in some ways of Ray Bradbury's "Let's Play Poison." King has not had it included in any of his collections because he feels he inadvertently copied an idea already explored in a story by Stanley Ellin. An elderly, woman teacher discovers evil entities taking over all of the children in her classroom. They can even cause their new child bodies to shape-shift into horrible monsters. This realization finally pushes the teacher over the edge and she commits a heinous act in her attempts to fight back.

"**Weeds**" (*Cavalier*, May 1976) is an interesting little tale once again told in the tradition of E.C. Comics; like a Joe Orlando science fiction story, to be precise.

Jordy Verrill is a dim-witted farmer who, on the Fourth of July, sees a meteorite impact on his land. He hurries over to it and in the finest, time-honored, lame-brained tradition of such movies as **The Blob**, he touches it. Even the most horrible moments are told with dark humor, so that we can have a good time with it, just as we did with "The Lawnmower Man." Jordy Verrill wasn't a smart man. He wasn't feeble or retarded, but he sure wasn't going to win an Quiz Kid award, either. When God hands out the smart pills, he gives some people placebos, and Jordy was one of those.

The horrifying aspects of this idea appeared in Clark Ashton Smith's "The Seed From The Sepulchre," while King goes for the bizarre, morbid humor in the idea. Sort of like laughing at someone who slips in a pool of blood.

"**The Reploids**," published in *Night Visions* 5 (1988), reads like the first half of a story or the first chapter of a novel. It introduces a character who turns out to apparently be from a parallel Earth. It's not very well developed.

"**Sneakers**," published in *Night Visions* 5 (1988), is about a pair of ghostly sneakers which turn up in a men's room stall. It's an oddball little idea which is carried off well.

"**Dedication**," published in *Night Visions* 5 (1988), is easily King's most controversial story. Rejected by magazines which would otherwise jump at the chance to boost their circulation for an issue by featuring a King story, it's basic premise is so bizarre that even reading it becomes an exercise in will. Most reviewers have danced around the subject of the story because describing it is difficult to do in an inoffensive way. While this is a detailed and well thought out story, it revolves around a cleaning woman's inexplicable compulsion towards the semen from the sheet on a certain man's bed in the hotel where she works. This somehow leads to the conception of her son, so that she feels that her son is the son of this writer.

"The Night Flier," published in *Prime Evil* (1988), is a story about a vampire who flies an airplane, and tells the tale of the reporter who figures out the cause of a series of inexplicable crimes. It's pretty straightforward without surprises; a fun horror story.

"Rainy Season," published in *Midnight Graffiti* #3 (1989), is another down home story set in Strange Maine as some might call the state which King is determined to give a haunted reputation to. A story with a very dark sense of humor, it's about a couple who move into town on just the wrong night and refuse to heed advice to bolt their doors and shutters during the night. The impression is left that when the carnivorous toads appeared, *someone* had to die and these two just happened to be the luckless sacrifices. A down and dirty horror story such as King does best. This story is significant because King had suffered a year-long bout of Writer's Block after finishing **The Tommyknockers**, and writing this one afternoon broke through that block for him.

"Home Delivery," published in **Book Of The Dead** (1989), is set in a weird universe where the dead don't die as established in George Romero's **Night of the Living Dead** films. Set in the same island community as King's "The Reach" (aka "Do The Dead Sing"), we're introduced to a young woman who's husband is lost at sea, but who nonetheless makes it home, much the worse for the wear. A bizarre subplot involves an alien satellite orbiting in space and a group of astronauts who encounter it, leaving the impression that perhaps the living-dead phenomenon is of alien origin. It's a good story and one of the better entries in that original anthology.

Michael R. Adams

DANSE MACABRE

The Danse macabre is a waltz with death. This is a truth we cannot afford to shy away from. Like the rides in the amusement park which mimic violent death, the tale of horror is a chance to examine what's going on behind doors which we usually keep double-locked. Yet the human imagination is not content with locked doors. Somewhere these is another dancing partner, the imagination whispers in the night—a partner in a rotting ball gown, a partner with empty eye sockets, green mold growing on her elbow-length gloves, maggots squirming in the thin remains of her hair. To hold such a creature in our arms? Who, you ask me, would be so mad? Well. . .? —page 366

The excerpt above provides a good description not only of what horror is, but of why some people are fascinated by it. **Danse Macabre** deals with many examples of horror in print and in film in many of the guises it has adopted over the past thirty years. In ten chapters King examines novels, films and even the old E.C. comic books. E.C. is dealt with only glancingly, through a haze of nostalgia. The one story King deals with in detail is "Foul Play," a very atypical tale, memorable for that reason.

This is not a complete overview of horror since 1950. In the final chapter King outlines what he overlooked. This book offers only a cross-section.

King explains the problem he had writing this book in the chapter entitled, "An Annoying Autobiographical Pause."

I think that only people who have worked in the field for some time truly understand how fragile this stuff really is, and what an amazing commitment it imposes on the reader or viewer of intellect and maturity. When Coleridge spoke of "the suspension of disbelief" in his essay on imaginative poetry, I believe he knew that disbelief is not like a balloon, which may be suspended in air with a minimum of effort; it is like a lead weight which has to be hoisted with a clean jerk and held up by main force. Disbelief isn't light; it's heavy.

The difference in sales between Arthur Hailey and H.P. Lovecraft may exist because everyone believes in cars and banks, but it takes a sophisticated and muscular intellectual act to believe, even for a little while, in Nyarlathotep, the Blind Faceless One, the Howler in the Night. And whenever I run into someone who expresses a feeling along the lines of, "I don't read fantasy or go to any of those movies; none of it's real," I feel a kind of sympathy. They simply can't lift the weight of fantasy, the muscles of the imagination have grown too weak. pages 104-1 05

This is what is at the core of the book—showing readers what is available to them in fantasy between the covers of some very special books. King will no doubt annoy some devotees in that he dismisses most of the output of the original *Twilight Zone,* but he doesn't just dismiss the series in a casual manner. Rather King explains how he feels it could have been improved, citing Jack Finney's book **The Third Level** as an example of where he felt the show should have stretched.

Other books have examined horror films and still many others have tackled horror fiction, but **Danse Macabre** blazes new trails by showing how the two interrelate and affect each other, as well as how they have all shaped

King's own perceptions of the form. This is no superficial treatment but goes right to the heart of the genre and gives it its due in a manner which is detailed, thoughtful and eminently entertaining.

THE MASTERS OF TERROR — Director GEORGE ROMERO (left) and screenwriter (and debuting actor) STEPHEN KING have made their first movie together, "CREEPSHOW," a Warner Bros. release.

COPYRIGHT ©1982 WARNER BROS. INC.

PRINTED IN U.S.A.

BK-A-2

MEDIA MAYHEM

In the fifteen years since **Carrie** was first published, over a dozen movie adaptations and a television mini-series have brought Stephen King's words to cinematic life. This doesn't even include the anthology adaptations of short stories on such series as **The Twilight Zone** and **Tales from the Darkside**. This is an unprecedented number of screen adaptations of an author's work to occur in such a short time. What's equally surprising is that most of them have not been box-office successes but new adaptations continually appear. An example of the hit and miss success rate of the films occurred in the summer of '86 when **Maximum Overdrive** was released to dismal box-office and poor reviews followed a month later by **Stand By Me** which became a certified hit and received the best notices of any film yet adapted from a King story.

A brief overview of the features should give an idea of why there such a pattern exists.

CARRIE (1976)

This is the film which brought both Sissy Spacek and Brian DePalma popular recognition and truly established their careers. The ghost of Hitchcock was present in this film, even to DePalma naming the school Norman Bates High. While DePalma captures the essence of the brutality of the high school in-crowd syndrome, he veers off in less certain directions with Carrie's mother (played by Piper Laurie). Although the novel makes it clear the woman's religious fanaticism is an outgrowth of her insanity, the film gives no perspective whatsoever. It's just there. When Carrie kills her mother, the film brings on a reprisal of biblical proportions, further blurring the focus of the story. Budget limitations prohibited the massive burning of the town described in the novel. This would not be the last time that a film chose to ignore the climax of King's book in favor of a different slant. Still, the shock ending the film uses works quite well and has itself been imitated in subsequent horror films. In spite of its flaws, *Carrie* still stands as one of the best screen translations of King's work.

SALEM'S LOT (1979)

Originally broadcast as a four hour mini-series (on two nights, a week apart, no less), it was only seen in its four hour version once until syndicated in 1985. When rerun it was trimmed to fit a three hour slot while cable and video presented a 90 minute version made for European theatrical release. The last contains a couple short scenes too violent to be aired on commercial television.

The story of a small Maine town being taken over by vampires actually filmed quite well under director Tobe Hooper. Some scenes are unfortunately truncated while others translated without the payoff. The biggest flaw, though, is the portrayal of Barlow looking like the classic film vampire Nosferatu, with a mouth full of teeth that make it impossible for him to speak any dialogue! That is almost made up for by James Mason in a delicious performance as the vampire's human, and very malignant.

Except for the fact that people start believing in the vampire a little too fast, the story is well told, particularly when the young boy returns from the grave. It's all very atmospheric and marks one of the rare instances in the last decade where a horror story has been presented on prime time network television.

THE SHINING (1980)

A stunning film which is marvelous to watch and actually works half the time. The Overlook Hotel is well realized by Stanley Kubrick, but unfortunately he has Jack Nicholson starting out as a slightly crazed character who steadily gets worse instead of as a normal man who is broken down by the hotel's ghostly influence. Scatman Crothers is brilliant as Halloran. Why Kubrick chooses to kill the character off when he comes to rescue Danny, the psychic little boy, is totally mystifying. The film ends in a maze instead of with the destruction of the hotel and its evil influence, as in the book. In fact the movie cuts off the entire climax, leaving it wide open for someone else to do a more faithful adaptation.

CREEPSHOW (1982)

The anthology horror film has been with us a long time and t. They have always been a mixed blessing. This one is no exception. This group of King short stories is linked by the framing device of a ghoulish narrator and an old mythical comic called *Creepshow*. The stories don't translate well to the screen.

"The Crate" is adapted from a previously published story about a man who finds out how to get rid of his nagging wife by feeding her to a little monster. It reads better than it plays.

"The Lonesome Death of Jordy Verrill" (published under the title "Weeds") is about weeds from outer space which grow on anything, even a person. Stephen King plays the title role and has lots of fun with the role.

The other two stories are originals, both riffs on the revenge theme. In one corpses come back from the sea to exact justice and in the other, cockroaches exact revenge in an extremely difficult to watch story if you're the least bothered by the pesky little things.

Overall the film is fun without being memorable or powerful.

THE DEAD ZONE (1983)

David Cronenberg *(Scanners, Videodrome)* comes down to earth to direct a film which avoids visceral shocks to concentrate on the strange and often downbeat story of a man who can see glimpses of the future. Johnny Smith is in an auto accident and lapses into a four year long coma. Upon awakening he finds that he has to recapture and rebuild nearly everything he'd achieved, but this is complicated by his newly acquired ability. Along the way he helps a sheriff solve a string of vicious murders before deciding to single-handedly end the career of a mad political aspirant in order to head off a future holocaust.

Christopher Walken perfectly captures the essence of this wounded and troubled man, even when he chooses a path which demands an assassination. A powerful and disturbing film, the odd decisions made in adapting the story don't really cripple it. For instance, Johnny's old girlfriend turns up as a member of the mad politician's staff just so that she'll be conveniently on hand for the climax. Otherwise its quite well done, certainly one of the three best translations of King's novels to the screen.

CUJO (1983)

This story of a woman and her child trapped in her car by a rabid St. Bernard works better as a film than I would have thought. The novel is pretty thin on plot. In fact, this is a much better film than it has any right to be considering the very weak book it' s based on.

In an interview once, King explained that you can't build up an audience's interest in a character and then just kill him off at the end of a long, torturous story, but that's exactly what he did in the novel when he kills the little boy off right after he's rescued. The film-makers decided this was a bad idea so the boy lives at the end. There's really nothing more to be said about this film.

CHRISTINE (1983)

This film was directed by John Carpenter and released almost simultaneously with the first paperback publication of the novel. It holds the record for going from book to movie the fastest as it was already going into production when the hardcover was first released. Unfortunately, this story of a car haunted by its previous owner just isn't all that gripping. It quickly becomes a revenge film when the car starts killing off a bunch of young toughs who have been harassing the car's new owner. The most interesting aspect of the film is the role played by John Stockwell, that of a jock who is portrayed as a person rather than a cliche. All in all, though, this is a pretty weak story which did pretty poorly at the box-office.

FIRESTARTER (1984),

Although a very close adaptation of the novel, somehow the film comes across as limp and lacking real impact. While George C. Scott as the Indian assassin Rainbird sounds like inspired, if bizarre, casting, his character is never really developed as in the novel. For instance, the film never reveals that Rainbird likes to look into the eyes of his victims as he kills them because he wants to try to see what they see as they die. He wants to kill the little girl, Charlie, because she's such an extraordinary specimen since she possesses pyrokinesis, the power to start fires. In the film when he says that he wants her, it comes across with a totally different meaning.

Since I always felt the climax of the book was predictable, I was hoping the film would try another approach. For instance, in the book it states that there was one other survivor of the experiments performed by The Shop, but that he had never manifested any abilities. What if he had been hiding his abilities? What if he had all of the powers that the others had exhibited? A climax in which he rescued Charlie and destroyed the shop would have been much more interesting.

CHILDREN OF THE CORN (1984)

Easily the worst and most inept of the adaptations of King to the screen. While the short story from which this comes cried out for a follow-up. The movie needed more plot, not just padding of the existing plot. The major problem is that the main characters of the story, a bickering married couple, are replaced with a young couple who are just boyfriend and girlfriend. He-Who-Walks-Behind-The-Rows has become something which one reviewer described as "gophers from Hell" rather than the monster glimpsed in the original story. Rather than explain where "He" came from, it just comes on to be dispatched by the hero. A dull script poorly filmed makes for a classic in bad cinema.

CATSEYE (1985)

Another anthology film which goes for a different kind of story than **Creepshow**. Two segments are suspense stories with no supernatural elements. They could have worked as episodes of **Alfred Hitchcock Presents**. The third story, about a little troll who tries to kill a child, is visually the most interesting but marred by unnecessary gags. The film's connecting thread, that of a cat who turns up in each story, doesn't work. It makes no sense because the opening story of the film, which explained the presence of the cat, was dropped. It revealed that the cat's previous owner was killed by the troll and now it's out to hunt it down. This would have played better as a television movie. Anthology films aren't popular with audiences because just as you're getting interested in a main character the story is over. They're good adaptations of the King stories, though.

SILVER BULLET (1985)

The otherwise fine script to this film was written by King but some of the best parts never made it to the screen. The director turned it into just another werewolf film in which Corey Haim plays a plucky crippled boy who outsmarts the beast. The film offers a great dream sequence in which a church full of people turn into werewolves where the makeup is vastly superior to the disappointing doglike creature seen in the climax. Gary Busey shines in his role as the boy's uncle who comes to believe his nephew's story about what the Full Moon Killer really is. It's a fun movie but by no means what it could have been.

MAXIMUM OVERDRIVE (1986)

Stephen King takes the bull by the horns and it gores him. In his directorial debut, King chose to take a short story and puff it up into a feature. In so doing we get a lot of machines wrecking havoc on the soft, squishy humans but after awhile it becomes a bit repetitious. Because he felt they slowed the film down, King threw out all the character scenes from the script so that what's left is loud and flashy but lacking in substance. Being both the writer and director, King seemed to get caught up in the logistics of filming machines going amuck and attacking people while overlooking that the people being attacked need more than superficial personality. In a situation where it looks pretty bleak as to their chances of survival, we never get under their skin to learn who's living there.

The pressures of filming for King are exemplified by the fact that even though the characters utter a lot of profanity, he didn't record a backup soundtrack to use when the film is sold to commercial television. In explaining why this happened, King states, "I forgot!"

STAND BY ME (1986)

This property was shopped to studios all over town and no one would touch it. Aside from the fact that Stephen King films have not been big moneymakers, production heads just didn't feel that a mass audience would be interested in a film about four 12 year olds. It reminds me of similar stories of how studios had decided that no one would want to see a film about old people (**On Golden Pond**) or a little kid and an alien (**E T**). When the film opened in August '86 it received glowing reviews. Excellent word of mouth from patrons caused the box-office to remain consistently good.

Based on the story "The Body," the film kept that title throughout production until it was wisely decided that it sounded too much like a horror tale rather than a coming of age story. The setting was changed to Oregon (where it was filmed) from Maine (where the original story is set). The cast is marvelous and the directing by Rob Reiner both powerful and sensitive. The adaptation is perfect, including the story within a story about the pie eating contest.

The framing story about the writer thinking back on this childhood adventure originally featured a different actor who was later replaced with entirely new footage with Richard Dreyfuss. The first actor can still be glimpsed, though, in the long shots of the writer sitting in his parked car.

The soundtrack for the film, like **American Graffiti**, consists of late Fifties rock and roll tunes to firmly establish the ambience of the period. Until **Stand By Me**, Cronenberg's adaptation of **The Dead Zone** had come the closest to capturing the sensitivity of King's characters. This film portrays the characters we read in the story. We feel their turmoil and angst just as strongly as they do. While King's reputation is largely that of a horror writer, **Stand By Me** portrayed a broader canvas of perspective.

CREEPSHOW II (1987)

The worst of all the films based on Stephen King stories, "The Raft" is the only previously published story which is adapted here. The other tales are all originals. The adaptation of "The Raft" is marred by the film's low budget and shoddy special effects. The blob which absorbs people looks like a plastic garbage bag floating in the water and the story has none of the tension communicated by the text. A new ending is added to the story which doesn't help. The film misses a sure bet when the sequence closes by showing a No Trespassing sign which should have also said: Violators will be eaten. Without that, the story falls flat. The rest of the film consists of revenge stories in which a wooden cigar store Indian comes to life and slays a gang of toughs who killed the old people (George Kennedy and Dorothy Lamour) who'd been running the store for decades. The story begs the question: if the Indian could come to life to avenge the old folks, why didn't it come to life to save them? There's also a tale of a woman who's relentlessly pursued by the body of a hitch-hiker she accidentally ran down. It drags on and on to an inevitable conclusion. The only story which really works is about a little boy picked on by a gang of toughs until the gang meets his collection of carnivorous plants. This last story takes place entirely in poor, modern day limited animation.

This film is a hodgepodge of warmed over, poorly thought out and badly realized ideas. Coming after the best Stephen King adaptation, **Stand By Me**, it is the worst of the bunch.

THE RUNNING MAN (1987)

Optioned for a film based on the Richard Bachman novel of the same name before word got out Bachman was a pen name for King, King's name was played up when the film was released even though it bears only superficial resemblance to his book. While the novel is a dark view of the near future when a life or death game show chase is the only way out of crushing poverty for the nation's underclass, the film is nothing more than mindless action adventure. In the film, Arnold Schwarzenegger is forced into the contest when he's framed as a criminal by the corrupt government. During the hunt he becomes involved with the underground and in the end we're led to believe the destruction of the game show will lead to the downfall of the government! The film portrays a Roman Coliseum-style audience who cheer whenever one of the contestants is killed. Why they would cheer the hunters over the hunted is never made clear as game shows have traditionally had the audiences rooting for the contestants. The film came under criticism because theater audiences cheered the deaths of the hunters with the same bloodthirsty enthusiasm as the studio audience in the film cheered the massacre of contestants. Life parodying art?

PET SEMATARY (1989)

King is a hands-on participant in the film-making process again. This time, rather than directing, he wrote the screenplay, consulted with the director and even helped get the film made in Maine. King had come under criticism in the past because films set in Maine were shot elsewhere. The locations are excellent here, and King does a fine job adapting his novel. Whether you like the film will depend on your enthusiasm for the novel itself. Like the book, the film tortures all of its characters and then kills them at the end without a glimmer of hope. It's a very bleak story of the disintegration of a man's family and life. While King has stated horror comes from caring about the people being subjected to awful incidents, that presupposes some chance of winning out. Here all we can do is sit back and ponder how horrible it will be before they're put out of their misery. Not even their poor cat escapes the cruel machinations of fate. One of the most disturbing scenes in the film is when Louis Creed executes his little boy by injecting a fast-acting poison into the boy's neck. The boy returns from the dead as a murderous zombie-child. It's a horror film which twists your insides.

ON TV

Tales From The Darkside:

"The Word Processor of the Gods" originally appeared in Playboy magazine under the title "The Word Processor," a title which works better than the more grandiose one King gave it in this adaptation. It's a very interesting short story which somehow didn't translate into a half-hour television episode. While the original story stresses the tragedy of the dead wife and child of the writer's brother, this adaptation instead details how awful the writer's wife and child are. This twists the focus entirely and turns it into a typical "magic typewriter" tale in which the self-centered writer achieves his dreams. It becomes a story of a cruel fate set right instead of the unhappy life of the writer being improved. It's what's missing from the adaptation that spoils the perspective.

The Twilight Zone:

"Gramma" was aired for the 1985 Halloween show. This is an excellent adaptation of what must have been a challenging story to translate to the screen consisting of an internal monologue of an eleven year old boy. Screenwriter Harlan Ellison cracked the visual codex to present the eerie, suspenseful and frightening incidents as witnessed by the little boy as his dying grandmother (a powerful witch in her day) reaches out with her mystical strength one last time to snatch victory from the jaws of death. This adaptation, directed by cinematographer Bradford May, makes much of lighting techniques to enhance mood and action. An effective and unsettling use of mnemonic voiceovers (which includes one vocalization by Ellison) helps fill in background on the dying woman who never utters a word, but who waits, silently, like a vulture watching its prey. The adaptation succeeds in capturing the essence of this story which, in other hands, might have fallen flat.

Other King films have been periodically announced as being in the works, including the on-again, off-again adaptation of **The Stand**, as well as the ABC mini-series based on **It.** ABC apparently bought the novel before they realized the focus of the story was the murder of children, a subject they are not eager to dramatize in a 10-hour mini-series. Several years ago Stephen Spielberg bought the film rights to **The Talisman,** a property the director apparently still considers a future film project. Since Spielberg talked about making **Always** for seven years before he finally filmed it.

THE NEW HORROR KING

Clive Barker was unknown in the genre of horror and dark fantasy when his six anthologies, **The Books of Blood**, were published in 1984 & 85. Although anthologies are notoriously difficult to market, Barker found a British publisher who not only accepted the series of six books, but allowed him to illustrate the covers for the hardback editions. The books were a smash in England and it didn't take long for word of this exciting new writer to reach America. Many writers in the genre, especially scribners such as Stephen King and Ramsey Campbell, were singing the praises of this new talent. Other writers were not so enthusiastic and found the graphic nature of many of Barker's short fiction to be not at all to their liking.

By the time that **Books of Blood** was being reprinted in the United States, Barker's first novel was being published in England, and **The Damnation Game** showed the writer broadening his range, which he demonstrated still further in **Weaveworld** two years later. Barker is a writer who has not cared to stand too long in one spot, quickly moving into the director's chair when two adaptations of his stories made by other hands turned out badly. Barker's first film, **Hellraiser**, was a hit and his second directorial effort, **Nightbreed**, follows in 1990. While dark fantasy has largely been the province in which he has worked, Barker has moved in many different directions within the wide boundaries of this genre, and the future promises further experiments by this talented writer.

—-JAMES VAN HISE

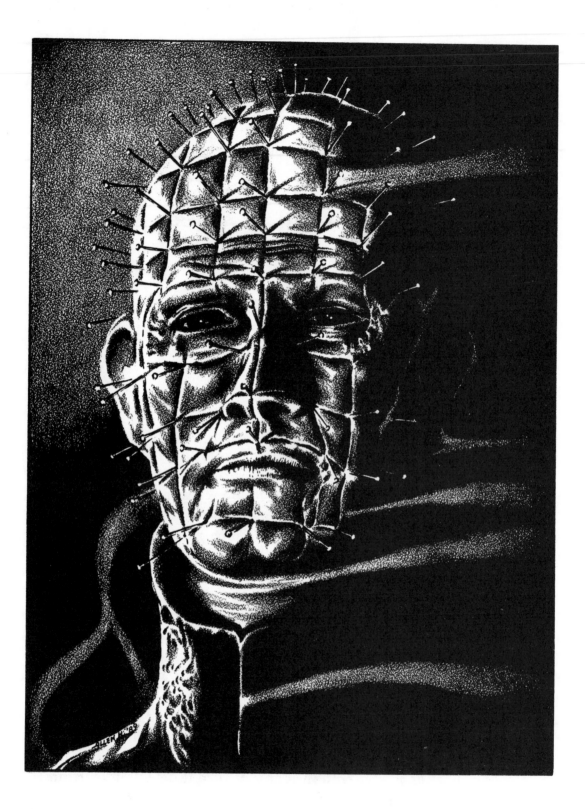

THE NEW KING

by Bob Strauss

Upon publication of Barker's fiction in the United States, the writer journeyed here to become acquainted with the new fans of his work, and to be interviewed by the American press who were anxious to learn more about this man whom Stephen King had dubbed "the future of horror." The following is one of those interviews conducted with Clive Barker on one of his first visits to these American shores. Wonder how he liked it here in "The Colonies"?

A new King of horror fiction is stalking the land, and he doesn't answer to the name of Stephen. He's Clive Barker, a babyfaced 37-year-old from Liverpool, England, and in less than four years he's become the scariest man in the world. The author of several plays, six bestselling short story collections known as **The Books of Blood** (reprinted in the U.S. under such titles as **In The Flesh** and **The Inhuman Condition**), the groundbreaking supernatural novel **The Damnation Game** and the equally inventive fantasy opus **Weaveworld**, and writer/director of the hit horror movie **Hellraiser**, (and of the current release, **Nightbreed**), Barker is a one-man dynamo of disturbing ideas, grisly images and—unusual in this often graceless field of childish fears and gross-out shocks—surprisingly well-wrought prose.

Old King Stephen has already acknowledged his successor. "I have seen the future of horror and it is named Clive Barker," King has said. "He is so good that I am almost literally tongue-tied. He makes the rest of us look like we've been asleep for the past ten years."

And although he's the type of guy who's content to work in the vineyards of other dimensions and graveyards of the semi-dead for (at least) the rest of his life—"John Updike I will never be," Barker likes to say—the gifted writer has more on his mind than merely scaring or sickening his readers.

"The underpinning of a lot of fantastic fiction—horror, science fiction, fantasy—is metaphysical," suggests the friendly, intellectually adventurous Barker in a speaking voice that reminds you of early Beatles press conferences (he grew up a few blocks from the actual Penny Lane). "They're the tales of the collective tribe, the fundamental metaphors of confrontation with things that may devour us or may offer us transcendence, and may be offering both in the same moment. At its best, fantastic fiction creates an immensely sophisticated, metaphorical language about very basic human issues. I'm not denigrating entertainment, but I hope that good horror fiction can be more than that. For me, it is only going to make sense if it somehow liberates you into a new truth of some kind."

In the fantasy realms of Clive Barker, liberations of many kinds—the body, the spirit, the longing for love—walk hand-in-hand with the threat of imprisonment, madness, mutilation and all manner of damnations. He shies away from such traditional horror icons as vampires and werewolves, preferring instead to explore the creepier possibilities of such recognizable human motivations as desires and the hunger for power. Barker's books are loaded with outre sexual couplings between the living, the dead, and those not quite either; and with mortifications of the flesh (a favorite motif of Barker's is the sadomasochistic piercing of skin with hooks, needles, et cetera).

"I do try," Barker laughs about his graphic preoccupation with physical pain and pleasure. Again, what the average shockmeister would use for mere icky ef-

CLIVE BARKER

fect, Barker employs with deeper allegorical significance. "A lot of horror fiction is about individualism and the loss of individuality," he says. "That has a great deal to do with how much each of us possesses our own body, and how much it's outside of our possession.

"Flesh is the fundamental problem into which we are born. It is the first paradox we are aware of, long before we know what the word paradox means. The very same nerve endings which present us with pleasure if stroked in the right way give us pain if that hand which strokes us decides to slap us instead. We're aware of that paradox real early; Mum will do it to us. We also learn at a young age that certain pleasures we can induce for ourselves—masterbation being an obvious one—are forbidden, secret, taboo. We're in classic Freud territory here, toilet training and the whole lot, all of which may seem a thousand miles from the stuff of fantasy and horror fiction. I think it's fundamental."

Barker's unflinching combination of psychosexual and horror themes (a typical example: **Hellraiser,** based on Barker's novella "The Hell-Bound Heart", is about a sexually obsessed woman who lures strange men to her house so her undead lover can kill them and bathe in their blood, which will gradually return him to corporeal human form and, by extension, her arms) has resulted in some conservative-minded critics accusing him of sensationalism and unwarranted titillation. To the author, finally bringing sex out of the genre's closet is just one of many strategies he uses to "renew fantastic fiction by stripping it, by de-romanticizing it, by taking away its knee-jerk conventions and seeing whether it still works without the cliches that have been so much a part of its recent history.

"I wrote an introduction to a collection of sexual horror stories called **Scared Stiff,**" Barker notes. "In it, I said that one of the reasons horror fiction falls shy of being considered serious writing is that there's a general belief these kinds of stories have sexuality as their subtext, and that by bringing that subtext into the more prominent position of text, you somehow call the bluff of the machine that made the thing work in the first place. You've pulled the hood off, so to speak, and people feared that in showing the workings, the magic wouldn't work any longer.

"I don't think that's true at all (it doesn't stop me, certainly). Any genre that requires the willful disregard of certain facts that we all know to make it work, is moribund by definition."

Besides his recognition of sexuality's role in human affairs, Barker applies many other facts as he knows them to his complex, highly entertaining fiction. A non-Christian who logically assumes most of his readers share the same view, he refuses to fall back on old standbys like crucifixes and holy water as remedies to his more monstrous creations. And he does not cleave to narrative notions that have grown from two thousand years of Western religious thought. For example, his first novel, **The Damnation Game,** has as its central villain a seemingly immortal being named Mamoulian who can animate the dead, create horrifyingly real illusions, possess other people's bodies and who, apparently, never forgets someone who owes him a debt.

Satan, right? Wrong. "The chief perspective for me, in that story, comes when Mamoulian says, 'Every man is his own Mephistopheles,' "Barker explains. "This is the 'Faust' story without the Devil, and the whole point is that it must be without the Devil. Mamoulian is not only just a guy, but a guy we can relate to because he's lonely, and all you have to take on board for this book to work is the single idea that he has these few special powers. That flies in the face of generic expectations; it says, 'Forget **The Omen.** Forget **The Exorcist,** that's not actually the way the world is.' "

CLIVE BARKER

With his second novel, **Weaveworld**, Barker tries to do for the invented world genre what he's so successfully pulled off in the horror field. The story of a secret universe woven into the design of an oriental rug, **Weaveworld** unfolds, for the most part, in the very real environment of economically depressed Liverpool. And that's just one of the ways Barker tries to revitalize the fantasy novel by exploding its conventions from within.

"It's an anti-fantasy fantasy book," he cheerfully proclaims. "I'm trying to avoid the typical structure of these stories, in which the invented world is somehow a place of escape where values are simplified and you know good from bad by the color of its eyes or the horse it rides on. I don't think it works if, when the story is over, you end up sighing for a world of simplified values and artificial solutions that only work for the period of time you're reading them. In other words, it's fiction as lie, as opposed to fiction as metaphorical truth.

"I wanted to see what happens if you take from an invented world the elves, the faeries, the wizards, the magic powers—all the crap that has accrued around the whole idea. What are you left with? The basic question asked by **Weaveworld** is, 'What is a working definition of Eden?' which is the first invented world we are offered as children. And if such a definition is possible, how do you write a fiction about the problem of Eden? The problem being—again, as we're taught when kids—that we lost it because of a sin that had something to do with knowledge.

"As I see it, we're taught by the wise apes in our community that we shall not look, that we did bad stuff, and the bad stuff was about wanting too much in the way of information. Being too curious, desiring too much. If those things are sick or bad, then I'll join the bad and the sick any time. I cannot make that work in my head, so I have to define Eden as being something else."

Regardless of his rigorous philosophical questings and grand theoretical experiments, Barker writes visceral, suspensefully involving stories that never fail to entertain. He discovered his imaginative gifts early in life. A pudgy, nearsighted child, he lived in a world of comic books and Edgar Allan Poe stories. Unable to compete in most sports, he made friends by telling them outlandish stories, inspired by his favorite literature. As he grew older, Barker studied art (he's illustrated the British editions of most of his books), and gradually gravitated toward writing macabre, *Grand Guignol*-style plays, two of which were produced at the prestigious Edinburgh Arts Festival. His most recent play, "The Secret Life of Cartoons," opened in London a couple years ago.

Barker ultimately realized that his true calling was in writing the same kind of bizarre tales—from a more complex, adult point of view, of course—he used to astound his pals around the schoolyard with. Ever growing as a prose stylist, a philosophical inquirer and an observer of human nature, Barker still sees his highest calling as that of a fantasist.

"It's just my dream to be known as an imaginer, as somebody who makes worlds," he insists. "When I was a kid, I had a book by Ray Bradbury. In it was a picture of Ray with stuff that he had imagined drawn all around his head: Mars, the illustrated Man and miracles of various kinds.

"I want that for myself. I want people to associate Barker with the real world reinvented in a literary or cinematic form. But in such a way that they can leave the moviehouse or put down the book knowing that they can begin to reinvent this," Barker says, tapping knuckles on a table that, to him, represents the definable world, "and our relationship to this.

"Works of the imagination are, finally, tools for change," he concludes. "They're not, and should never be, substitutes for reality."

NAUGHTY BITS

by Cliff Burns

One aspect of Clive Barker's work which has made it controversial in some quarters is the explicit nature of some of it. While not every Barker story indulges in graphic depictions of violence and bizarre sexual activity, some of it marches fearlessly into realms where others fear to tread, and describes what is found there. Cliff Burns, a young writer who has been making a name for himself in small press publications, lifts the veil on some of the more disturbing scenes in Barker's fiction and reveals what he finds.

"In extremis, he clawed at the polluted mirror before him, and through the dusky air saw gobs of the child's flesh come away. There was a rush of bluish matter—like its mother's stuff—the chill of which slapped him back from dying, and he drove his fingers deeper into the beast's face. Its size had been gained at the price of durability. Its skull was wafer thin. He made a hook of his fingers and pulled. The beast howled and dropped him, the filth of its workings spilling out. . . "

—from **Weaveworld** by Clive Barker

Ah, music to the eyes, isn't it? As you read the words, can't you picture the scene in your mind? Don't you actually experience physical sensations, imagine yourself mauling a face that has the consistency of runny plasticine?

That's Clive Barker when he's running on all cylinders putting the pedal to the metal and creating good, straight ahead, hard-driving horror.

Here's another good one:

"Ian knew he was beyond salvation from the beginning, because he'd died this way in his sleep on a hundred occasions and Daddy never got there in time. The mouth was wider even than he'd dreamed it, a hole which he was being delivered into, head first. It smelled like the dustbins at the back of the school canteen, times a million. He was sick down its throat, as it bit the top of his head off."

That was from "Rawhead Rex," a nasty bit of writing that appears in the third volume of Barker's World Fantasy Award-winning series **The Books Of Blood.**

To those of you as yet unfamiliar with Clive Barker's work (yeah, right), you are hereby warned: *approach with caution*, the author is armed and dangerous. Barker, like director David Cronenberg—whom he admires—is not content to merely scare. . . he must also horrify. And to that end, his will be done. He is not above the old pie-in-the-face shtick; but Barker's pie is a rancid stew of offal that overpowers the sensibilities and sends our preconceptions scurrying for cover.

Make no mistake, Clive Barker wants a response from you, the reader, and he isn't too particular about what kind of reaction it is; just as long as it's heartfelt and, better yet, *extreme.*

Barker writes about bodies that are (sometimes literally as in "The Body Politic") in revolt against their human operators. Like Cronenberg, he seeks "the new flesh," an unprecedented hybrid of man and beast that is not imprisoned by intellect or cowed by conscience. Barker sees us, his fellow human beings, as an untrustworthy, suspicious, unsavory lot with very little to recommend us. It is time to improve the breed. Of course, in order to do that there must be experiments, and some of them will no doubt fail. We may accidentally spawn half-aborted monsters and then find that our hoary creations don't appreciate our endeavors on their

behalf. . . as Doctors Frankenstein and Jekyll, among others, discovered—always just a tick too late.

Barker's monsters are of a different kind; his have forsaken cosmetic surgery and catgut, they make no attempt to mimic human shape. They drool flesh and brandish strange, stunted limbs and drag themselves across the ground, leaving long wet trails behind them. Frequently it is only their mewling cries that reveal their human ancestry. These are self-made monsters; for their sins—even if they are only sins of association—they have been turned inside out and when they lurch out of the shadows they are caricatures of humanity: a fetid, flapping collage of entrails and sinew.

"She half-turned in the bed, eyes closed, as if rolling over in her sleep. Then—horribly—she said his name. Her mouth didn't work as it had; blood greased the word on its way. He couldn't bear to look any more or he'd scream, and that would bring them—whoever did this—bring them howling at him with their scalpels already wet. They were probably outside the door already; but nothing could induce him to stay in the same room. Not with her performing slow gyrations on the bed, still saying his name as she pulled up her nightdress."

—**The Damnation Game** (1985)

The Damnation Game was Barker's first full-length effort, a book which earned him a good deal of critical acclaim but also, as an added bonus, a nomination for the much-coveted Booker Prize. It is Barker's most difficult book, but also, I feel, his finest hour. It does seem to take an awfully long time to get going, but right about page 100 it finds its stride and from there induces a spell of queasy fascination right up until the end—where it tapers off again, unfortunately. Still, it is one of the finest horror novels of the Eighties; a provocative and thoughtful read.

It concerns Marty Strauss, a resident of Wandsworth Penitentiary, who's just had his first real bit of luck in six years. He is being released early in order to take up a position in the household of Joseph Whitehead, pharmaceutical mogul. What starts out as a second chance at life becomes a series of harrowing encounters with a representative of Doom and Despair; he is Mamoulian, a once-great enchanter whose last days are preoccupied with the everlasting terrors of the Void, the vast gulfs to which the soul-less are consigned after death. He has an old grudge to settle with Whitehead and he'll not be cheated by the magnate. . . not again.

Are you ready for necrophilia? Cannibalism? Bubbling toilets? Then **The Damnation Game** is for you. If you prefer your horror a little *lighter*, well, then maybe you'd better haul your favorite Stephen King book off the shelf and read it through again.

The two writers share precious little in common. King's style is relaxed, conversational. Barker is more lyrical, darker, bloodier. King's horrors come from without; Barker's from within. King's books, in the past at least, have frequently featured some truly fine writing and some extremely scary moments. But King, for all his diatribes against Reagan, Republicanism and gun freaks is essentially a conservative man with a strong sense of right and wrong. His heroes are imbued with moral purpose and follow strict codes of conduct; more often than not they survive their encounters with THE ULTIMATE EVIL, becoming better, stronger Americans in the process. And while all of this may be *affirming* and *positive*, it also gets a bit predictable and boring.

In interviews and in conversations, King is ingenuous and engaging. He appears tickled pink that his little tales give people the creepy-crawlies. It's all good fun to

CLIVE BARKER

him. This guy likes his beer and his baseball and for entertainment he goes and watches autopsies being performed.

No, no, of course he doesn't.

But Clive Barker does. That's what it says—right here. Which leads us to wonder if Barker is the victim of an overzealous advertising man or if he's a genuine, dyed-in-the-wool wingnut. I don't know him personally, so I don't think I'm the one to say. I do know his work; I think I've read just about everything the man's written. I know he's a gifted writer who affects me as few writers do. . .

Oh, I know that Chris Lacher, **New Blood**'s inimitable editor, swears high and low that Richard Laymon was kicking ass when the splatter punks were still fantasizing about hacking Annette Fullsome into itty-bitty pieces for slow dancing with that jerk Ted Longdong at the Freshie Dance. I could remind him of Philip Jose Farmer's legendary **Image of the Beast**, published originally in 1968. Yes, of course Barker has forebears. But while authors like Laymon and Farmer may have done it first, Barker does it *better*. They assume strong standpoints, affix themselves firmly on the side of Good and by so doing objectify the horror; Barker approaches the task somewhat differently. He presents us with protagonists who have been compromised; they are somehow already sullied by the time the story begins. Thus, we don't really know what motivates them or where their allegiances lie. They are paradoxical and unstable and all too susceptible to the allure of Evil.

"What do the good know?" The Candyman, a murderous legend granted flesh in "The Forbidden," asks rhetorically. "Except what the bad teach them by their excesses?"

It is a statement that brings to mind Blake's famous dictum that "The road of excess leads to the palace of wisdom."

Barker wants to explore through excess, using horror to create moments of pure *frisson*. It comes as no surprise that in an essay on King, Barker discusses horror as a source of self-illumination. Thanks to Barker's machinations many of his characters *do* eventually see the light, or at least a hopeful glimmer that signifies a kind of understanding—usually just before they get their throats torn out. Oh, yes, they must pay a hefty price for that grim knowledge. They are made to suffer ghastly mutilations, and have heinous indignities inflicted on them; it's all part of the learning process:

"In desperation Boyle fought back, but the man's passion lent him ungovernable strength. With one insolent hand holding the policeman's head, he tore at Boyle's trousers and underwear, leaving his buttocks exposed. . .

. . . 'Stop,' he murmured into the wall, not to his attacker but to his body, urging it not to find pleasure in this outrage. But his nerve endings were treacherous; they caught fire from the assault. Beneath the stabbing agony some unforgivable part of him rose to the occasion. . . "

How many male readers are shifting uncomfortably as they read this passage from "The Age of Desire"? How many of us hold a secret fear of something similar happening to us? Our bodies violated but at the same time responding to the violation.

Sex is power.

It lays waste to our defenses. It over-rides good sense, short-circuits the higher functions. Our universe contracts until it approximates the contours of our bodies; our hearts thud concussively as we grind into each other, our vocabulary reduced to paleolithic grunts—

"Her body was seething, her shaved sex opening and closing like some exquisite plant, purple and lilac and rose. . . "
—"Jacqueline Ess: Her Will and Testament"

"The dress billowed up a little higher and he stared, fixated, at the part of Marilyn he had never seen, the fur divide that had been the dream of millions.

"There was blood there. Not much, a few fingermarks on her inner thighs. The faultless gloss of her flesh was spoiled slightly. Still he stared; and the lips parted a little as she moved her hips, and he realized the gline of wetness in her interior was not the juice of her body, but something else altogether. As her muscles moved the bloody eyes she'd buried in her body shifted, and came to rest on him."
—"Son of Celluloid"

In **Weaveworld**, Barker's most commercially successful book and his personal favorite, an ectoplasmic nasty gets her/its jollies by raping men and then giving birth to their polluted off-spring. Yechhhh!

Weaveworld is, by turns, kinky and enjoyable, though maybe a bit slick in spots. It is truly a "dark" fantasy, darker than King's **Gunslinger** and more literate and original than **The Talisman.** Unfortunately **Weaveworld** and Barker's newest book, **Cabal,** seem to indicate that the Englishman is mellowing, perhaps acceding to the wishes of the majority of horror fans who like to see the lines between good and evil strictly delineated. **Weaveworld** boasts heroes in abundance but no *anti*-heroes, and its villains, with the exception of Immacolata—an intriguing creation and a credit to Barker's prowess as a writer—prove to be villainous through and through. It is a tame book by Barker's standards, both in content and form. The battle scenes are fairly bloodless, the plot line unencumbered by unsightly convolutions. It is a fast read, perhaps the best introduction to his work I can suggest. From there, I'd tackle **The Books of Blood** (Volumes 1-VI) and then have a go at **The Damnation Game,** bypassing the lamentable **Cabal** completely. **Cabal,** like a lot of other novels out there, would have made a damn fine short story. Barker must not agree, otherwise why would he adapt **Cabal** into **The Nightbreed,** a feature film?

Well. . . Clive Barker is certainly not infallible. He is perfectly capable of delivering up a dud. **Cabal** is pretty terrible and he must be held at least partially accountable for **Hellraiser II,** which should have made everyone's Ten Worst List. His stories sometimes give the impression that they could use another spin through the typewriter; just one more quick polish.

Barker's record is still enviable. Most of his stories do the job and that job is finding new ways to get our goat. They make us uncomfortable. They make us wonder. They make us sick and they make us believe. In spite of its surreal trappings, "In The Hills, The Cities," *works*; bringing to mind the mythic power of a Ballard or a Burroughs. Like Ballard's "The Drowned Giant," Barker's tale makes no attempt to impose credulity; it begins without offering a caveat that an unnerving and totally original vision is about to be imparted. You can tell, this one wrote itself. It is timeless the way that only the best tales are. And, oh yeah, the two main characters in the story are homosexual lovers. Wouldn't you know it?

Go ahead, bitch about the writhing pudendas and the bestiality and the pederasty. But give Barker credit for the sheer diversity of characters he has introduced us to: the ex-cons, the street-wise punks, the homos, the freaks, the geeks. . . and the women.

Especially the women. I would be hard-pressed to name a writer who has so bravely gone where so few male horror writers have gone before: creating female characters that are believable and who say believable things and act in a manner befitting sentient beings with fully-functional brains.

They are not mouthpieces for outraged feminism or cowering pretty things; they are chubby cynics who work in rundown movie theatres trying (and failing) to imagine a better life. . . and lost souls, shorn of their identity by a surgeon's insensate blade:

"She'd wanted to spit their suspicions in their faces; tell them that she and her uterus were not synonymous, and that the removal of one did not imply the eclipse of the other.

"But today, returning to the office, she was not so certain they weren't correct. She felt as though she hadn't slept in weeks, though in fact she was sleeping long and deeply every night. Her eyesight was blurred, and there was a curious remoteness about her experiences that day that she associated with extreme fatigue, as if she were drifting further and further from the work on her desk; from her sensations, from her very thoughts. Twice that morning she caught herself speaking and then wondered who it was conceiving of these words. It certainly wasn't her; she was too busy listening."

That was from "The Life of Death," a slice from the life of a woman who decides to make a friend of Death and then becomes its lover—truly a marriage made in Hell. But her own life is so empty that she bares her throat to The Reaper willingly; she is ready to go on, whether to something better or worse she can not know. Any place is better than here.

We can all relate to that feeling. It is born of our dissatisfaction and our impatience and our feelings of insecurity and inferiority. It fuels our myriad neuroses and is the cause of many sleepless nights. It is the price we pay for thinking of the unthinkable—death. Heaven. Hell. Or. Worse.

The Void.

The Void pervades Barker's writing. Whether or not this makes it one of *his* mortal dreads, I don't know. More likely the Void serves as a precarious metaphor, bespeaking of lives spent in quiet desperation, consisting of a succession of uncomfortable silences, anonymous days of hurrying and waiting, hurrying and waiting. . .

It's easy to forgive Mamoulian for wanting to take Whitehead into The Void with him. Wouldn't it be nice to have some company in Eternity even if it was your mortal enemy? Don't we feel for the cancer in "Son of Celluoid" for aspiring to be "more than a humble cell," possessing and killing, struggling to stay alive to the very end? Nothing can be worse than *not* being: not moving, not seeing, not thinking, just *dead* and *buried*. Worm food. I would do anything to avoid that. So would you. Clive Barker knows that.

He knows that you like to try on your wife's dresses when she's not around. And he knows that you once took the hamster out of its cage and left it on the floor just to see what the cat would do to it. And he knows that you drive around at night with your lights off, looking for animals to run down. And he knows that your once-sacred heart is scarred with sin. And he knows you feel a tremendous sense of guilt for every bad thing you've ever done or said and you're seeking absolution or, at the very least, the satisfaction of knowing that if you're bound for the Pit you won't be alone.

Don't worry. Clive Barker will be there. Holding your hand—his grip rough, cold and clammy. You're falling, endlessly, hopelessly, falling forever and ever amen. . . And you see that he's there beside you and he's trying to catch your eye and you can't help it, you look and—He's showing you his naughty bits.

101

THE BOOKS OF BLOOD

Reviewed by Gus Meyer and James Van Hise

Clive Barker's BOOKS OF BLOOD launched him to international acclaim when they were first published in 1984. Copies were quickly imported into the U.S. by dealers and fans and articles were being written about them long before they finally began being published in America in the fall of 1986. In this series Barker set out to explore as many different facets of horror as possible, such as one often finds in anthologies. The one major difference was that rather than two dozen writers each exploring a different facet, Barker took it upon himself to do it all.

"Every body is a book of blood;
Wherever we're opened, we're red."

So begins every volume of Clive Barker's thirty-story collection of grim and grisly tales. This dose of dark wit hints at what is to come: horror, laden with a heavy helping of twisted humor and strong, often visceral imagery. The imagery, more than the humor, is the strong point of Barker's work. He enables us to *see* the horror in his stories quite vividly and, on occasion, to taste it as well. The underlying wit, however, is a vital component of the work as a whole.

The collected stories are framed by the story of Simon McNeal, who becomes, quite literally, "The Book Of Blood." This opening tale, although short, is Barker in a nutshell. In it, the supernatural intrudes upon lives already gone awry, that of a psychic researcher hoping desperately to contact the "other side," and McNeal, a clever con artist who is merely giving her what she wants. The underlying sexual tension between these two holds the story together; when the dead, angry at McNeal's mockery, mete their punishment upon him, it serves to bring the two people, and their separate lives, together. As is often the case in Barker's stories, there is a gap or a lack in the characters' lives, and the irruption of the supernatural into their worlds is frequently embraced as an alternative to drudgery and despair. At the very least, Barker's characters are drawn to the horror that besets them whether they wish it or not. His approach to horror, even when not overtly sexual, is erotic in its basic drive. Doctor Florescu, finding McNeal after his punishment, follows the bloody writing on his body with her hands: *"She would trace, with infinite love and patience, the stories the dead had told on him."*

Their desire, therefore, has been consummated, in a sense, by the direct intervention of the underworld. The words engraved upon him, we are told, comprise the narratives that follow. Although the stories are varied, there is little attempt made to justify them with the opening story; only one tale deals directly with the concepts outlined in it. The only real linking material between the stories is the presence of death, on-stage or off, and the inventiveness of Barker's writing. (There is little attempt to establish ghostly authorship of any story, except in "Scape-Goats.")

The writing is deft, and gripping, often painting with a few strokes the most overwhelming visions Barker can conceive. This, then, is an overview, story by story, of those visions, and of their varying intensity. Most are strong; a few are compromised. None fail to move the mind or the stomach in some way, great or large.

"The Midnight Meat Train" is the story of Leon Kaufman, a New Yorker disillusioned with the city he once loved from afar. Kaufman derives small pleasures from life; saying "f—k it" to himself is perhaps the most daring of these. Life, and the city, have let him down. The suggestion of monster as the perpetrators of some gruesome subway murders does not appeal to him, since this would let the "human monsters" of the city, and the city itself, evade responsibility. Still, he is headed on a collision course with those monsters, once he falls asleep on the train of the title.

Contrasted with the small, commonplace Kaufman is the butcher, Mahogany. Proud, almost arrogant in his work, he has a sense of mission that Kaufman lacks, but his work has been suffering, which he tried to avoid. He is, in fact, a complacent killer, and it is just that complacency which proved his downfall.

Kaufman's unwitting approach to their meeting gives way to a morbid curiosity once he realizes the gravity of the situation, and then, once he faces Mahogany, to a surprising presence of mind. His defeat of the butcher, another proof of the banality of evil, gives way to a deeper horror when he finally faces the butcher's masters. They come to feed on the night's human harvest:

" . . . *gracile hands were laid upon the shanks of meat, and were running up and down the shaved flesh in a manner that suggested sensual pleasure. Tongues were dancing out of mouths, flecks of spittle landing on the meat. The eyes of the monsters were flickering back and forth with hunger and excitement.*"

Kaufman, of course, is elected to replace the butcher. Through the horror he experiences, his faith in the city is restored. He becomes an important figure in its secret workings, not entirely willingly, but accepting the job in awe and wonder. A life once empty and cheated becomes renewed through fear. The reader feels Kaufman's disorientation, his bewilderment and pain, and ultimately his resignation to the strange new world revealed to him in the depths of the subways of New York.

"The Yattering And Jack" is a horror comedy, of sorts, in which the roles of tormentor and tormented are reversed. The Yattering, a minor demon assigned to the case of one Jack Polo, is itself driven over the edge by the apparent imperturbability of its intended victim. Its constant and ever mounting efforts are in vain. One even begins to sympathize with the Yattering. Cursed with a less-than-human intelligence, it cannot begin to imagine how to confound the unflappable human, and breaches protocol by appealing to his superiors, in this case represented by Beelzebub. (Barker describes the archdemon as part wasp, part elephant; his visual inventiveness takes a hellishly whimsical turn.) This only places it in deeper trouble, causing it to take out its frustration on Polo's cats.

Soon enough, it is revealed that Polo is aware of the demon, and playing a deadly game designed to make it overstep its bounds and thereby forfeit everything. This undercuts the slapstick humor of the Yattering's efforts, which include a re-animated roast turkey, for it reveals that Polo is willing to place his family in jeopardy to win out over his adversary. His wife has already killed herself, offstage, before the beginning of the story proper, and the final confrontation not only makes a shambles of the remaining family's Christmas dinner, but leaves one of Polo's daughters in a rather questionable mental state. In a sense, the clever and manipulative Polo stands revealed as the true monster of this story, and the Yattering as his hapless victim.

In **"Pig Blood Blues,"** one pig—the ex-cop Redman—ventures into unknown territory, where he ultimately faces a carnivorous sow. This is not a laughable concept. Anyone who has ever met a real pig knows that they are a far cry from love-able Porky. Spared the spectacle of anthropophagia by porcine marauders, I still re-call Ambrose Bierce's chilling depiction of wild swine consuming the dead on a Civil War battlefield in his story "The Coup de Grace." Their tastes are, to say the least, eclectic. In "Pig Blood Blues," the sow holds sway over an entire boy's de-tention center, perhaps through some psychic power, or perhaps through sheer dint of gravity. The reader enters this strange realm along with the outsider, Redman, whose fascination with the strange boy Lace, provides another—if somewhat tenu-ous—link with the sow, for both, it seems, want the boy for reasons of their own. This passes through Redman's mind quite quickly, however. There is little effort to develop any real parallel between the pig and the policeman beyond the obvious slang connection. Still, the story is memorable for its strangeness, and the gripping sense of place Barker brings to the pigsty. Its look and smell reach beyond the page. Here, the escaped boy, Henessey, still hangs, rotting and half consumed, while his spirit, apparently, occupies the pig which devoured him. The story is a bit of a set piece, for all of its strengths. We receive some background on Redman, but little insight into his mind. He is little more than a convenient viewpoint char-acter. He comes to work as a shop teacher, is drawn into the center's secrets, ob-serves some other sketchily drawn characters, and winds up as a victim.

The pig, however, holds our attention in its big scene, where we learn of her hunger for human flesh. Two boys are bringing her bacon (cannibalism does not cause her any moral qualms), a poor substitute for her true desire. The basic im-petus behind the story, the *idea* of a man-eating pig, gives a charge to this scene. The sow waits for her tribute.

"*. . . her eyes glinting like jewels in the murky night, brighter than the night be-cause living, purer than the night because wanting.*"

The human characters here may be a bit flat, but Barker takes a certain pleasure in getting into the mind of the sow. It is tempting to wonder if Barker's sympathies might lie, not with the victims in his stories, but with the various agents of fate who bring them to their ends.

In **"Sex, Death And Starshine,"** Barker's own background in the performing arts lends credence to this story of a haunted theatre, the Elysium, and of the final production to grace its stage. As promised by the title, sex opens the story; death ends it, but it does not end the lives of its characters. As actors, they go on in death to 'play life.'

The characters, even the quick sketches, have a life to them that the wooden Redman of "Pig Blood Blues" lacked completely. The focus here is on Terry Cal-loway, the director of a foredoomed production of "Twelfth Night," and his pro-blems in getting the play on the boards. The primary obstacle he encounters is in the person of Diane Duvall, a soap opera star stuck in a Shakespeare comedy to boost ticket sales. She has no place in the play, but Calloway can do little about this, for not only is she essential to the box office, she also complicates matters by being the primary source of the sex already mentioned. Calloway is in a double bind for these very reasons.

Fortunately for the production, if not for its participants, the Elysium Theatre has a guardian angel of sorts. The charming Richard Lichfield takes a personal in-terest in the affairs of the theatre, having once performed there with his wife in the past. Both he and his beloved Constantia are quite dead, but this does not lessen their determination that she is better suited to the lead in "Twelfth Night" than the lamentably talentless Diane. Their machinations to assure a successful opening

CLIVE BARKER

night result in a full house comprised entirely of corpses, the physical death of the entire troupe, and a fiery finale to the venerable theatre's existence. This is not in any sense a tragedy. The play itself is better served than it had been in decades. Lichfield's philosophy is simple but eloquent: *"The dead must choose more carefully than the living. We cannot waste our breath, if you'll excuse the phrase, on less than the purest delights."* To Lichfield, art is more vital than life itself. Most of the dead join Lichfield and take the show on the road, accepting the beauty of his outlook. Only the theatre administrator, the stage manager, and Diane Duvall leave corpses behind. The rest take up the mission to carry art to their fellow dead. Barker states his position here most clearly: *"Who better to applaud the sham of passion and pain they would perform than the dead, who had experienced such feelings, and thrown them off at last?"*

There is a real joy of art for art's sake here. The humor in "The Yattering And Jack" seems contrived by comparison. The thesis that death is preferable to sex is amply illustrated in the scene where the dead Diane returns to bestow her sexual favors on Calloway one last time. Rejected by him once he realizes her condition, she kills him, freeing him to concentrate on his art. Her own passion, being merely physical, does not sustain her body for long at all. Whereas in other Barker stories sex and death are hopelessly intertwined, here they are diametrically opposed. (This does not stop Diane from making a game attempt to prove otherwise.) The whole affair seems to suggest that sex is an impediment to higher aspirations. This does not come off as prudish in Barker's hands. As Lichfield and his new recruits stand by the road, about to begin their tour, it is difficult not to feel that this story, rare among the Books of Blood, has a genuinely happy ending.

"In The Hills, The Cities," the last story of the first Book of Blood is a set piece for one of Barker's most boschian visions. The witnesses to the strange spectacle of the duelling cities are two bickering gay lovers on a trip through Yugoslavia. Having discovered their basic incompatibility, they are stuck with each other for the duration, but soon find out that hell is more than simply "other people." Or perhaps it is: thousands of people from rival cities form immense human sculptures, to perform a ritual of gigantic proportions. This idea is almost impossible to visualize. Judd, the hard-nosed right wing journalist, and the vacuous Mick, his latest acquisition, are hard pressed to understand the events they are suddenly faced with, high in the Eastern European hills. So, to a certain degree, might the readers of this story find it difficult to imagine just what the cities of Popolac and Podujevo might look like once assembled for their wrestling match. Still, it is primarily the carnage that ensues when a city falls that Judd and Mick encounter. This is hard enough for them to take. Their encounter with the other city, driven mad by the death of its friendly rival, leaves them briefly awestruck, and permanently dead.

One could perhaps see this story as an analogy for all human conflict. The basic drive here seems to be the visual impact of the idea, however, and I doubt that Barker had any sort of political message in mind when he set this tale to paper.

For **"DREAD,"** education comes to the forefront in this story. An inquiry into the roots of philosophy, as it were. The mysterious student Quaid, seemingly the holder of some deep knowledge of fear, entrances the impressionable and aptly named Stephen Grace with his cryptic words. Grace follows, not knowing where Quaid will lead him, not realizing, until too late, that Quaid is a master manipulator with only his own interests in mind.

Quaid seeks to examine the state of dread, which he believes to be a state preceding the development of personality. To see its primal face, he humiliates people around him, debasing them cruelly with their own innermost fears. To get to Cheryl Fromm, an avowed vegetarian who rejects his theories, Quaid becomes her lover, then uses that advantage to lock her in a darkened room with no food but a well-cooked steak. He reveals this "experiment" to Grace through a series of still photos taken with a hidden camera, shortly before subjecting Grace to a similar torture, fashioned to mesh with Grace's own dread. Grace's last lucid thoughts, before the ordeal leaves him an idiot, are a realization of Quaid's true motive.

"... *Quaid... was obsessed with terrors because his own dread ran deepest. That was why he had to watch others deal with their fears. He needed a solution, a way out for himself.*"

(This observations could stand as an extreme statement of why people rear horror fiction in the first place.)

Grace's subsequent reduction to a childlike state seems to negate Quaid's thesis, however, for the destruction of his personality frees him from dread completely. Quaid, having failed in his "researches," is finally revealed to carry a deep-seated terror of his own. By a final twist of fate, the simplified Grace becomes the happy agent of Quaid's doom, wearing the very form that drove Quaid to his actions.

"Hell's Event" moves at a rapid clip, much like the footrace that forms its framework. The narrative shifts between the banal exchanges of the newscasters covering the charity event, and the point of view of the trainer Cameron, who discovers that one of the racers is an envoy of hell, out to win control of civilization for its infernal masters. The final stretch of the race is quite suspenseful, and the story builds to a well-pitched climax.

With **"Jacqueline Ess: Her Will And Testament"** put on the Liebestod from Wagner's "Tristan und Isolde" while reading this one. Love and death do not elude each other here, but collide head-on in one of Barker's warped but happy endings.

Jacqueline Ess, in a moment of deepest despair, discovers her hidden strength: the ability to change others physically according to her will. Unfortunately, this works only in the most literal fashion possible. Her wish that her obnoxious doctor "become a woman" wreaks havok on his body, ripping him open and leaving him dead on the floor. She suppresses this memory for a time, but it soon comes back to her, and she realizes the awesome power she holds. Breaking all ties, becoming a wanderer, she sets out to learn how to most effectively wield this power, self-determination her goal.

Somewhere in the course of her wanderings, Jacqueline takes up with the lawyer Oliver Vassi. Half of the narrative of "Jacqueline Ess" takes the form of Vassi's "Testimony." Ess and Vassi become lovers; even after he discovers her power, he still accepts and loves her. In fact, his love for her becomes obsessive, sending the rest of his life into ruin even before she leaves him.

Jacqueline, of course, leaves him on her quest to sharpen and apply her unusual abilities. This is where the dream really begins as she searches to consolidate her strength. Vassi, in turn, searches for her, disconsolate, while the man Jacqueline chooses as her tutor plays his own twisted games. Eventually, Jacqueline realizes that she loved Vassi as much as he loved her and they gravitate towards each other's arms.

This story is one of Barker's best, a truly erotic mingling of sex and horror. Ess and Vassi both come across as credible characters, moved but not defined by their desires. The contradictions of desire are considered as well. Vassi watches Jacqueline sleep, shortly before discovering her secret, and muses that, *"One knows, in those moments, that one does not exist, except in a relation to that face, that personality."*

And this, in fact, is the fate of both Vassi and Ess, to lose themselves, each in the other, in a staggeringly literal metaphor for sexual love.

In **"The Skins Of The Fathers"** a revisionist creation myth, this, with a perfectly reasonable explanation for the proliferation of masculine violence in the world. The demons of this story are strangely beautiful and mysterious, the fathers of men, doomed to be reviled by their own creations. Barker lavishes loving detail upon his descriptions of them.

"Pyramidal heads on rose colored, classically proportioned torsos, that umbrellaed into shifting skirts of lace flesh. A headless silver beauty whose six mother of pearl arms sprouted in a circle from around its purring, pulsating mouth. A creature like a ripple on a fast-running stream, constant but moving, giving out a sweet and even tone. . . "

The plot, meanwhile, is vaguely Western; the demons dwell in the Arizona desert near the town of Welcome, and the action largely involves an aroused populace going forth in wretched ignorance to do battle with their betters. The people of Welcome are vulgar American grotesques, broad caricatures in Barker's hands. Once again, his sympathy lies with the seemingly monstrous.

"New Murders In The Rue Morgue" is a belated sequel to the story with which Poe, single handedly, invented detective fiction, but it is not, in essence, a detective story. Barker is primarily concerned with examining, anew, the dynamics of the horror revealed at the end of the original tale. What resonant chord of fear was struck by the revelation that the killer was an ape with a straight razor, bent on passing for human? Whatever impact this may have had in the 1830's, Barker brings up to date, as a descendant of C. Auguste Dupin finds himself faced with a bizarre duplication of his ancestor's adventure. Here, however, the ape becomes, almost, the hero, as it struggles to adopt humanity, and succeeds, surprisingly, far better than its human counterparts.

In giving this the '80's treatment, Barker throws in a bit more sex than Poe was liable to work with and, although this might seem to some an awkward bit of almost Freudian reductionism, it does make sense since this is, after all, the area of endeavor where man and beast share the most common ground.

A projectionist friend of mine doesn't much care for **"Son Of Celluloid."** "Nobody's written the definitive haunted movie theatre story yet," he contends. "Luckily for me, I've got plenty of time to work on it while I'm projecting." So, until he completes his magnum opus, we're left with "Son of Celluloid" as a prime contender in that very specific subgenre.

In this tale, a hunted cop-killer dies in the back of a movie house. My friend detects a glitch here already.

"This guy dies behind the screen, right? So where are the speakers? Any theatre that old has speakers behind the screen. The setting here is obviously not a place with Dolby mounted on the side walls. It's an old dump. It should have speakers behind the screen, but this reads like the screen is right up *against* the wall. Speakers or no speakers, there should be some accessible space behind it, but this guy dies and rots there—they mention the smell—and nobody even checks it out."

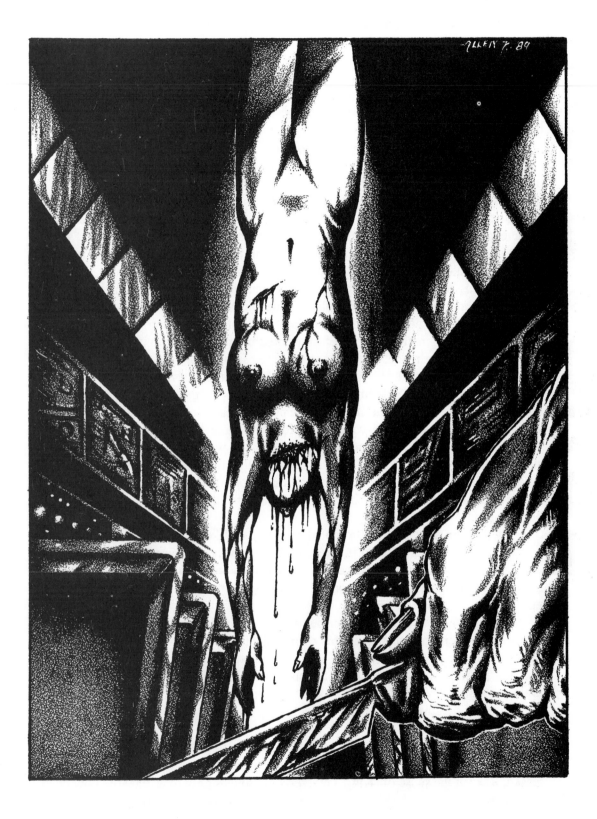

CLIVE BARKER

I venture to suggest that the theatre, being converted from an old mission, might not conform to standard theatre architecture. He's not convinced, but he lets the matter drop.

"So when this guy dies, he's overwhelmed by all these images that have somehow accumulated behind the screen, right? This goes directly against my own theory of psycho-filmic accumulation, but that's not important, and I'm sure not giving away any of my ideas to this Barker guy, anyway. But that's what happens when the killer kicks. Killer kicks—good title, almost an early Kubrick, but not quite. . . and later, it turns out that his cancer survives his death and takes forms derived from all those pictures built up over the years, and kinda' goes berserk with the idea, right?"

I agree with him, but fail to see the problem.

"Well, nothing wrong there, really, as far as plot devices go. I've seen flimsier in my time, believe me. But then it assumes this desire for adulation, supposedly inherent in the images themselves, and goes around trying to subsume—excuse me, to eat—various victims. In other words, these projected images are supposed to have an inherent desire within them. That's baloney."

Intrigued by the theories of this unshaven nightown with a Budweiser in his hand, as well as his use of the word "baloney," I listen without comment.

"What this story is really about is American iconography. The main forms adopted by the cancer are those of John Wayne and Marilyn Monroe. But whatever adulation those two people might have desired during their careers cannot by any stretch of the imagination have been imprinted upon each frame of each print of every film they ever made. And the force of their images derived from their actual personalities, but from the vicarious desires of their audiences, projected on to the images just as the images themselves are projected upon the screen. That's where Barker goes screwy. It's the *audience* whose desires filled that backscreen area with unfulfilled wishes. The cancer should have taken those forms to fulfill the wants of the audience, in a mad loving sort of way, whether the characters in the story wanted it to or not. Right? So. . . the actual manifestations of the cancer are pretty good. It's scary, right, and that's all that counts—I'm just picking on points that would have been different if I'd written the damn thing. Actually, over all, it's not that bad."

So what, then, I wondered, prompted his initial dislike of the story?

"There's no projectionist in it. I mean, all right, it takes place late and the projectionist has probably gone home already, but he's not even mentioned. Give me a break! Those images don't get on the screen by themselves, you know. At least, not usually."

Not usually? He acts a bit mysterious around this point, but refuses to talk. I try to pry some more information on his own project out of him. Does his story deal directly with the psychic energies of a movie audience?

"In a sense, yes, but that's only the surface." He arches an eyebrow in a well practiced smirk. "What's beyond the screen is totally different."

And that's his final word on the subject.

For **"Rawhead Rex,"** Barker dips back into the pagan past in this story of a pre-Christian, inhuman being imprisoned underground since medieval times. Released, Rex (in the sense of 'King') reasserts his sovereignty over the area now occupied by the village of Zela, a country location increasingly overrun by Londoners fleeing from urban blight.

Rex is a living embodiment of primal appetites. The god, perhaps, of the blustery men in "Skins Of The Fathers." He thrives on rapine, pillage and the flesh of children. He is the ultimate manifestation of all that is vile in man, macho taken to an archetypal extreme:

"He'd never been a great thinker. Too much appetite: it overwhelmed his reason. He lived in the eternal present of his hunger and his strength, feeling only the crude territorial instinct that would sooner or later blossom into carnage."

Bound for centuries, he has nonetheless left his mark on the countryside; in distant memory of his immense size, the local pub is named "The Tall Man."

The story is fairly straightforward action and gore, but, as is usual for Barker, these matters have behind them a weight of verisimilitude. Rex is no mere monster on a rampage. His reawakening is felt throughout the village even before he makes a public appearance. Declan Ewan, the verger (a clerical caretaker and attendant) of St. Paul's Church, feels something stir inside him on the day of Rex's return. When they meet he finds in Rex the god he has been seeking, in vain, for many years, and gleefully abases himself before his new master like a heretic Renfield.

As is often the case with ancient mysteries, however, there is an even deeper mystery that predates it. As Rex gives shape to the bloody pagan deities that preceded Christ, *"a sexless martyr, doe-eyed and woebegone,"* so does a stone hidden behind the altar give form to an even older religious impulse, perhaps the original one. Reverend Coot senses it at about the same time that Declan Ewan has his first intimation of Rawhead: at the altar for morning prayer, he experiences an electrical sensation, accompanied by an erection, for the power of a goddess lies within the stone, and is awakened by the proximity of her old enemy. It is left to Ron Milton, whose son is eaten by Rex, to discover the image of the Mother Goddess, an emblem of concentrated female essence, and to try to use it in the battle against Rex. This is a case of polar opposites: Rawhead is a vicious force of destruction, male in the extreme, while the primal Venus figure represents the forces of creation and regeneration. They face each other as the village of Zeal burns, Rex having discovered the flammability of the "blood" of the metallic beasts used for transport by the humans he despises.

"Rawhead Rex" is a pretty visceral tale, and quite literally, for Rex's favorite delicacy is the innards of children. Rex, being almost elemental in his nature, has little going for him personally in the way of characterization, but the subsidiary characters who face him make up for this lack. Declan Ewan, as mentioned, goes completely off the deep end in his devotion to Rex, and devotes his newfound energies to defiling the church he has tended for years. Ron Milton, a vacillating weekend villager, is transformed by the death of his son into a man determined to kill the beast despite the impossibility of the task. Even Thomas Garrow, the farmer who unwittingly frees Rex, gives us, in his few remaining moments, an inner glimpse of a man given to working the soil.

"Rawhead Rex" is a rollicking read, and one of the standouts among Barker's stories.

"Confessions Of A (Pornographer's) Shroud" is a far cry from Casper the Friendly Ghost, at least insofar as the vengeful spirit in this story hasn't much of a sense of humor. Barker does, however, thoughtfully explain to us by way of demonstration, a possible reason for the traditional appearance of spectres.

Ronald Glass, a milquetoast accountant (two words that invariably accompany each other) and staid Catholic, flies into a rage when he discovers that he's been the unwitting dupe of a porno ring. To forestall any trouble from him, his former associates set him up as a Smut Lord, ruining his family and his career. Glass dispatches two of his tormentors to their graves, but encounters a slight hitch in the commission of his revenge against their ringleaders, Maquire: his own untimely murder.

Glass' quest for revenge develops not so much out of hot-blooded rages as out of his bookkeeper's meticulousness. Everything must be balanced in his books. And so he lingers in his body, trying to figure out how to proceed with his plans despite this handicap, until the idle banter of two morgue attendants suggests a means of escape from his cold flesh. His spirit seeps out through the bullet hole in the middle of his forehead, and takes possession of the nearest thing to hand, which just happens to be the sheet covering his corpse. This, too, poses certain practical problems, but Glass perseveres. He simply can't stand to leave any loose ends lying around.

Glass' assumption of a fabric body presents an image both comic and surreal. To his credit, we feel the determination he feels, and the difficulty he experiences. At the mercy of the wind and dogs, aided only, perhaps, by the incredulity of his intended victims, Glass struggles on, becoming ever more and more soiled and torn, holding his warp and weave together through sheer strength of will.

In a final irony, his attempt to confess, in the Catholic sense, fails. By the time he has carried out his mission, he has not the strength to get the attention of the priest, who is busy taking provocative pictures of a young female parishioner in the vestry: another pornographer, however amateur. In the end, nothing remains but a dirtied cloth on the stairs of the church, a parody of the shroud of Turin, suitable only for cleaning up some questionable stains.

"Scapegoats" is a rare excursion into first-person narrative for Barker. The narrator turns out, like William Holden in **Sunset Boulevard**, to have died of drowning *before* telling the story, but here, at least, the trick is accounted for by the framing device of **The Books Of Blood.** The question raised by this is simple: why do most of the dead who left their stories engraved on McNeal's flesh take such pains to cast them in the third person? Do all ghosts have literary ambitions? A minor point, but one worthy of consideration.

The narrator and her three companions would seem to be jaded jetsetters of some sort, adrift somewhere off the Hebrides; their yacht, their ennui, their passionless sexual liaisons, all seem to suggest that they are possessed of some wealth and a great deal of time to waste. Their inept seamanship would seem to confirm this.

The narrator, Frankie, seems particularly disaffected. Her tone is flat, even when fear strikes her.

The setting, also, reeks of lassitude. The uncharted island these weekend seafarers run around on seems, at first, to be lifeless. Even the flies on the island, when discovered, do not move when they are trod upon, and when the only other inhabitants of the island are found, they turn out to be sheep. The sheep mirror the lost humans: slack, uncaring, with barely enough energy to be bewildered by their surroundings. The heat of the island, the sickly sweet stench that rises from it, the apathetic lapping of the waves on the trash-littered shore, all contribute to the aura of emotional emptiness that surrounds the characters.

Frankie does not exactly accept her ultimate demise with good grace, but neither does she contest it; she lets it happen, almost passively, perhaps not even distinguishing between her vacuous, petty life and the swaying depths of her watery grave. This is a perfect mood piece. In "Scapegoats," Barker once again makes us wonder whether death might not be preferable to life, and gives us characters who might think that it is, if only they could summon sufficient conviction to express an opinion.

"Human Remains" is a twist on Narcissus, in the person of Gavin, a street hustler of indeterminate sexual persuasion who just happens to be graced with, we are told, a perfect face. This is a boon in his line of work, but somehow fails to cover over the core of emptiness within him. In fact, it is this ache of loneliness, felt acutely as he admires his reflection in a mirror, that drives him out one night for one last score, and leads him to his fate.

Unbeknownst to the hapless Gavin, his evening's pickup, a middle-aged scholar, is burdened with a living wooden statue that requires frequent bathings in blood to keep it alive, a sort of arboreal Elizabeth Bathory. Gavin, blissfully unaware of this, leaves the scholar's apartment, attributing the man's strange and disturbing behavior to an attack of guilt and nothing more. He does not know the fate he has escaped, or the reason why: the statue, having glimpsed his face, has decided to *become* Gavin. Gavin becomes haunted by the vaguely-shaped being, and is plagued by reports of his own strange behavior, until circumstances finally force them together.

Gavin eventually becomes complicit in this being's assumption of form; already self-admiring, he is drawn by the opportunity to observe himself from without, even though it means the unavoidable reduction of his already negligible humanity. Perhaps the accompanying loss of responsibility and feeling attracts him most of all, as the copy soon transcends the original, leaving him as dull and wooden as the statue once was.

Thematically this is much like Harlan Ellison's short story "Shatterday," but doesn't delve as deeply into the emotional undercurrent of the characters nor generate as much conflict between them on a personal level.

In **"The Body Politic"** we find something beyond the scope of all previous "creeping hand" stories. In most entries in this subgenre, the actions of the hand are usually ascribed to some aspect of the personality of its owner, or sometimes its former owner, usually a psychotic of some sort; transplants often transfer the problem from one person to another, until the disgruntled hand goes off on its own, to wreak whatever havoc it may. Here, the hand itself has its own motivation: quite simply, it wants to assert its individuality, free from the restraints of the rest of the body, and of the tyrannical mind above. This is a variation on the fear of loss of bodily integrity, and Barker takes it to a new extreme. First of all, it is no mere individuality that is sought by the right hand. This hand is a manual megalomaniac, intent on raising an entire army of hands, a grandiose scheme of conquest that mocks, by exaggeration, the simplicity of your average disembodied hand. In simple pragmatic terms, one hand sneaking around behind the drapes is not a very formidable opponent, but a full-scale flock of them might very well be just that. Charlie's right hand liberates its first disciple, Charlie's left hand, with a handy kitchen knife, and sends it out to gather recruits for a five-digit blitzkrieg. The ensuing scene in a YMCA, where men struggle in vain against their suddenly autonomous hands, is truly horrific.

In staying with Charlie and delegating the job of conscription to its subordinate, the right hand makes a large tactical error. The other hands, once gathered, need their leader; they are followers, and have no plan of action. This gives Charlie a considerable advantage over them, which he exercises spectacularly.

So, ultimately, even a mass uprising fails. But Barker does not stop there: what about the rest of the body? One character, while fleeing the rampaging hands, has his legs severed by an oncoming train. Later, his legs visit him in his hospital room before going off to enjoy their newfound liberty, leaving him to wonder:

". . . did his eyes envy their liberty. . . and was his tongue eager to be out of his mouth and away, and was every part of him, in its subtle way, preparing to forsake him? He was an alliance only held together by the most tenuous of truces. Now, with the precedent set, how long before the next uprising? Minutes? Years?

He waited, heart in mouth, for the fall of Empire."

In **"The Inhuman Condition"** a group of young thugs torments, for entertainment, an old derelict, a simple exercise in viciousness that would ordinarily be forgotten by dawn, if not for the fact that their youngest member, Karney, steals a length of knotted rope from the old man's pockets. Karney is the only one of this gang who has any rudimentary sort of conscience; he steals the rope out of a fascination for puzzles, and because it strikes him as the least significant of the old man's possessions. But he is wrong there, for the knots bind strange creatures, who are to exact old Mr. Pope's revenge for his senseless beating. The unwitting Karney becomes the agent of his friends' deaths, and must ultimately face the old man and his beasts in a violent final confrontation laden with surprising revelations.

Lovers rarely get a second chance, but in this storm drenched Southern Gothic, **"Relations"** Sadie and Buck Durning reunite thirty years after their last tryst, in an attempt to find out what went wrong. They haven't aged much at all in those three decades; Buck still bears the gaping chest wound inflicted on him by Sadie's .38 caliber pistol in 1955, while Sadie seems remarkably well preserved for a woman who has been electrocuted as punishment for killing her husband. Of course, they *are* dead, but some power, either heavenly or infernal, offers such terminal lovers a second chance at the set interval of thirty years. (Barker notes, quite wryly, that few couples exercise this option. But then, Sadie and her lustful ex-husband are both, in their ways, quite obstinate.) They return to the site of Buck's demise, Room Seven of the Cottonwood Motel in White Deer, Texas, only to find it occupied by another couple. Here, complications ensue.

The couple in question consists of John Gyer, an up-and-coming hellfire and brimstone evangelist with a fondness for the last book of the Bible, and his long suffering wife, Virginia. It is Virginia's weariness with her husband's self-righteous and self-regarding ways that sets the tone for what is to follow. To further complicate matters, she can see the ghosts of Sadie and Buck. This infuriates Gyer to no end, since he feels that he alone should see the spiritual world, and his puritanical rage reaches a fever pitch when he finds his chauffeur, Earl, in a compromising position with the oddball but lively daughter of the drunken motel owner.

The farce continues to escalate, however, for Sadie and Buck's attempted reconciliation falls to pieces fairly quickly. Buck, left to fend for himself after Sadie's stormy departure, finds that he can assume physical form in the presence of the half-drugged Virginia. He attempts to force himself on her, only to discover that, despite his remarkable ability to assume flesh, he has been left impotent by thirty years as a spirit. Finally, all these elements converge in a final fateful plot twist, which counts as another of Barker's oddly happy endings.

"Down, Satan!" is a short mood piece focusing on faith gone awry. The wealthy man Gregorius despairs of salvation, trying everything to assure himself a place in heaven, but nothing sets his spirit at ease. At last he decides to draw the attention of God by placing his soul in the utmost peril imaginable: he decides to make a pact with the Devil. Surely this horrendous act will warrant divine intervention. But Satan, too, will not come at his beck and call, so he expends all his wealth and energy in building a Hell on earth. His obsession escalates until something profoundly evil does, in fact, manifest itself, but it is nothing more than Gregorius himself, lost in an inferno of his own design, completely forgetful of his original motivation.

"The Age Of Desire" offers a grisly scene at a research lab, baffled police, a question raised with no apparent answer: what happened? The dead doctors were working on their own time, on their own project, and no records exist beyond the blurry and shocking videotapes of their final experiment. The nature of the injection given to their subject, causing his subsequent rape and murders of the researchers, can only be guessed, but when the readers finally meet the subject, it becomes painfully apparent that he has been given a lethal dose of the world's first truly effective aphrodisiac. Jerome has been rendered polymorphously perverse by the drug, giving everything in the world around him an erotic aura that drives him to further acts of violent, fitful lust.

Unlike the mad (or messianic) protagonist/narrator of J.G. Ballard's "The Unlimited Dream Company," Jerome's state is not creative, but is profoundly destructive, as he forces his unwanted attentions on anyone who catches his fancy. In his frenzied state, he takes quite literally the most banal romantic cliches, thereby elevating them to horrific status. He feels himself to be on fire as he plunges towards his doom like a speedfreak with satyriasis, and when he wants someone to "give him their heart," that is precisely what he desires. Jerome is, in the end, a pitiable figure, trapped in a chemically induced literalization of a state of compulsive sexuality.

"The Forbidden" takes us from order to disarray, the path taken by the Spector Street Estate development; once a clean, sharply structured machine for community living, it has become as good as a slum, half boarded up, half occupied by the misplaced poor and their offspring, descending from the rational structure imposed by its architects to the irrational, nightmarish embodiment of its inhabitants' most primal, pagan fears.

Of course, from the air, Barker observes, its structure is still apparent, but on the ground such patterns cannot be seen, and the patterns that rule the citizens of Spector Street come from somewhere even deeper. Into this deceiving region of hell comes one Helen Buchanon, a shallow academic working on her thesis: "Graffiti: the semiotics of urban despair," a topic chosen out of her complete ignorance of the real suffering of the lower classes. She believes, quite foolishly, that by reading the "signs" of the wall writing, and applying her undoubtedly half-digested version of Roland Barthes' philosophy to them, she can produce some sort of intellectual masterpiece. She has no real motivation to understand anything; she merely wishes to establish her academic credentials and show her aloof, supercilious husband that she is his intellectual match.

She falls deeper and deeper into this unknown world, led by ever more fascinating graffiti, and by her pathetic attempt to befriend the young mother Anne-Marie. She finds a remarkable piece of representational art in an abandoned flat, a painting of a frightening, wild-haired man whose mouth encompasses, with vicious teeth, an entire doorway. Helen is drawn to view this artifact again and again. She cannot begin to understand what meaning it is intended to convey. With her convoluted, naively self-important intellectual delusions, she cannot even imagine that the figure is an actual portrait. The truth dawns ever dimly on Helen's mind even after Anne-Marie's child is brutally murdered. The real existence of the Candyman, a childhood bogey brought into existence by the primordial despair of the Spector Street slums, must grab her by the face in order to make her accept its truth. She resists it, but eventually returns to accept it, seduced by the prospect of something more essential than the pointless cocktail chatter that has been the round of all her days.

One might imagine a grisly end overtaking Sean Penn and his ex-wife in **"The Madonna,"** but it would only be wishful thinking. Instead we find Jerry Coloqhoun, a small time grifter with big plans and an unpronounceable name, waiting to interest a wealthy investor in his latest scheme. The investor, a Mister Garvey, does not seem too keen on the idea, but listen carefully, just in case. (In reading Barker's stories, I cannot help but notice that many of his character names seem to be derived from actors or writers. Does Barker follow baseball and its scandals as well?) Jerry's plan to somehow renovate an abandoned bath-house has no real point to it, and Garvey is about to dismiss it out of hand, when the obscure structure of the building baffles them both and they become separated in the darkness.

Garvey encounters a beautiful, naked girl who lures him farther and farther into the maze, where he has an experience so bizarre that he can barely remember it. Later, he becomes quite paranoid and is convinced that Jerry is being used by some unknown enemy to destroy Garvey.

Jerry, then, becomes confounded by the harassment he soon experiences at the hands of Garvey's thugs. He was only trying to turn a quick profit with his half-baked scheme, and had no idea that the structure in question housed some mysterious, supernatural secret. The Madonna of the title, a powerful mother Goddess, brings to mind other stories in **The Books of Blood** which pit masculine and feminine principles against each other: "Skins of the Fathers," "Rawhead Rex," even "Jacqueline Ess: Her Will and Testament." Here, the presence of the feminine principle wrecks a veritable sea-change upon the men who come into contact with her and her daughters. Garvey, finding himself changing beyond his control, torments Jerry in the hope of discovering information that Jerry does not possess. In his cruelty, he strives desperately to retain his vision of masculinity, of the sort which Barker obviously holds in contempt, but ultimately fails. Jerry, driven to the Madonna in his flight from Garvey, also suffers the same permutation, but comes to accept it as a viable change from his previous meandering way of life.

"Babel's Children" is a story about large decisions. It is also the only story with no overt horrific aspect to it, although the implications of the situation outlined in it are rather awful when considered in full. The heroine (if such she is), Vanessa, finds herself in this situation by benefit of her own haphazard decision making process, making her an idea participant in the project she stumbles upon.

The compound she enters seems insane: guards dressed as nuns, surveillance cameras disguised as religious statues, seemingly senile inmates playing games with frogs. Still, she finds herself a prisoner in this apparent asylum in the middle of nowhere, and no satisfactory explanations are offered by the commander.

Soon, she is co-opted into vague conspiracies by the inmates, who also cloud the real reasons for their incarceration, but even these yo-yo back and forth with no solid resolution. When one of them tells her that their games control the fate of nations, she thinks he is insane. But eventually the truth overwhelms. The rulers of the world are more concerned with appearances than with decision making, and have entrusted the hard work to a think-tank that has, over two decades, gone quite off the deep end. Still, this odd arrangement seems, to Barker, to be preferable to letting our despots and potentates do their own thinking, and Vanessa is drawn into the random process of global management with quiet resignation.

"In The Flesh" is the only story which further explores the vision of the afterlife put forward by Barker in his framing sequence. Here, a dreaming convict finds a mysterious city in a desert of black sand, filled with a bewildering variety of abandoned rooms whose purpose becomes more clear as he becomes more deeply involved with his cellmate's strange obsession.

Cleve, a small time dope peddler with a bit of poor luck, would prefer to serve his time out reading books on sin. His new cellmate, Billy Tait, is hardly more than a boy, and Cleve is charged by the powers-that-be to watch out for him. Cleve is quite capable of looking out for himself, but the added burden is an inconvenience he can do without. The dreams start soon after Tait moves in, but it is not until Tait begins acting quite oddly that Cleve begins to make a connection between him and them. Tait, it seems, committed a crime with the specific purpose of getting into this particular institution, for this is where his grandfather is buried. The grandfather, Edgar St. Clair Tait, killed all his children but one, and claimed he had done so to rid the world of his own "bad blood." Billy Tait, whose mother escaped the slaughter of her siblings, has discovered the dark powers that run in the family, and hopes to learn from his departed ancestor how to use them. The elder Tait, however, has other goals, having decided after fifty years of death that life as a monstrous being is much preferred.

Cleve is somehow drawn into this power struggle, and strives to find out the meaning of the mysterious desert city before one Tait ensnares the other. The aura of mystery here, and the claustrophobic prison setting, make "In The Flesh" one of Barker's more gripping stories.

A slight confusion of identity provides the twist in **"The Life Of Death,"** a story of a lonely woman, scarred by surgery, who comes to believe that Death, in the person of a charming but morbid stranger, has taken a fancy to her and made her his favorite. The center of attraction is an old church scheduled for demolition, which turns out to have, in its basement, a charnal pit from the days of the Black Death. Elaine Rider ventures into the pit by night to find a scene right out of Brueghel:

"The sealing of the crypt, closing it off from the decaying air, had kept the occupants intact. Now, with the violation of this secret chamber, the heat of decay had been rekindled, and the tissues were deteriorating afresh. Everywhere she saw rot at work, making sores and suppurations, blisters and pustules. She raised the flame to see better, though the stench of spoilage was beginning to crowd upon her and make her dizzy. Everywhere her eyes traveled she seemed to alight on some pitiful sight. Two children laid together as if sleeping in each other's arms; a woman whose last act, it appeared, had been to paint her sickened face so as to die more fit for the marriage-bed than the grave."

When Elaine's friends begin to sicken and die, she comes to believe that Death has chosen her as his agent, rendering her immune to the plague so that she might spread it. The story is primarily a psychological study of a disturbed woman. It is ambiguous, to say the least, whether or not the deaths of Elaine's friends have any connection to her and the plague pit. Elaine does, however, consummate her relationship with Death, although not precisely as she might have hoped. This is an oddly powerful story, and one of Barker's most memorable.

"How Spoilers Bleed" waxes politically correct in a cautionary tale. The spoilers in question are those destroying the Amozonian rain forest, and displacing or decimating its native populations. The trio of adventurers featured in this tale are cursed by the tribe whose ancestral home they are appropriating, and find themselves, each in turn, afflicted with a most sanguine problem. The most hardened of the three, Locke, maintains his *sang froid* until his turn comes 'round, and he embarks on a trip back to the village to seek the shaman who cursed him. Unfortunately for him, a new set of spoilers has arrived on the scene and dispensed a slight dose of small-scale genocide, leaving him to face his fate with no hope of redemption.

"Twilight At The Towers" encroaches on John LeCarre's territory, but it's a safe bet that LeCarre never imagined a deep-cover spy quite like Barker's protagonist. He is faced, like a character from Phillip K. Dick, with the knowledge that his essential nature is quite different from what he assumed it to be; on the other hand, after long struggle and incomprehension, he comes to accept the transformation of his world, and it is perhaps fitting that he seems to be named for science fiction's prophet of apocalyptic spiritual change, J.G. Ballard. Ballard is a British agent, assigned to the case of a Russian agent in search of asylum, who finds that he and the Russian are counterparts in deeper ways than he might have at first imagined. Barker piles revelation upon revelation in this story, building to an exciting climax, and, once again, a bizarrely happy ending.

"The Last Illusion" rounds out the collection, as psychic private eye Harry D'Amour strives to protect a dead magician's body from his enemies for a prescribed period of time. This Is no simple task, since the late Swann, famed illusionist, was a real magician, presenting his conjurations as mere prestidigitation as a brazen insult to the infernal powers he wrestled his abilities from. D'Amour has his hands full in this cluttered adventure, since Barker throws in everything including the kitchen sink.

"The Book Of Blood (A Postscript): On Jerusalem Street" is the final word, symmetry served. McNeal, the titular book of blood, long past his youthful humanity, referring to himself in the third person, meets, with quiet resignation, an assassin sent to collect his skin for a wealthycollector. It hardly ends here, for the skin written on by the spirits has unusual properties when separated from its original owner. The collection ends, as it began, on a stretch of Highway of the Dead.

The journey has been a long one, yet it seems, in retrospect, all too short. Barker's visions have leapt off the page leaving an aftertaste of horror and wonder. Clive Barker is a master, far more concise in his terrible musings than King, more visceral than Campbell, cutting to the heart of horror like a surgeon of fear. With McNeal disposed of, it seems a shame that **The Books of Blood** have ended, but Barker moves on in novels and films. The dream, however fitful, is not yet over.

THE NOVELS

Clive Barker made his mark on horror with the short story, one of the first of which, "In The Hills, The Cities," won the 1985 World Fantasy Award. But Barker has largely left the realm of the short story aside to concentrate on novels where he has made new strides in largely different directions.

THE DAMNATION GAME

In the eyes of many, Clive Barker redefined the realms of the dark fantasy short story in his **Books of Blood** anthology. Some were expecting something on the order of a thunderclap when he presented his first novel, but that's not quite what he achieved. What Barker has presented is a tale of an old conflict dating back to the second World War. The opening section of the book, "Terra Incognita," introduces two characters identified only as the Card-Player and the Thief. They meet in the war-blasted ruins of Vienna, where the Thief has come in his trek of survival as he has lived by his wits throughout the war, profiting and looting as best he could to stay alive. But this time he's made a mistake and come to a city which has nothing left in it worth stealing, until he hears about the Card-Player, a man who never loses. There's an air of mystery surrounding the man as those who do lose to him seem to invariably die, and their bodies spirited off. But the Thief is searching for a challenge and cannot help but be drawn to him.

Forty years later, these two characters, the Card-Player and the Thief, are revealed to be Mamoulian and one Joseph Whitehead. While the opening section ends with the beginning of a card game, we learn through unfolding events that Mamoulian allowed Whitehead to win and helped him gain wealth and success on an international scale. All he wanted in return was for Whitehead to kill him. Whitehead failed to understand this and instead ultimately just cast Mamoulian out when his usefulness seemed to have ended, thus creating a bitter enemy.

Into the middle of this walks Martin Strauss, a convicted thief himself paroled into the custody of Joseph Whitehead, who is looking for just the right kind of bodyguard. Soon Strauss comes to learn what Whitehead fears when he sees Mamoulian perform superhuman feats to breach the electric security fences on Whitehead's estate.

At one point Whitehead confesses his growing fear to his right hand man, Mr. Toy, when he says, "I can bear the night itself. It's not pleasant, but it's unambiguous. It's twilight I can't deal with. That's when the bad sweats come over me. When the light's going, and nothing's quite real anymore, quite solid. Just forms. Things that once had shapes. . . "

The tone of the novel is generally eerie and disturbing as Strauss finds himself in the middle of this rich man's problems without understanding what those problems are until it's almost too late.

Other characters drift in on this un-placid sea, including the billionaire's daughter, Carys, who spends much of her time on a heroin induced high with drugs supplied by her father. Her relationship with her father is bizarre and never clearly defined. Does he supply her with drugs because he doesn't want her to suffer addiction withdrawal or because he knows she'll remain home so long as he keeps her supplied with drugs? There's one scene which even suggests a sublimated in cestuous relationship, but this isn't explored beyond one disturbing interlude where Joseph Whitehead's mask of the dutiful father seems to slip.

Although the hero falling in love with the rich man's daughter is a cliche, it happens here but works within the context of the story since the hero suffers more than his share of loss in order to win her.

Strauss is not your standard literary hero, as he's been in prison for five years and upon release is allowed to visit his ex-wife, who has not fared so well during his confinement. She seems a rather pitiful figure compared to the beautiful woman Strauss had often remembered during his long nights in a prison cell. In fact, the portrayal of their relationship is brutally honest, depicting as it does the dissolution of a marriage and of the mutual love once felt between these two. Ultimately one is uncertain which to feel the more sorry for.

But Strauss is forced by circumstances to rise to the occasion, even when he realizes his antagonist, Mamoulian, possesses supernatural abilities. But then so does, Carys, Whitehead's daughter. Unexplored is the tentative hint that Mamoulian may actually be Carys' real father as he had lived in Whitehead's household for years and was responsible for driving Whitehead's wife to suicide.

Although Mamoulian comes across as a very satanic figure, his actual origin reveals him to be a man to whom the secret of immortality was passed hundreds of years ago, in exchange for killing the man who gave him the secret. Only with the passage of time does Mamoulian come to realize that immortality is its own curse. Although Mamoulian could border on being a sympathetic character given half the chance, he goes out of his way to commit hideous acts forced to bring Whitehead's wrath down on him. One of the worst involves Mamoulian's unique ability to raise the dead, which continue to decay while under his command. During a raid on Whitehead's estate, Mamoulian has his henchman, Anthony Breer, slay all of the guard dogs, including the pups, and then he brings them back to life to attack a group of party guests, slaying some and driving the others off. The crowning horror is when Strauss finds the bitch with her pups, who are still trying to suckle on their mother's dead and withering flesh.

Anthony Breer, the henchman, is a disturbing character all his own. A child-killer, he tries to commit suicide but is brought back from the brink by Mamoulian—or at least that's what he thinks. Breer doesn't realize until very late in the game that he's been dead for some time and animated only by Mamoulian's peculiar talent. When he tries to rebel, Mamoulian breaks the spell and Breer realizes the truth, but his raging spirit fights to keep going long enough to exact revenge on his former master. Due to an unpleasant habit Breer has, he is often referred to in the story as the Razor-Eater. In the following scene, Mamoulian's two new henchmen (two born-again Christians whom Mamoulian turned to his control without killing them), see Breer return after he'd been supposedly disposed of.

"Tom caught sight of the Razor-Eater before Chad. His unruly stomach rebelled at the mingled stench of sandalwood and putrefaction, and he threw up on the old man's bed as Breer stepped into the room. He'd come a long way, and the miles had not been kind, but he was here.

"Mamoulian stood upright from the wall and faced Breer.

"He was not entirely surprised to see that rotted face, though he wasn't sure why. Was it that his mind had not quite relinquished its hold on the Razor-Eater, and that Breer was somehow here at his behest? Breer stared at Mamoulian through the bright air, as if awaiting a new instruction before he acted again. The muscles of his face were so deteriorated that each flicker of his eyeball threatened to tear the skin of its orbit. He looked, thought Chad—his mind high on cognac—

like a man full to bursting with butterflies. Their wings beat against the confines of his anatomy; they powdered his bones in their fervor. Soon their relentless motion would split him open and the air would be full of them."

This takes place in a setting where Mamoulian has gone to have the final conflict with his old enemy, in a place called the Hotel Pandemonium, which is introduced by Barker with the following passage:

"Hell is reimagined by each generation. Its terrain is surveyed for absurdities and remade in a fresher mold; its terrors are scrutinized and, if necessary, reinvented to suit the current climate of atrocity; its architecture is redesigned to appall the eye of the modern damned. In an earlier age Pandemonium—the first city of Hell—stood on a lava mountain while lightning tore the clouds above it and beacons burned on its walls to summon the fallen angels. Now, such spectacle belongs to Hollywood. Hell stands transposed. No lightning, no pits of fire.

"In a wasteland a few hundred yards from a highway overpass it finds a new incarnation: shabby, degenerate, forsaken. But here, where fumes thicken the atmosphere, minor terrors take on a new brutality. Heaven, by night, would have all the configurations of Hell. No less the Orpheus—hereafter called Pandemonium—Hotel."

This is definitely not your usual clash between good and evil, and while its approach is not to every horror fan's taste, it is interesting and unusual with quite a few disturbing surprises along the way.

WEAVEWORLD

Barker shifted gears in a largely new direction in this novel, creating what he termed an anti-fantasy novel in which the fantasy world he creates is not a wonderful place where everyone goes to live happily ever after. Barker makes certain of that.

The novel starts off deceptively like the very kind of epic fantasy novels that Barker is doing a bounce off. Cal Mooney is an ordinary enough young man who lives in Liverpool with his father in a pleasant cottage. When one of their homing pigeons escapes, he gives chase to the spot it's drawn to. This spot is near the home of an old woman who has been hospitalized and whose possessions are being sold off. When an antique carpet is unrolled in the yard of the house, a freak of circumstance enables Cal to glimpse another world in the weave of the cloth. This is an enchanted carpet whose magic hides an entire other-worldly valley and its surviving populace who have been sheltered here in a state of suspension to elude an ancient foe.

But another old foe, the beautiful Immacolata, and her merciless henchman, Shadwell, have been searching for the carpet and are close to finding it. Her one goal is to destroy the Weaveworld and revenge herself on the people there who cast her out. Shadwell is along to help her carry out her goal and make a profit on the deal as well.

Immacolata is a witch of sorts and has enchanted henchmen as well. These are her three weird Sisters, whom she'd strangled in the womb, and whose vicious spirits she now commands.

Cal's glimpse of the Weaveworld leaves him a changed man whose one great goal in life is to find and re-experience what he saw, and which for a time he fears was just a dream; a wishful illusion. Cal is the descendant of a well-known poet who'd been known as "Mad Mooney," and Cal feels that he has more than just a little of this ancestor's blood in his veins.

Barker masterfully portrays Cal's fever over what he's glimpsed, and his need and hunger to experience it again: *"And all because he'd seen something wonderful, and he knew in his bones that his life would never be the same again. How could it? He'd climbed the sky and looked down on the secret place that he'd been waiting since childhood to find.*

"He'd always been a solitary child, as much through choice as circumstance, happiest when he could unshackle his imagination and let it wander. It took little to get such journeys started. Looking back, it seemed he'd spent half his school days gazing out of the window, transported by a line of poetry whose meaning he couldn't quite unearth, or the sound of someone singing in a distant classroom, into a world more pungent and more remote than the one he knew. A world whose scents were carried to his nostrils by winds mysteriously warm in a chill December; whose creatures paid him homage on certain nights at the foot of his bed, and whose peoples he conspired with in sleep." One gets the feeling that Barker is describing some of his own creative soul in this passage.

The weakness of the Weaveworld and its controlling powers is revealed by the fact that only one guardian remains, a dying old woman, Mimi Laschenski. When Immacolata tracks the old woman down to her hospital room she expects a powerful conflict to learn the location of the rug, but Mimi is so old and infirm that her brief defensive spells are quickly breached. Even the witch Immacolata is dumbfounded that the Weaveworld could have been left this defenseless.

But enter Suzanna Parrish, Mimi's granddaughter and inheritor of Mimi's powers. Although Immacolata defeats Mimi, Suzanna proves to be a more troublesome foe, even with her nascent and unpracticed abilities.

Suzanna and Cal soon meet and form an alliance against Immacolata, but their battle is uphill all the way, with the possession of the rug shifting from one side to the other throughout much of the story.

At one point, Suzanna finds an old book of fables which bears the inscription: *That which is imagined need never be lost.* That she and Cal are kindred spirits quickly becomes evident when she realizes what this book of fables is and what it once meant to her, and once again we hear Barker speaking from his heart.

"Yet the stories moved her. She couldn't deny it. And they moved her in a way only <u>true</u> *things could. It wasn't sentiment that brought tears to her eyes. The stories weren't sentimental. They were tough, even cruel. No, what made her weep was being reminded of an inner life she'd been so familiar with as a child; a life that was both an escape from, and a revenge upon, the pains and frustrations of childhood; a life that was neither mawkish nor unknowing; a life of mind places— haunted, soaring—that she'd chosen to forget when she'd took the cause of adulthood."*

The lure of the fantasy world is also explained by Barker when the spell holding the Weaveworld in the rug is broken and it is revealed for the first time in decades, with Cal there to witness the glorious event.

"True joy is a profound remembering; and true grief the same. Thus it was, when the dust storm that had snatched Cal up had finally died, and he opened his eyes to see the Fugue spread before him, he felt as though the few fragile moments of epiphany he'd tasted in his twenty-six years—tasted but always lost—were here redeemed and wed. He'd grasped fragments of this delight before. Heard rumor of it in the womb-dream and the dream of love; seen its consequence in sudden good

CLIVE BARKER

and sudden laughter; known it in lullabies. But never, until now, the whole thing entire.

"It would be, he idly thought, a fine time to die.

"And a finer time still to live, with so much laid out before him."

This book is populated with marvelous and memorable characters, both people of the Weaveworld (called The Gyre) and mortals (called "Cuckoos" by the re-awakened inhabitants of the Weaveworld).

Much of the action first takes place in our world, where Shadwell, with his jacket that makes dreams come true, tracks down Cal and the rug. Shadwell's jacket, a gift of magic from the witch Immacolatta, requires an expert salesman like Shadwell to use it to its utmost, as what he sells are dreams, and what he gives is temporarily satisfying but ultimately intangible and unreal, leaving only crushing disappointment in its aftermath. It serves very much as a metaphor for people who grasp at the threads of pointless dreams—selfish dreams instead of honest dreams—in the belief that these cherished delusions will solve all of their life's ills, and how ultimately they must always be disappointed by the emptiness of the illusion.

This is a fantasy which grows darker as it proceeds. When the Weaveworld is resurrected in all its glory for one brief night, and then hidden again, the fear that drove these people into hiding is revealed, and the tools for their undoing are revealed as well.

When the Weaveworld is resurrected one last time in a valley far in the sparsely populated highlands, Shadwell moves in for the kill, forsaking his previous plans and blinded by the fantasy of possessing it for himself. When he cannot, he embarks on a mission to disinter the old enemy of the people of the Gyre, The Scourge, and bring it back to destroy what remains of the Weaveworld and its people.

While most epic fantasies deal with the fantasy overwhelming the mundane reality, this book goes in the opposite way, showing that reality is more powerful than fantasy when the two collide. Although not truly a horror novel, it has its horrific moments along the way, particularly with the three weird sisters in the earlier part of the book, and with The Scourge in the latter. But these are effective in contrast to the tone of the rest of the story, serving as counterpoints to the world of the Gyre and the people from there.

This is an amazing adventure and displays Barker at the peak of his craft, balancing a long, complicated tale and keeping all the elements airborne without faltering once along the way. This is by no means a "splatter" tale or anything of the kind, but instead shows the writer embarking in new directions and exploring altogether different terrain rather than plowing familiar ground. It's a story of special wonders wherein the unreal and the magical are often shattered and broken, but not at the cost of the strength to dream.

This book contains Barker's richest and best realized characterizations and uses the expanded length (over 700 pages) to its best effect. Barker said as much in an interview in the August, 1988 issue of **Science Fiction Eye**. In responding to the interviewer who felt that the novel had a lighter touch in that it wasn't a horror novel, Barker replied: "Lighter in one sense because it's not as visceral. But in another sense, I think that when the bad things happen to the characters in **Weaveworld**, they are very bad. I think in part because I hope the characters are more approachable than they have been in previous books, it may be that the harm that is done to them will be all the more significant. Harm which is healed for the first time in the books. The book moves towards moments of epiphany and optimism and life confirmation. It's an Eden book, finally. It's a book about our dreams of Eden, our hopes for Eden. I think it's the first really optimistic thing that I've done."

CABAL

This short novel runs through a fast-paced 200 pages and moves in unpredictable directions. It opens with a young man, Boone, who is apparently being confronted with evidence of his horrendous crimes by his psychiatrist, Decker. Horrible murders have been committed and Decker is trying to get his patient to face up to his crimes. The twist is that the psychiatrist is the real killer, and he's just using his patient as a handy scapegoat. Whereas such a piece of information would be a surprise ending from other writers, this fact is revealed early as the real surprises lie in entirely different directions.

Set in Canada, it follows the trail of Boone who flees, trying to make sense of his life and figure out what's going on. A chance encounter leads him to Midian, a necropolis where the living dead, who call themselves Nightbreed, live peaceful existences until their presence there is inadvertently revealed by Boone. Even after Boone dies, he becomes one of the supernatural residents of Midian, and is ultimately responsible for both the realm's destruction and its salvation.

The "nightbreed" of Midian are not the ordinary living dead as they have to be bitten by one of the nightbreed in order to return from the dead when killed. Boone describes what this experience is like when he says: "Being dead isn't bad. It isn't even that different. It's just. . . unexpected."

The people of Midian are sort of friendly versions of the zombies found in the **Night of the Living Dead** movies. The characterizations of the people here are only sketched in, unlike what you'd expect to find in a novel. We know little of Boone's background and nothing of what made Decker into a homicidal maniac. Even Lori, Boone's faithful girlfriend, is little more than a cypher, and she's one of the three pivotal characters in the story.

The prose lacks a lot of the heat and energy we've come to expect from Barker and reads like a movie treatment. Coincidentally, this story has been turned into a film being released under the title **Nightbreed**, which Barker is directing himself. The cabal of the book's title refers to Boone, and what he ultimately becomes in order to become the savior of the realm whose destruction he inadvertently brought about. No doubt it was decided not to call the film **Cabal** since a certain number of people unacquainted with the unusual word would otherwise think it said "cable" and assume it was a movie about HBO or something.

Although this book has a lot of interesting ideas in it, they aren't very well developed and it reads like it should have had another draft of it done to expand on the details and flesh out the characterizations more. It's definitely one of Barker's weaker stories from a writing standpoint, but it does offer a variety of interesting ideas which aren't fully developed. Apparently Barker thinks so as well, because certain plot threads remain unresolved at the end and it's clear that more tales of the Nightbreed will be forthcoming, in one form or another.

CLIVE BARKER

SUMMARY

Clive Barker's novels have demonstrated not only a willingness, but an eagerness to explore new frontiers. Unlike the novels of Stephen King, which often cover similar themes and explore the lives of similar characters, each of Barker's novels are singular in their intent and overlap not at all with any of the others, as though he says what he has to say on one theme and then moves into an entirely new area. Even stylistically his novels are quite different, so it's difficult to discuss Barker in terms of an individual style, the way one can discuss Stephen King and other writers. Perhaps Barker's unwillingness to plow familiar ground has prevented him from becoming the popular success in the United States that was predicted for him, although his books, beginning with **Weaveworld,** have broken out into the range sought by popular audiences, and the multimillion dollar deals made for his forthcoming efforts indicate that American publishers expect him to forge ever onward and upward.

FLICKERING FRIGHTS
by Bob Strauss

HELLRAISER

Dissatisfied over UNDERWORLD and RAWHEAD REX, the first two films based on his stories, Barker chose to adapt and direct the adaptation of "The Hellbound Heart" himself. The result was HELLRAISER, and in the following interview Barker discusses the challenges of directing his first motion picture.

Nobody raises Hell quite like Clive Barker.

In less than six years, with the best-selling **Books of Blood** short story collections and **The Damnation Game**, his first novel, the 37-year-old English author has staked out an indelible world of perversity, supernatural terror and poignantly misapplied passion that has revitalized horror fiction while at the same time turning most of the genre's creaky narrative conventions on their pointy little ears. Stephen King has all but relinquished his crown to the young Liverpudlian, admitting in print that Barker writes rings around anyone else in the field and dubbing him "The future of horror fiction."

So what does this friendly, unassuming, slightly disheveled guy who talks like an intellectualized Ringo Starr do to scare the bejesus out of legions of readers in Europe, Japan and, increasingly, America? For one thing, he keeps you guessing. You'll never see such scare-story archetypes as vampires or werewolves stalking through a Barker book, and even if you do, you can bet they won't be dispatched by anything as simple as a crucifix or a silver bullet. You will find a lot of living dead—or more often, half-living—folks in the pages of Barker's fiction, but their presence is as much to attract as to repulse you. Barker is a genius at investing his monstrous characters with complex motivations and vivid psychological lives. More often than not, they're as concerned with expressing and receiving love (no matter how demented their definitions of love might be) as they are with ripping open flesh—hence the bizarre, often graphic intertwining of sex and gore imagery that is a Barker hallmark. Beyond that, both Barker's protagonists and villains often find themselves, consciously or not, dealing with fundamental metaphysical issues: escape from prisons either manmade, mental or mystical, discovering truths beyond the perceptions of their senses, confronting God or eternal damnation, usually in one and the same form.

"I feel I write happy, optimistic stories," Barker said of his blood-drenched tales of magic and madness. "I write a fiction of transcendence, metaphors for transcendence. The upside is that people get new information about the way that they are in relation to their flesh, their desires, their vulnerability, their spiritual potential. The bad news is," he added with a hooligan grin, "this stuff will kill you."

And kill people it does, sometimes over and over again, in Clive Barker's world. For the first time, Barker brought his purgatorial milieu of razor-pierced flesh and postmortem eroticism from prose to visual life with **Hellraiser**, a film based on his novella "The Hell-Bound Heart." Set in a decaying London house that is at once a confining trap, an ineffective mortuary and a gateway to a terrifying universe where pain and pleasure are indistinguishable, Barker's film directing debut tells the story of a married couple (Andrew Robinson and Clare Higgins), whose chances for happiness were ruined when the husband's amoral brother

(Sean Chapman) seduced the bride-to-be shortly before the wedding. Sexually obsessed with the subsequently deceased adventurer ever since, Higgins' character is delighted to find his spirit haunting the old family home; unfortunately, his body has been decimated by the sadomasochistic masters of the terror dimension, and he can only return to human form via a slow process of bathing in blood. Lots of blood.

The picture is not for the squeamish, obviously. Yet it's a surprisingly assured maiden effort—well-acted and shot, and dripping with the same kind of icky, twisted ambiance that's found in Barker's books—from a man who's never had any great desire to make movies.

"I felt I'd got cornered into directing," Barker explained. "The other two movies that have been made from scripts I'd written (**Underworld** and **Rawhead Rex**) were terrible. If they had been great pictures—in other words if my screenplays had been made, as opposed to there being only seven of my lines left, like in the first movie—I probably wouldn't have directed before my mid-forties.

"But, I figured, I've got to do this now to see whether I *can* do it. If I can't, I'll shut the hell up and let other people make the films, for better or for worse. If I do something that's successful, though, then maybe I'll be justified in telling other people in the future what I think they might be doing wrong, and at least have enough of their respect that they'll listen to me."

Barker feels he has succeeded. "For a picture that cost what it cost, I'm real happy with **Hellraiser**," he said (budget estimates run at a paltry $2.5 million). "For a picture which was my first, I'm real happy with it. It has some of the book's intensity and eroticism. What I set out to do was to make a solid, commercial movie that had the feel of one of my written pieces. Yeah, I'm satisfied that I pulled that off."

Barker likes to point out that he was not totally unprepared for the job. After writing six **Books of Blood** (reprinted in the U.S. under such titles as **In The Flesh** and **The Inhuman Condition**) and two novels, directing several plays (including two at Scotland's prestigious Edinburgh Arts Festival) and illustrating a number of his own and others' publications, Barker had most of the experience a good visual storyteller needs. But the one thing he wasn't ready for was the sheer amount of time a movie demands of its director.

"There's only one real difficulty about film directing, and that's energy," Barker sighed. "I mean, this is a f—-ing exhausting procedure. I've got lots of energy. When I write I work twelve-hour days, and **Weaveworld** was a nine-month book. A lot of commitment, and a lot of time. But writing is an absolute solitary occupation, and film-making is this zoo where everybody's got something to say and the question is, 'Can we all have a vision of the picture which is roughly consistent?'

"So you're dealing with people who need cosseting, persuading, calming, motivating, subduing and so on. Each of them needs a different kind of handling to get the best from them. And all of them need to be infused with your vision. It's ten weeks of 18-hour days. I hadn't anticipated how demanding that would be. But, at the same time, how rewarding. Clearly, we had a very happy time of it. The producers let me do things my way, and there were very few tears and tantrums. I never raised my voice once in the entire ten weeks."

Barker was aware going in of one other major difference between writing and film-making. "I wanted the people who liked the particular qualities of my prose to be able to see the same thing on screen," he revealed. "Inevitably, that required a certain amount of playing around with what the censors would allow. There's usually some kind of sexual energy going on in the stories, and they're certainly very visceral in places. I had to find a way to turn those images from the books into something that would be acceptable on the screen. The tightrope was between avoiding shooting stuff which I knew wouldn't even be allowed in the picture and trying to dramatically justify what I did shoot. Not like coming up with a gross thing, then trying to dramatically justify it. The way it works is that within a dramatic context, I want to push things to the limits. So I usually just forge ahead, trying not to consider what the critics or producers or censors might think.

"Of course, with the books, that works fine. The editors just say go for it. But then, you're not spending a lot of money generating those sentences. If I spend half a day shooting a scene that I'm not even sure will get into the movie, that's not clever thinking. It's good Michael Cimino thinking, but not for a guy who wants his first feature to be a financial success."

Despite his sincere attempts at self-restraint, Barker ran afoul of censors in the United States, Canada and England with one **Hellraiser** scene. In a film where a man graphically regenerates from protoplasm to wholeness—literally from the gooey inside out—**Hellraiser**'s distributors had Barker reshoot a flashback sex scene they felt was too hot, perhaps because both participants were alive and quite healthy at the time. "Too real-looking, was the actual complaint," Barker chortled.

A pudgy, near-sighted youth, Barker was the classic fantasy-loving kid, self-sufficient in his own world of comic book dreams and made-up stories. Regardless of his acute insight into human nature and the prodigious literary gifts he's still developing, Barker has no intention to venture outside the realms of fantastic fiction. In this lifetime, anyway.

HELLBOUND: HELLRAISER II

In the wake of the popular success of HELLRAISER, it was inevitable that a sequel would be spawned, particularly since Barker had created a universe rich in invention and populated with bizarre characters which fans wanted to learn more about. With that in mind, HELLBOUND was written, featuring everything you always wanted to know (but were literally afraid to ask) about the Cenobites, including how to make a Cenobite! The following chapter goes behind-the-scenes with the people who brought the sequel to HELLRAISER to the screen.

Hellraiser, Clive Barker's enormously successful tale of love, lust and demonic dealings is one of the most successful horror films released over the past decade. Opening to excellent critical notices and outstanding business throughout the world, the New World International release has collected a cluster of awards, including the prestigious Grand Prix De La Section Peur at the 16th annual Avoriaz Fantasy Film Festival in France earlier this year.

Hellraiser II: Hellbound reunites the two female stars of the first film in a nightmare quest into torment and terror. Acclaimed British actress Clare Higgins once again portrays the scheming Julia Cotton, who uses the blood of innocents to return from beyond death, and Ashley Laurence repeats her role as Julia's stepdaughter, Kirsty, who must plumb the depths of Hell and confront the awesome powers of the Cenobites.

Filmed over a nine-week schedule at Britain's Pinewood Studios in 1988, this sequel also features Ken Cranham, Imogen Boorman, William Hope, Doug Bradley and Sean Chapman. Written by Peter Atkins, from a story by Clive Barker,

131

CLIVE BARKER

Hellraiser II: Hellbound is produced by Christopher Figg, directed by Tony Randel, and is a Film Futures Production for New World International.

TONY RANDEL

Within hours of first meeting during the shooting of **Hellraiser**, Clive Barker and Tony Randel developed a unique rapport that has resulted in Randel making his directing debut with **Hellraiser II: Hellbound.**

"I have tremendous respect for his instincts on the way **Hellraiser** was cut," enthuses Barker. "Tony has immense editorial skill and a wonderful grasp of the horror genre. When producer Christopher Figg and I started looking for a director for the sequel, we needed someone who would show great passion for the material, and we agreed that Tony was the ideal choice."

"Tony's strengths as a film-maker are different from those of Clive," Figg explains, "and he has brought those new skills to the sequel, while at the same time expressing a great enthusiasm for the picture."

"I could never have made **Hellraiser** the way Clive did," agrees the tall, soft-spoken Californian, "because that is a very personal film for him. **Hellraiser** is a unique picture: It's a very contained, tight drama about a family, and it works in it's structure brilliantly.

"Of course I was a little nervous about following in Clive's footsteps — he's a tough act to follow. **Hellraiser II: Hellbound** is set in the same world, but with a slightly different personality. I can't make the same kind of film that Clive would. I'm hoping that what I bring to the sequel will show through and be as entertaining and interesting for an audience as the first one."

So how does someone with an avowed fascination for the films of Charlie Chaplin and the silent movie era find himself taking audiences on a nightmare journey to explore the depths of Hell?

Tony Randel was born in Los Angeles in 1956. Like so many other inhabitants of that West Coast city, he developed an interest in film-making at an early age, becoming a regular movie-goer and experimenting with his parents' 8 mm camera.

When he started college he expected to major in Accounting, but quickly discovered how much he hated it: "I soon dropped out of Accounting and moved across to film," he explains. "It wasn't even like being in school, so I decided to stick with it."

His tenacity was rewarded when, upon leaving college in 1979, he started work in the mail room at producer/director Roger Corman's New World Pictures. Corman, renowned for his skill in achieving impressive results on a shoe-string budget and for his ongoing commitment to developing new talent, soon moved Randel to New World's visual effects facility where he worked in the editorial department for nine months on **Battle Beyond the Stars.**

During that time, while methodically logging the footage being shot, Randel started to learn the techniques of optical effects work, a skill that he subsequently utilized and developed on a string of low-budget science fiction films, including **Escape From New York, Galaxy of Terror, Forbidden World,** and the highly acclaimed **Android.**

From there, Corman moved him on to editing trailers, where he worked on fifteen campaigns in eighteen months, culminating in his co-editor credit on the feature **Space Raiders:** "It was a new movie starring Vince Edwards, but used old visual effects footage from all the films I had filed when I was working in the ef-

132

fects editorial department," explains Randel. "I had the best knowledge of anyone what had been shot at the New World effects facility.

"Roger then sold New World and offered me the job as head of post-production for his new company, which was called Millennium. I stayed there for four months, editing trailers on several successful campaigns for such films as **Deathstalker** and **Suburbia**."

Randel was then offered a job at the new New World Pictures, overseeing their post-productions facilities and doctoring such pictures as **Godzilla 1985**. "We took the original Japanese version and totally restructured it," he laughs. "We cut out about half an hour and shot about twelve minutes of new material with Raymond Burr and effects footage from **The Philadelphia Experiment** and made it seem like a sequel to the original.

"I then went on to get involved in the actual development and making of movies at New World. I was appointed the studio representative on **Hellraiser** because I have a good feeling for horror films. I came to Britain about mid-way through the shooting and stayed right through post-production. It was a good experience and I got along very well with Chris and Clive.

"When we were finishing up **Hellraiser** I already thought we should start developing a sequel, even before the film was released. At that time I hadn't thought about directing it, but when I discussed it with Chris and Clive they thought it was great idea."

"Tony brings a freshness to the material," Barker points out, " and a passion for science fiction that tinges some of the material in a very interesting way. **Hellraiser** was a medium-budget horror movie with an emphasis on the bizarre, the outlandish and the surreal. Tony has taken the sequel in a slightly different direction, and we have opened up the storyline and actually visit the Hell from which the Cenobites were raised."

Randel strongly believes it was important to maintain a continuity of actors and crew between the two films. "If you come into a sequel with all new people you are asking the audience to get used to everybody again, and taking a very big risk that they never will.

"The one thing I wanted to do with **Hellbound** was make a picture that was a little bit broader than the fist one. The things that fascinated me about **Hellraiser** were the Cenobites and how little was revealed about who they were. This time I wanted to examine them more, without giving too much away: Who they are, how you become one, and what it means to be a Cenobite. I also wanted to examine this place we call Hell, and in **Hellraiser II** we do get a glimpse of it."

Although he admits to a great fondness for the films of Chaplin and Hitchcock and German Expressionist pictures such as **The Cabinet of Doctor Caligari**, Randel has always nurtured a love of science fiction and fantasy films: "The most important movies I've seen in my life are **2001: A Space Odyssey** and **Star Wars**. Perhaps more than any other picture, **Star Wars** has influenced the film-makers of my generation."

Tony Randel is committed to ensuring that **Hellraiser II: Hellbound** will continue its successful predecessor's ability to combine high-powered scares with a strong emphasis on plot and characterization:

"There is probably a higher body count than in the first film and just as much blood. There are certainly more visual effects: We have four or five matte paintings, blue-screen composites, stop-motion animation and rotoscoping to create the center of Hell.

"I'd like audiences to come away from the film still thinking about it," he continues, "examining the feelings and desires of people in the picture and the types of relationships we have explored.

"Don't worry, though, the horror fans will not be disappointed; **Hellraiser II: Hellbound** delivers everything the audience expects — and more."

CLIVE BARKER

"The first picture was, in many ways, a gore-hound movie. It was the picture I wanted to see on 42nd Street, but couldn't. It came out of my own passion for modestly budgeted horror films with an emphasis on the bizarre, the outlandish, and the surreal, plus a conscious desire to take the imagery just a little bit further— pushing those limits."

That is how Clive Barker describes his directing debut on the enormously successful horror thriller, **Hellraiser**. So why then has Barker taken on the role of executive producer for the sequel, **Hellraiser II: Hellbound**? "I didn't direct this time because I had responsibilities to my publishers to deliver a new novel," he explains. "However, I had a very strong creative involvement and there is a great sense of continuity—and that continuity would have been there, whether I directed or not. It's based on my story and I feel that it is very much in the tradition of **Hellraiser.**

"Christopher Figg and I often spoke about making a sequel if **Hellraiser** worked, but we weren't prepared for it to work to the extent it has, both critically and commercially. I was certainly aware that the first story left open ends, some of which were quite deliberate. Others were there because we didn't have the resources to follow some of the ideas through to their logical conclusion. **Hellraiser II: Hellbound** will answer some of those questions, but it also opens up a new level of possibilities. . ."

Many of the elements which made **Hellraiser** a box office hit worldwide have been retained in the sequel. The Lament of Configuration puzzle box is described by Barker as "still the most important element in the sequel," and once again it acts as the catalyst for a terrifying quest through the corridors of Hell. "We also explore the theme of the disintegration of the family unit and, of course, the very popular Cenobites reappear from the first film. These and other elements are carried over from my published novella, 'The Hellbound Heart,' where the title of the new film comes from.

"During interviews or at autograph sessions, people would keep coming up to me and saying. 'Tell us more about the Cenobites' or 'What did the box mean?' Well, they're going to get some of the answers in **Hellraiser II**. What we've been able to do with the slightly higher budget and our experience on the first film has allowed us to develop the mythology. I like the idea that you can carry the momentum forward.

"One of the great things about **Hellraiser II: Hellbound** is that it starts off at a run. When I'm writing short stories I can actually begin in the middle of things and then track back. It's much more difficult to do that in movies. We tried to do a little bit of that in **Hellraiser** in the sense that there was all that flashback material with Frank and the box..

"I like that approach. The first film was a teaser— there were many things in there that we never got around to explaining. It's like the shimmering image of the Emperor in the first **Star Wars** picture. You end up thinking, 'Who is this guy?'

and then you have to wait until part three to find out. So I see **Hellraiser II** as being both an advance of the first picture and a filling in of detail."

Born in 1952 in LIverpool, Clive Barker is an award-winning short story writer, best-selling novelist, illustrator, playwright, screenwriter and film director. He has always been a big fantasy fan, and no less an authority than Stephen King has described him as "the future of horror."

"I don't ever remember a time that I wasn't genuinely interested in horror in some form or another," says Barker. "It was always the grisly bits of fairy tales that I was interested in. I've always liked fantastical literature of some kind, and I've always liked the darker aspects of that."

After his early success with plays like "The History of the Devil", "Frankenstein In Love", and "Colossus", he made an auspicious literary debut with six volumes of short stories entitled Clive Barker's **Books of Blood.** These were followed by two acclaimed novels, **The Damnation Game** and **Weaveworld**, and the screenplays for **Underworld** and **Rawhead Rex**, the latter based on his own published story.

Both critical and commercial reaction to **Hellraiser** led to a string of tempting offers from Hollywood, but Barker turned them all down to concentrate on developing his own movie projects. Film Futures, the production company he owns with Christopher Figg, is already preparing its next production, based on the supernatural exploits of Barker's fictional private detective, Harry D'Amour. "It's my screenplay and I will also be directing. We are also developing a number of other projects, including another horror film, **Cabal** (aka **Nightbreed**), scripted by Peter Atkins and based on my novella. I'm still very keen to continue doing this stuff."

On **Hellraiser II** he was content to hand over the directorial reins to newcomer Tony Randel. "**Hellraiser** was a 'raw' picture," explains Barker, "made by somebody who didn't have a filmic education. I came at the picture to make a no-holds-barred horror movie. Tony brings to the sequel an informed understanding of special effects and that is reflected in the look and style of the movie.

"We needed someone fresh to come in and say, 'Hey, we haven't had the box do this,' or 'What about if we had a Cenobite do that?' Tony had displayed a passion for the material in his involvement on the first picture, he had evidenced his grasp of our particular version of the horror genre, and he knew many of the production team. He'd been in close liaison with Christopher and myself, and he'd worked closely with Richard Marden in the editing room. It was just a matter of convincing New World that Tony should take, what in many people's view, was a retrograde step—back to creativity!" laughs Barker.

"He has a passion for science fiction that tinges some of the material in very interesting ways. Tony has taken it in a slightly different direction, and knowing he was going to be involved in the project allowed scriptwriter Peter Atkins and myself to formulate the kind of narrative that was most suitable."

Barker was also responsible for bringing fellow Liverpudlian Atkins on board to write **Hellbound**. "I'd worked with Peter in the past in the theatre," says Barker, "and we like the same kind of horror movies and have a passion for the same kind of art. It was a natural combination and we really sparked ideas off each other.

"This time we've opened up the story," continues Barker, "we see Leviathan, the great Lament Configuration; we travel to the Hell from which the Cenobites were raised, and we have even got a how-to-make-a-Cenobite sequence. I always thought that Kirsty would go into Hell for her father, but the question was whether she would find him when she got there. . ."

Barker is adamant that **Hellraiser II: Hellbound** illuminates many of the concepts that he was happy to leave as mysteries in the first picture, while at the same time offering a more sophisticated interpretation of the bizarre ideas originated in the first film: "We want the people who came to **Hellraiser** to feel all the 'pleasures' of the first picture, and a few more besides.

"I know there are bad sequels around, pictures that almost undo the good work of the original. But because Tony was involved in the first film, and because the same team worked on **Hellraiser II**, it's going to have a continuity, which is very important.

"Without doubt, audiences will have some of their questions answered," agrees Barker, "and I think they'll find the spiral of weirdness begun in the first picture continuing. In **Hellraiser** we were in the real world, but raising Hell. This time we are going on the great adventure and plumbing the fiery depths. For audiences that had a good time with the first picture, I think we've got a lot more of the same kind of thrills, but we've got a lot of new ideas, as well.

"I'm excited because I feel the story, indeed the whole Hellraiser mythology is capable of being reinterpreted in many different ways," explains Barker.

"Of course, I'd love there to be a **Hellraiser III**—I have a very clear idea of what we would do with that. There's a **Hellraiser II** because the first one did so well, and the next one in very much in the hands of the audience. If they have a good time with **Hellbound** then the next one is waiting in the wings. As long as we can continue to invest the images and the mythology with something fresh, something new, then there's nothing wrong with sequels."

Hellraiser II: Hellbound ably confirms Barker's belief that sequels need not be inferior to the original

CHRISTOPHER FIGG

Figg is justifiably proud of **Hellraiser**, which marked his debut as a producer. "The first picture was very successful in America and the international markets. To date it has grossed more than $16 million in the States, and we've done a very respectable one million pounds of business in Britain. On top of that, it was the most successful foreign picture released in 1987 in Hong Kong. Spain and Australia had very strong openings, and it broke box office records in Europe—particularly in France, where it was the number one film.

"With this worldwide success, there will be automatic audience recognition of the sequel and marketing **Hellbound** will not be as difficult as it was for the first picture. We can exploit the elements that were successful in **Hellraiser** while at the same time expanding them for the sequel."

Christopher Figg was born in 1957 in Aylesbury, England. After producing a number of plays and short films while attending a university, he went on to appear in several small acting roles in movies, before changing sides of the camera and becoming third assistant director on **The Mirror Crack'd**. He worked his way up as an assistant director on a number of successful films, including **Evil Under the Sun, The Ploughman's Lunch, The Dresser, Another Country, A Passage to India** and **Mr. Corbett's Ghost,** finally teaming up with first-time director Clive Barker to make **Hellraiser**.

According to Figg, "**Hellraiser** worked because it had characters the audience could empathize with, a clever and unexpected script, and of course, some moments of fantasy and horror unlike anything seen on the screen before."

It therefore comes as no surprise to discover that the enterprising young producer has done his best to ensure that all these successful elements are retained and developed in **Hellraiser II: Hellbound**.

"We've kept many of the key elements from Hellraiser," agrees Figg. "The characters are still motivated by family ties. Kirsty goes to Hell to save her father; Julia, the wicked stepmother, still wants to control things to her advantage, and we discover Frank incarcerated in the Hell he has created for himself. We also learn more about Pinhead, one of the most successful images from **Hellraiser**. This time we reveal something about his past, where he is going, and why he is in the condition he is in.

"We have not tried to outdo the gory aspects of **Hellraiser** though, as I don't think we want to go any further than the first picture and anyway, we would never have been able to do it. I hope the gore-hounds will come along to **Hellraiser II** expecting the blood and not be let down. But at the same time, they will experience something that is a different work altogether. The sequel takes us much more into fantasy, while still delivering the shocks for the horror fans."

It comes as a surprise to learn that **Hellraiser II** proved to be a much more difficult project to set up than the first picture: "Clive and I pitched the sequel idea to New World and they liked it, but it still took a long time to set up, which is not unusual with an effects picture such as this.

"However, we were in the middle of budget discussions when 'Black Monday' hit the world's stock markets. We were also anxious to start as soon as possible, not just because **Hellraiser** had been such a huge hit, but to insure that we could get Clare Higgins to reprise her role as Julia before she had to move on to another project. It was difficult to juggle the schedules of cast and crew who we wanted to hold over from **Hellraiser**, but in the end we had all the same heads of departments, plus Clare, Ashley Laurence, Sean Chapman, Doug Bradley and others in the cast."

Although Figg admits they had a little more money to spend on the sequel, they had to be very careful when budgeting because of the fluctuating exchange rate. "Some people say that it might have been cheaper to make the picture in America, but I refute that. It's not cheaper. In Britain the technicians are keen and enthusiastic, and despite the weak dollar we still got much better value for money than we could have got over there.

"The decision to film at Pinewood Studios made sense. We shot over five stages plus a special effects stage. We were able to create a bigger canvas than on the first picture and Mike Buchanan's sets were wonderfully fantastical—particularly the Center of Hell and Frank's chamber, which involved complex fire effects."

So did working with another first-time director pose Figg a new set of problems? "Absolutely not," he replies. "We brought Tony Randel in because he showed a great sensitivity for the first film, as well as understanding the genre, the market, and the audience extremely well.

"Of course, Clive was still closely involved in **Hellraiser II**—he wrote the original story, collaborated closely with scriptwriter Peter Atkins, and was very influential during post-production. We had to make a few compromises story-wise, to accommodate character changes as we'd seen them develop from **Hellraiser**, and also to set the direction for a possible third picture, which will hopefully treat the material in a different way again."

PETER ATKINS

Peter Atkins admits that he enjoyed **Hellraiser** immensely, which is a good thing because, although he didn't realize it at the time, he would soon be asked to write the sequel.

"Clive invited me to write **Hellraiser II: Hellbound** because he didn't have the time to do it himself," explains Atkins. "He had read some of my fiction and thought I could do the job.

"With **Hellraiser II** it was such a relief to see a horror movie that was serious, without being solemn. Particularly as there have been so many recent entries in the field that were tongue in cheek, or gross-out for the sake of being gross-out. It was a pleasure to see a work that took itself seriously and wasn't afraid to expect the audience to do that as well".

Both Atkins and Barker were fully aware that the sequel had to live up to audience expectations, as well as their own. "Clive provided me with a very thorough outline of the story," Atkins reveals, "who was in it—and whether they were dead or not. I proceeded from there.

"**Hellbound** is an extension of **Hellraiser**; we picked up thematically, structurally, and gross-outly from the first film. If **Hellraiser** is about a hedonist achieving what he desired and finding out that it wasn't what he wanted, then the sequel is about a voyeur who is also disappointed when he achieves what he thinks he wanted."

"I'd worked with Peter in the past in the theater," says fellow Liverpudlian Barker, "and we like the same kind of horror movies and have a passion for the same kind of art. It was a natural combination and we really sparked ideas off each other."

"Tony Randel wasn't involved in the first draft of the script," Atkins explains, "but from the second draft onwards I worked very closely with him and he brought a great vision to the final script."

Peter Atkins hopes that audiences will remember the horror in **Hellbound**, but also the human drama that has been the core of both films. Meanwhile he is busy adapting Barker's novella "Cabal" for the screen and thinking about **Hellraiser III.**

"The third film is even bigger and grosser," he laughs. "Without giving too much away, certain story lines are thoroughly resolved by the end of **Hellraiser II**, but there is at least one major character whose story, while *temporarily* resolved, has very much more to do in the third one."

IMAGE ANIMATION

"In **Hellraiser II: Hellbound**, we learned from our mistakes on the first film and were able to go back and do certain things better this time," admits special makeup effects designer Geoff Portass. "We made a few changes to the Cenobites, although the most obvious is to Chatterer, who becomes Chatterer II in a sequence where he has his eyelids pulled off. This was so that Nicholas Vince, who couldn't see a thing in the first film, could control his movements in the sequel."

Geoff Portass and Bob Keen started Image Animation two years ago, after working together on such movies as **Lifeforce** and **Highlander**. "**Hellraiser** was our first major project," explains Portass, "and we created the Cenobites, the Engineer, and all the blood, guts, and slime."

138

More recently, the company has created the effects for **Waxworks**, **The Un-holy**, **Lair of the White Worm** and various television commercials and music promos, and Bob Keen is making his directing debut with another horror film, **Changer**, which Image Animation will create the effects for.

"There aren't a great number of ground-breaking effects in **Hellraiser II**," Portass points out, "but we tried to take our experience on the first picture and improve on it. The most complex effect on the film was the skinless Julia makeup where the skin rips off. It was difficult to produce a skinned woman and at the same time a skin that fitted her perfectly. Instead of going for anatomically correct detail, we actually went for a look that Tony Randel called 'sexy'.

"We also created a new Cenobite for the film. Ken Cranham, who plays the Channard Cenobite, was very lucky that we learned from our mistakes on **Hellraiser**, where we did separate piece makeups on the Cenobite actors. Ken's makeup was an over-the-head mask, which we glued to his face. However, it still took us four or five hours to get him ready. He usually fell asleep in the chair and we just stuck the pieces on and painted him.

"All the actors were interested in what we do, so they were prepared to sit still for hours and endure the process."

On **Hellraiser II** there were almost fifty separate effects (which could be broken down further) and, at its largest, Image Animation employed a team of 35 people. However, with only nine weeks of pre-production, it was still a rush to have everything ready for the start of shooting. "Money is always the biggest problem on any film," according to Portass. "You always want to do the best possible job you can.

"**Hellraiser** was a modern Gothic horror movie, whereas the sequel is more of a chase movie. It's paced differently, and although I think audiences will get the scares, they will also be enthralled. Tony Randel had quite a large input with the effects. We discussed various ideas before the picture started, and then we were allowed to develop our own concepts. Ninety nine percent of the time, Tony was happy with the finished results."

With most of its employees aged in their early twenties and the youngest team member only 16, Image Animation actively welcomes anyone who is interested in special effects to show them their work. "Obviously, we get a lot of people who, after having seen **Hellraiser**, think we only deal in blood and guts," says Portass, "which we don't. We want to see something original, something that would excite us. We will always give someone an interview, look at their work, and try to be as constructive as possible. We simply can't afford to turn away talented people."

CLARE HIGGINS

"It's the blood they remember," laughs Clare Higgins, "the blood and the way I narrowed my eyes just before bashing someone's head in with a hammer!"

Despite her initial trepidation about appearing in a horror film (after all, she had once fainted during a public screening of **The Exorcist**), Clare is obviously delighted to be playing Julia Cotton again. "How could I resist playing the Queen of Hell?" she asks.

"I saw about half of **Hellraiser**—the rest of the time I just covered my eyes. It terrified me, and I was in it, so I think we must have accomplished what we set out to do. After **Hellraiser**, people would nervously come to me and ask, 'Are you?', and when I said 'Yes', they would tell me how much they enjoyed the film. It was great."

In **Hellraiser**, the accomplished British actress played Julia as a sympathetic character. "At the beginning of the film she seems very secretive, but we only learn later that she is hiding a burning secret," explains Clare. "I hope you understood her reasons for being an unpleasant character, because you see the depths she was prepared to plumb for love. She ends up a very disappointed woman."

At the end of the first picture she had the life sucked out of her body by her not-quite-fully-fleshed lover, Frank. Now, in **Hellraiser II: Hellbound**, Julia uses the blood of innocents to return from beyond death and seduce Channard (played by Ken Cranham) with the pleasures of Hell.

"Julia is a lot meaner, much more evil, in the sequel," says Clare. "Tony Randel and I discussed the character and we had rehearsals—which was a great help, as Julia is a difficult character to play. She just gets nastier, and nastier, and nastier. If anybody sympathizes with her this time then I've done something wrong. I think **Hellraiser II** will be scarier, more evil and more disgusting. Julia is evil incarnate in the sequel. In the first film she started off as a human being and there's no way that she's human in **Hellbound.** Just pure nastiness.

"However, I have less visible blood letting in the new film, which is a bit of a shame, because that's what everybody talks about from the first one. But I don't think anyone will be disappointed. **Hellraiser II** is a total fantasy. We are no longer in suburbia—this time we're in Hell!"

Clare Higgins was born on November 10th (she prefers not to reveal in what year) in Norwich, England. She comes from an academic family. Her mother is a teacher and her father a maths lecturer, but she left school at 16. "I was working in this wine bar in Norwich, which was next door to the local theater," she recalls. "And these actors used to come in and scream their heads off, calling each other 'darling' all the time and talking about how wonderful they were. I loathed them. But I decided to go and see what they were doing. It turned out to be an amateur performance of 'Pygmalion' and I was just captivated. I thought, 'Well, if they can do it, so can I'. About a week later I applied to drama school."

After three years of learning her craft, she left in 1979 and went straight to the Royal Exchange Theatre, Manchester, to play the lead in "The Deep Man". More prestigious stage parts followed, including Isabella in "Measure For Measure" and her acclaimed portrayal of Stella in "A Streetcar Named Desire".

When not appearing in the theater, she was busy carving a niche for herself in BBC television plays such as "Pride and Prejudice", "Unity", "Byron", and her memorable performance as Christine Barlow in the ten-part dramatization of A.J. Cronin's "The Citadel", in which she co-starred with Ben Cross.

More recently, her television credits have included Anglia Television's "Cover Her Face", "Foreign Bodies" for Thames TV, and the pivotal role of Fizzy Targett in Channel 4's comedy about cults and pyramid selling, "Up Line". "The whole thing was weird," says Clare, "but I really liked the scripts. I thought they were wonderful and that the series really worked."

In 1984 Clare made her movie debut in **Nineteen Nineteen**, which starred Paul Scofield, and since making **Hellraiser** she has co-starred in Phillip Saville's tale of bizarre sex and murder, **The Fruit Machine**. "I'm not sure if this is what **Hellraiser** did for me," laughs Clare, "but I play a pretty nasty woman who goes around picking up young boys and taking them to Robert Stephens' house. I have my wicked way with one of them and Robert's character has his wicked way with the other. It was a very good script, and I got to be pretty mean and evil in that as well."

It's been a busy year for Clare between both Hellraisers. She appeared in the BBC-TV play "Beautiful Lives" and found time to return to London's Royal Court Theatre in a play about Nicaragua. Clare admits she would like to do more stage work, if her schedule permits. "I've only done one play in two years, and I'm dying to do more—that is, if anyone will have me after **Hellraiser II!**"

She has also been hard at work on a mammoth television adaptation of Frederic Raphael's "After the War", to be shown in ten one-hour episodes in early 1989. The series follows the friendship of two young men who meet at boarding school in England during the Second World War. Clare describes he character, Rachel, as a victim of her times. "If she had been born in the 1980s she'd have been okay. She is very passionate, a little amoral, and wide open to everything. I loved working on it—we started in the 1940s and followed these people's lives through to the late 60s."

So, after working closely with Clive Barker and the first picture, how did Clare find first-time director Tony Randel's approach to the material? "Clive and Tony are very different personalities, but they have both got the same sort of minds underneath—if you know what I mean," she laughs. "They both understand and enjoy the script, which I find deeply worrying."

Working on a special effects oriented picture like **Hellraiser** didn't seem to offer her too many problems as an actress, as she explains. "I don't find it difficult to work with special effects at all, because after a while you begin to think of them as other actors. The only problem is that they involve a lot of waiting around on the set.

"The most difficult thing I had to do in **Hellbound** was walk down the wind tunnels with a jet engine blowing at me, keep my eyes open, and look evil at the same time. There's a lot of wind in this movie," she adds with a laugh, ". . .and blood. . .and slime. . .and gore. . ."

With her role in **Hellraiser II: Hellbound** set to firmly establish her in the minds of audiences as the British *femme fatale* of the 80s, is she not worried about being type-cast? "For quite a long time I played a lot of good characters, and I got sick to death of it. So I have no worries about being typed."

She believes that **Hellraiser II** is more horrific than the first picture, but it is also more fantastical. "It's a lot of people's nightmares, and because of the added fantasy element the story is no longer contained, as it was in **Hellraiser**. This time we are in Hell, and anything can happen.

"I hope Julia comes across as a really evil, mean bitch of a woman. I really want everyone to hate me." She pauses for a moment, then adds somewhat wistfully, "Still, I did miss the hammer killings."

ASHLEY LAURENCE

Ashley Laurence admits that she was a little disappointed that nobody recognized her after **Hellraiser.** "The only time it occurred to me was when I was out with my boyfriend in New York and he happened to be wearing his Clive Barker T-shirt," she explains. "Although I was standing right next to him, people came up to him and asked if *he* was involved with **Hellraiser**! I guess I just don't look the same when I'm not covered from head to foot in blood and slime."

Luckily for the young actress, still in her early twenties, **Hellraiser II: Hellbound** did not quite turn out as uncomfortable for her as the first picture, despite being occasionally covered in blood by Geoff Portass and his Image Animation team.

"Clive Barker said that I got the part in the first film because I can scream. But I hope it was also because I'm willing to take risks as an actress. It's really hard to show your emotions when you are surrounded by technicians and everyone's watching you." However, Ashley obviously enjoyed the opportunity to reprise her role as Kristy Cotton in **Hellraiser II.** "It was good to be working with the same team again," she agrees.

In the sequel, Kristy has not long escaped from the clutches of her Uncle Frank's reanimated corpse and the dark desires of the Cenobites when she awakens in a psychiatric hospital. But she soon discovers that the nightmare is not over yet, and she must once again venture into Hell's corridors to save her new friend Tiffany (played by Imogen Boorman) and release her father's tortured soul from eternal damnation.

"Kristy is a much stronger character in this picture," Ashley states. "After all she went through in **Hellraiser**, she's learned a great deal. Now she must gather her wits about her and go on the offensive because she has to protect Tiffany, who is also dependent on her."

Ashley Laurence was born in Los Angeles and began her acting career in school plays and local theatre groups. She soon made the transition to the professional stage where she honed her craft in a wide variety of plays from "Harvey" and "Bye Bye Birdie" to the more dramatic challenges of Shakespeare's "Macbeth" and "The Taming Of The Shrew."

It was not long before she made the successful move to television, becoming a regular on a daytime soap opera and making guest appearances in such series as **Spring Madness**, **McMillan** and **Highway To Heaven** before her motion picture debut in **Hellraiser**.

After **Hellraiser** was finished, Ashley returned to California to study Fine Art at college. She is a remarkably accomplished oil painter, with a style not too far removed from that of Clive Barker's. However, for the time being at least, she is happy to concentrate on two careers at the same time. "After the first film I needed to recuperate. By doing other things I'm starting to feel more confident as both an artist and an actress. But painting will never replace acting for me."

Prior to the start of **Hellraiser II**, she was set to appear in **Apt Pupil**, a film adaptation of the Stephen King story. "I did one day's filming with Nicol Williamson, and then the whole project closed down!"

So almost a year after she finished **Hellraiser**, did she find it difficult to pick up her role as Kirsty again for **Hellbound**? "No, it wasn't difficult at all because, for me, **Hellraiser II** is the same film as the first one. I play the same character in similar situations again. However, after this one, I don't think I was to do any more horror films for quite some time."

IMOGEN BOORMAN

"I learned a lot on this film," the young actress explains, "particularly on the technical side. And although there's a lot of waiting around on film sets, I'm used to that." For 16-year-old Imogen Boorman, film-making is not always as glamorous as her school friends think, especially when you are making a special effects picture like **Hellraiser II.**

"The worst thing I had to do was pretend to fall off a catwalk in Hell," explains Imogen. "They rigged me up on wires about fifty feet in the air. I was just hanging on to this little board while the camera was in the ceiling shooting down at me. I had to imagine I was in Hell and keep looking at a piece of sticky tape and pretending it was Clare Higgins. Luckily I don't suffer from vertigo!"

Although still in her teens, Imogen (who is not related to her more famous film director namesake, although they both originate from the same area of Southeast England), always has an impressive number of film and television credits.

Born in Kent, England, she wanted to be an actress from the age of four. She was only eight when she began her career at Maidstone's Hazlittl Theatre (where, incidentally, Joan Collins made her debut in repertory many years earlier). Imogen made her professional debut playing one of Mcduff's daughters in "Macbeth" - "We all got killed. . . it was *very* bloody," she laughs.

Two years later she starred in the BBC-TV film **Frost In May.** Imogen followed this with roles in two episodes of the BBC's science fiction series **Tripods**, the TV-movie **Lime Street** starring Robert Wagner, during which she became a close friend of the late young actress Samantha Smith, and she made her motion picture debut as Alice's sister in **Dreamchild.**

In **Hellraiser II** Imogen portrays Tiffany, the enigmatic mute puzzle-solver who Channard uses to open the portals to Hell. "The danger with playing a mute is that you don't realize if you're acting all on one level. Tony Randel wanted me to convey a lot of emotions with just my eyes, and he began by explaining every glance and reaction to me. But as the filming went on he let me decide how Tiffany would react in a given situation."

WILLIAM HOPE

Canadian actor William Hope portrays Kyle Macrae, the young doctor who befriends the distraught Kirsty and discovers that there are doorways into the Outer Darkness. "Kyle is a young, sympathetic psychiatrist who's charming and slightly off-best," Hope states. "As a character he is functional in registering Kirsty's panic and fear, being sensitive to that, and rebuilding her confidence. I just tried to make him as real as possible. In better circumstances I like to think that he and Kirsty might have formed a long term relationship."

Born in Montreal, Hope started acting at school and in 1974 decided to travel around Europe. Arriving in London he joined the National Youth Theatre and later trained at the Royal Academy of Dramatic Art.

"After that my career seems to have totally opened up in Britain," he says. "There's a lot more stage work and it has a reputation of producing the finest actors in the world."

After four years of uninterrupted repertory theatre, he moved into television with roles in ATV's **Flickers**, opposite Bob Hoskins, four episodes of BBC-TV's **Nancy Astor** and the mini-series **Lace** and **Master Of The Game.** Hope made his film debut in Franc Roddam's **The Lords Of Discipline**, which he followed with **The Last Days Of Patton, Going Home** and a starring role in **Aliens** as the doomed Gorman, the inexperienced Lieutenant who gets in way over his head.

DOUG BRADLEY

"The success of Pinhead took me completely by surprise," admits actor Doug Bradley. "It is an extraordinary image, and I don't know of another image anything like it in the horror field. When I first looked in a mirror and Pinhead was looking back at me, I felt it was actually quite beautiful."

Prior to **Hellraiser**, Bradley's acting experience was entirely in the theatre. He began his career working with Clive Barker in the Fringe Theatre in Liverpool and later in London. "In Clive's 'The History Of The Devil' I played the Devil and I was Dr. Frankenstein in 'Frankenstein In Love.' It was a good pedigree for the **Hellraiser** movies."

The first time Bradley saw what Pinhead was going to look like was at the initial makeup test a few weeks before **Hellraiser** began filming. "It was decided then to add the black contact lenses over my blue eyes, which I think really completes the image and takes away the last vestige of Doug Bradley completely."

As filming progressed on the first film, Bradley admits that he began to feel less and less like a conventional horror film monster. "People have said to me that they find the character sad and there's certainly a strong nobility about him.

"In **Hellraiser** I got this strange feeling of a sense of kinship between Pinhead and Kirsty, with Pinhead having a caring, almost fatherly, attitude towards her; almost wanting to protect her. This carries over into **Hellbound**, where it is Kirsty who reminds him of his humanity."

Perhaps more than any other image, Pinhead has become associated with the Hellraiser films, appearing on posters, displays and merchandising around the world, much to Bradley's delight. "The image of Pinhead seems to have pretty much encircled the earth. I begin to wonder if there isn't a town or country on the planet that hasn't seen him by now!"

SEAN CHAPMAN

In **Hellraiser II**, London-born actor Sean Chapman returns as the evil Uncle Frank, still lusting after his niece, Kirsty, and trying to find a way out of Hell.

"Frank has been in a personal Hell of 150 years duration," explains Chapman. "This consists of being locked up in a castle-like chamber in the company of three naked, writhing, female ghosts who he is not allowed to touch.

"For Frank, that's a pretty nasty Hell, and I like to think that he summons up Kirsty into his room to free him."

Chapman made his motion picture debut in the 1977 German comedy **The Passion Flower Hotel** (aka **Boarding School**), which starred Nastassja Kinski. He followed it with roles in **Scum, Quest For Fire, Party Party, The Fourth Protocol** and **For Queen And Country** in which he plays one of three paratroopers returning from the Falklands and having to readjust to British society.

Chapman enjoyed **Hellraiser** because he firmly believes that it broke new ground as far as horror movie-making goes: "I loved Clive's original ideas, and I think a number of them are reflected in the sequel.

"In **Hellraiser II** the character of Frank is less important because the story moves forward into so many new dimensions," he points out. "However, I think **Hellbound** is an equally impressive picture and is, if anything, even more original than the first one."

KEN CRANHAM

Most actors would not find it much fun getting up at three A.M. on a winter's morning, arriving at a near-deserted studio, sitting in makeup for six hours while your face and hands are given a bluish hue and bloody wires are imbedded in your flesh. Then, to cap things off, a 16-foot-long pink tentacle is attached to the top of your head, you are suspended on wires twelve feet above the studio floor and asked to give a performance! However, that's what Ken Cranham had to endure while playing the new Cenobite in **Hellbound.** And he says he enjoyed every minute of it.

"I had so much glue and rubber on me it was unbelievable," he laughs, "but you get used to it eventually. And the flying wasn't so bad - just as long as I didn't look down!"

Ken portrays the obsessive Doctor Channard who has spent a lifetime attempting to unlock the secrets of the Lament Configuration puzzle box and experience for himself the pleasures of Hell.

"I supposed Channard is a misguided person much in the same way Julie was in Hellraiser. But he is also a classic mad surgeon figure who gets punished for his curiosity into the occult and ends up in the hierarchy of Hell. He eventually gets his wish and is transformed into a Cenobite. It is his final fulfillment."

Ken Cranham was born in 1944 in Dunfermline, Fife, in Scotland. "My parents were struggling young people who were married during the War. We didn't have anywhere of our own to live until I was five years old."

Eventually the family moved to London, and Ken first became interested in acting at school. "They couldn't get anyone to appear in the school plays," he recalls. "All the kids wanted to play football, so the teachers actively encouraged us to appear on stage." He made his acting debut with a small role in Shakespeare's "Henry IV Part I."

"Everyone told me how good I was in it, which was the first time I was aware of being praised for anything. There was a lot of energy and hope around in the 1960s, and the teachers were very supportive."

His varied film credits include **Oliver, Brother Sun And Sister Moon, Joseph Andrews** and **Stealing Heaven**, where he played a shifty Bishop. But Ken is certain that nothing could have prepared him for his role as Channard in **Hellraiser II,** "Except maybe a visit to the butchers!" he jokes.

"I stopped going to see horror films around the time of **Alien,** which is when the genre peaked for me. Although I couldn't convince anyone to keep me company, I did see **Hellraiser** and was very impressed by Clare Higgins' bloodletting."

Although Ken Cranham is aware that his role as the ruthless Channard is the latest in a long and distinguished line of movie mad doctors delving into 'things man was not meant to know,' he believes that it is his performance as a Cenobite that audiences will remember from **Hellraiser II.**

"This sort of film, which is basically a special effects film, is like any other text. If you act it well, it works. Once you've got all that makeup on, you experience a great freedom. It gives you opportunity to stop being yourself, to open up and really express yourself. I had a chance to do something totally different with a character, which is what being an actor is all about.

"**Hellraiser II** goes further than the first film. It has a more bizarre, surreal element to it. In my own childhood I was fascinated by such things; I loved the

Chamber of Horrors. Now my 12-year-old nephew thinks this is the best career move I've ever made!"

CHRISTOPHER YOUNG

From the opening frame of Clive Barker's **Hellraiser,** the soundtrack is imbued with an evocative strings melody, punctuated by an ominous bell-like tolling which prepares the audience for a decidedly different kind of horror film.

The memorable music score for **Hellraiser** was the work of American composer Christopher Young, who once again contributed his unique terror tones to **Hellraiser II: Hellbound.**

Perhaps more than any other movie genre, the horror film must use music to sustain a mood and atmosphere in an audience to be entirely successful. Over the past few years, Christopher Young has been consolidating his position as one of the leading composers in this challenging field with an impressive list of horror, science fiction and fantasy titles to his credit. These include **Haunted Summer, Flowers In The Attic, Trick Or Treat, Invaders From Mars, A Nightmare On Elm Street Part 2: Freddy's Revenge, Torment, Def Con 4, Barbarian Queen, Wizards Of The Lost Kingdom** and **The Power.** Young also contributed additional music to **Deathstalker II** and **Godzilla 1985.**

His growing expertise in this field is reflected in his television credits as well, with music composed for the new **Twilight Zone** series and the ABC-TV specials **In The Closet, Under The Bed, Mad Doctors** and **Witches, Warlocks & Wizards.**

Hellraiser III is currently held up by the sale of New World Pictures, although a script has been written by Peter Atkins, who would also probably direct. In the meantime, Marvel Comics will be publishing a quarterly **Hellraiser** comic book exploring the bizarre world created in the films.

THE COUCH POTATO BOOK CATALOG 5715 N BALSAM, LAS VEGAS, NV 89130

The Phantom
The Green Hornet
The Shadow
The Batman

Each issue of Serials Adventures Presents offers 100 or more pages of pure nostalgic fun for $16.95

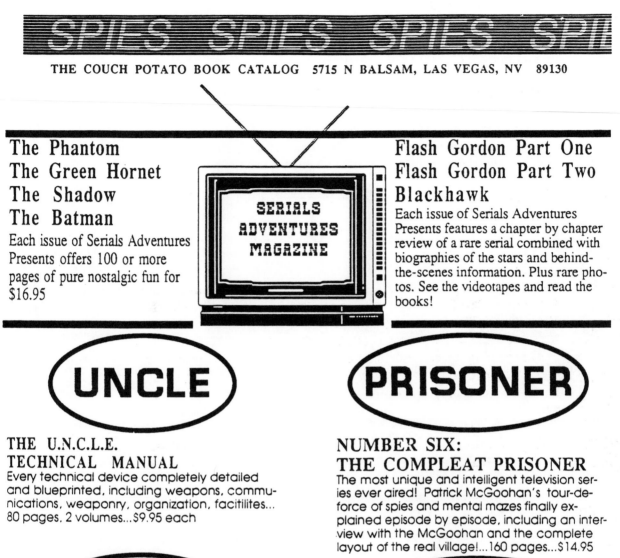

SERIALS ADVENTURES MAGAZINE

Flash Gordon Part One
Flash Gordon Part Two
Blackhawk

Each issue of Serials Adventures Presents features a chapter by chapter review of a rare serial combined with biographies of the stars and behind-the-scenes information. Plus rare photos. See the videotapes and read the books!

UNCLE

THE U.N.C.L.E. TECHNICAL MANUAL
Every technical device completely detailed and blueprinted, including weapons, communications, weaponry, organization, facitilites... 80 pages, 2 volumes...$9.95 each

PRISONER

NUMBER SIX: THE COMPLEAT PRISONER
The most unique and intelligent television series ever aired! Patrick McGoohan's tour-de-force of spies and mental mazes finally explained episode by episode, including an interview with the McGoohan and the complete layout of the real village!...160 pages...$14.95

THE GREEN HORNET
Daring action adventure with the Green Hornet and Kato. This show appeared before Bruce Lee had achieved popularity but delivered fun, superheroic action. Episode guide and character profiles combine to tell the whole story...120 pages...$14.95

WILD, WILD, WEST
Is it a Western or a Spy show? We couldn't decide so we're listing it twice. Fantastic adventure, convoluted plots, incredible devices...all set in the wild, wild west! Details of fantastic devices, character profiles and an episode-by-episode guide...120 pages...$17.95

THE COUCH POTATO BOOK CATALOG 5715 N BALSAM, LAS VEGAS, NV 89130

TREK YEAR 1
The earliest voyages and the creation of the series. An in-depth episode guide, a look at the pilots, interviews, character profiles and more...
160 pages...$10.95

TREK YEAR 2
TREK YEAR 3
$12.95 each

THE ANIMATED TREK
Complete inone volume $14.95

THE MOVIES
The chronicle of all the movies...
116 pages...$12.95

THE LOST YEARS
For the first time anywhere, the
exclusive story of the Star Trek
series that almost was including
a look at every proposed adventure and an interview with the
man that would have replaced
Spock. Based on interviews and
exclusive research...
160 pages...$14.95

NEXT GENERATION
Complete background of the
new series. Complete first season
including character profiles and
actor biographies...160 pages
...$19.95

THE TREK ENCYCLOPEDIA
The reference work to Star Trek including complete information on every character, alien race and
monster that ever appeared as well as full information on every single person that ever worked on the
series from the stars to the stunt doubles from extras to producers, directors, make-up men and came-
ramen...**over 360 pages. UPDATED EDITION. Now includes planets, ships and devices**...$19.95

INTERVIEWS ABOARD THE ENTERPRISE
Interviews with the cast and crew of Star Trek and the Next Generation. From Eddie Murphy to Leo-
nard Nimoy and from Jonathan Frakes to Marina Sirtis. Over 100 pages of your favorites.
$18.95

THE ULTIMATE TREK
The most spectacular book we have ever offered. This volume completely covers every year of Star
Trek, every animated episode and every single movie. Plus biographies, interviews, profiles, and more.
Over 560 pages! Hardcover only. Only a few of these left. $75.00

TREK HANDBOOK and TREK UNIVERSE
The Handbook offers a complete guide to conventions, clubs, fanzines.
The Universe presents a complete guide to every book, comic, record and everything else.
Both volumes are edited by Enterprise Incidents editor James Van Hise. Join a universe of Trek fun!
Handbook...$12.95   Universe...$17.95

THE CREW BOOK
The crew of the Enterprise including coverage of Kirk, Spock, McCoy, Scotty, Uhura,Chekov, Sulu and
all the others...plus starship staffing practices...250 pages...$17.95

THE MAKING OF THE NEXT GENERATION: SCRIPT TO SCREEN
THIS BOOK WILL NOT BE PRINTED UNTIL APRIL OR MAY. Analysis of every episode in each stage, from initial draft
to final filmed script. Includes interviews with the writers and directors. 240 pages...$14.95

Boring, but Necessary Ordering Information!

Payment: All orders must be prepaid by check or money order. Do not send cash. All payments must be made in US funds only.

Shipping: We offer several methods of shipment for our product.

Postage is as follows:

For books priced under $10.00— for the first book add $2.50. For each additional book under $10.00 add $1.00. (This is per individual book priced under $10.00, not the order total.)

For books priced over $10.00— for the first book add $3.25. For each additional book over $10.00 add $2.00. (This is per individual book priced over $10.00, not the order total.)

These orders are filled as quickly as possible. Sometimes a book can be delayed if we are temporarily out of stock. You should note on your order whether you prefer us to ship the book as soon as available or send you a merchandise credit good for other TV goodies or send you your money back immediately. Shipments normally take 2 or 3 weeks, but allow up to12 weeks for delivery.

Special UPS 2 Day Blue Label RUSH SERVICE: Special service is available for desperate Couch Potatos. These books are shipped within 24 hours of when we receive your order and should take 2 days to get from us to you.

For the first **RUSH SERVICE** book under $10.00 add $4.00. For each additional 1 book under $10.00 and $1.25. (This is per individual book priced under $10.00, not the order total.)

For the first **RUSH SERVICE** book over $10.00 add $6.00. For each additional book over $10.00 add $3.50 per book. (This is per individual book priced over $10.00, not the order total.)

Canadian and Foreign shipping rates are the same except that Blue Label RUSH SERVICE is not available. All Canadian and Foreign orders are shipped as books or printed matter.

DISCOUNTS! DISCOUNTS! Because your orders are what keep us in business we offer a discount to people that buy a lot of our books as our way of saying thanks. On orders over $25.00 we give a 5% discount. On orders over $50.00 we give a 10% discount. On orders over $100.00 we give a 15% discount. On orders over $150.00 we give a 20% discount. Please list alternates when possible. Please state if you wish a refund or for us to backorder an item if it is not in stock.

100% satisfaction guaranteed. We value your support. You will receive a full refund as long as the copy of the book you are not happy with is received back by us in reasonable condition. No questions asked, except we would like to know how we failed you. Refunds and credits are given as soon as we receive back the item you do not want.

Please have mercy on Phyllis and carefully fill out this form in the neatest way you can. Remember, she has to read a lot of them every day and she wants to get it right and keep you happy! You may use a duplicate of this order blank as long as it is clear. **Please don't forget to include payment! And remember, we** *love* **repeat friends...**

▪▪▪▪▪▪▪▪▪▪▪▪▪▪▪▪▪▪▪▪▪▪▪▪▪ORDER FORM▪▪▪▪▪▪▪▪▪▪▪▪▪▪▪▪▪▪▪▪▪▪▪▪▪▪▪

_____The Phantom $16.95
_____The Green Hornet $16.95
_____The Shadow $16.95
_____Flash Gordon Part One $16.95_____Part Two $16.95
_____Blackhawk $16.95
_____Batman $16.95
_____The UNCLE Technical Manual One $9.95 _____Two $9.95
_____The Green Hornet Television Book $14.95
_____Number Six The Prisoner Book $14.95
_____The Wild Wild West $17.95
_____Trek Year One $10.95
_____Trek Year Two $12.95
_____Trek Year Three $12.95
_____The Animated Trek $14.95
_____The Movies $12.95
_____Next Generation $19.95
_____The Lost Years $14.95
_____The Trek Encyclopedia $19.95
_____Interviews Aboard The Enterprise $18.95
_____The Ultimate Trek $75.00
_____Trek Handbook $12.95_____Trek Universe $17.95
_____The Crew Book $17.95
_____The Making of the Next Generation $14.95
_____The Freddy Krueger Story $14.95
_____The Aliens Story $14.95
_____Robocop $16.95
_____Monsterland's Horror in the '80s $17.95
_____The Compleat Lost in Space $17.95
_____Lost in Space Tribute Book $9.95
_____Lost in Space Tech Manual $9.95
_____Supermarionation $17.95
_____The Unofficial Beauty and the Beast $14.95
_____Dark Shadows Tribute Book $14.95
_____Dark Shadows Interview Book $18.95
_____Doctor Who Baker Years $19.95
_____The Doctor Who Encyclopedia:The 4th Doctor $19.95
_____Illustrated Stephen King $12.95
_____Gunsmoke Years $14.95

NAME:_____

STREET:_____

CITY:_____

STATE:_____

ZIP:_____

TOTAL:_____ SHIPPING_____

SEND TO: COUCH POTATO,INC.
5715 N BALSAM, LAS VEGAS, NV 89130

If your lo____ ____ the early
issues yo___
By Roy ____
_Buz Saw____ ____wyer #5
By Ale___
_Jungle J____ ___ngle Jim 6
_Jungle J____
_Rip Kirl____
By Lee___
_Mandra____
_Mandra____
By Pete___
_Modesty____ ____Modesty#7
_Modesty____
By Ha____
P V #1 ____ N. ($5.00)
By Arc___
_Secret A____ ____ Agent #5
_Secret A____

(All abo____ ___alk and Al
Williams____
___ TH____
(The fo____ ____ original
strip fo____
___ TH____
___ T____

___ (E____ ____red
and/o____
and/or $14.95 for THE MANDRAKE SUNDAYS.
and/or $14.95 for THE PHANTOM SUNDAYS.
Shipping and handling are included.

Name: _____

Street: _____

City: _____

State: _____

Zip   Code: _____
Check or money order only. No cash please. All payments
must be in US funds. Please add $5.00 to foreign orders.
I remembered to enclose:$_____
Please send to:
Pioneer, 5715 N. Balsam Rd., Las Vegas, NV 89130